DEADLY INSTINCTS

A NOVEL BY

RACQUEL BROWN GASTON

WWW.RSGPUBLISHING.COM

A Novel By

Racquel Brown Gaston
www.rsgpublishing.com

Printed in the United States of America
Copyright © Racquel Brown Gaston, 2012

ISBN -13: 978-0-9825735-0-1
ISBN -10: 0-9825735-0-2

Published by RSG Publishing, LLC
7045 Berry Road, Box 191
Accokeek MD 20607

Book cover design and inside layout by www.mariondesigns.com

Dedication

To my husband, Niaka Jermaine Gaston, a promise fulfilled and in honor of my father, Glen "Pecke" Brown, the biggest hero I've ever known.

Acknowledgements

I'd like to thank my creator for the abundance of blessings he continuously bestows upon me. A special thanks to my husband and best friend who believed in me more than I believed in myself. Thank you for your encouragement and unyielding support. Thanks to our son for being a constant reminder of life's greatest joy. Thanks to my family for being the strong pillars upon which I stood to reach my dreams. Thanks to my friends – you are my sweet savory. To my students and colleagues - I adore you and I am forever humbled that we have crossed paths.

I'd like to thank my friends whose expertise in their craft contributed to this novel. Thank you Marion Designs Inc., my formidable editors and the rest of the team that made this moment possible.

Last, but not least, a very special thank you to my mother and my grandma who sacrificed their lives so I could have mine.

Thank you all.

—*Racquel Brown Gaston*

CHAPTER
ONE

The naked woman's body lying in the alley behind the dumpster was not easily noticeable. She appeared to be in her late 20's. She had a caramel complexion and a lean figure. Her five foot-four body was toned, flawless and even had a shimmer. Her nails were manicured and polished. Her hair, golden bronze, was carefully pulled back, as if to ensure that no strand was out of place.

Elizabeth squinted her eyes, as she slowly returned to consciousness. It was nighttime. In a near distance, she heard yelling.

"Bitch, your stink ass betta get the fuck off my corner! Read the goddamn sign bitch! Blake and Liberty! You know dis is my spot! Don't let me beat your ass straight outta Brooklyn."

Elizabeth panicked. *I'm in East New York?*

She tried to get up and run but was unable to do so. She was horizontal on the ground facing upward. The muscles in her body did not react kindly to her temporary concrete bed. She needed a painkiller or a muscle relaxer. With all of her strength, she pushed herself up into a sitting position. She extended both arms behind her and against the side of the dumpster. Elizabeth reached for an invisible handle and positioned herself to stand. Her weakened legs alone were insufficient to support her, forcing her back to the ground. As she hit the cool concrete, the gravel on it pinched her bare buttocks. She sprinted outward and up onto both legs.

"Ouch," Elizabeth brushed off the gravel, and whatever else was on her buttocks, as she tried to control her staggering. She grabbed her head and planted her feet onto the ground making a mental note not to fall over. Elizabeth had the feeling that a feather weighed more than her at that moment. She immediately recognized that her entire body was exposed. Elizabeth quickly hunched over and covered her private area with her palms. She turned her attention to locating her belongings but her blurred vision made everything seem to be moving in a circular motion. It forced her to concentrate. The frightened Elizabeth squinted as she moved forward continuing to hide her naked body. She was alone. When she finally noticed her clothing, Elizabeth breathed a sigh of relief. She leapt toward her red-laced boy shorts panties. She could have won the world record for getting all of her belongings back in place on her body in a matter of seconds.

Elizabeth grabbed her bag and ran in the direction of the light. A familiar sight smacked her in the face. She came to a sudden halt. Abandoned houses with loose and hanging shingles were visible. Many of their windows were broken and boarded. Buildings were charred. The cars were stripped and burnt. Plastic covered by tape replaced some car windows. The pavement was cracked in multiple places. Grass was the cement that held the pieces of pavement together. Sharp edges replaced the pavement's smooth lines. Pebbles replaced portions of the concrete. Plastic bags, soda cans, sticks, pieces of boards with exposed nails and manholes outnumbered the working girls on the corners. Elizabeth's worse fear was confirmed. She had been here before. Like the other times, she did not have the faintest idea as to how she got there or how long she was there. She clutched the upper part of her left breast as if to subdue the raging heart.

She trembled as her memory took her back to that dreadful day a couple of years ago.

Elizabeth fixed her eyes on the plaques, trophies and awards in the office: Boston
University School of Medicine Distinguished Alumni Award, The Association of Women Psychiatrists' Distinguished Service Award, American Psychiatric Association Exemplary Psychiatrist Awards, Forensic Psychiatrist of the Year. She also noticed framed articles on the wall from the Journal of Clinical Psychiatry, written by as well as acknowledging Dr. Klauss as among the most prominent in her field. Elizabeth needed not go on browsing the wall as she had an idea as to whose office she occupied.

She remembered stories from her friend Diane who had used Dr. Klauss as a witness for the State of New York. It was common knowledge in the psychiatric and legal world, according to Diane, that if one was a patient of Dr. Klauss, that person was likely at the brink of no-return. Diane and Elizabeth were the very best of friends. They were so close that they deemed each other the title and responsibility of sister. They were intertwined in each other's life.

"How are you so in tuned with the world of psychiatry Diane? Shouldn't you be focused on your career as an Assistant District Attorney?"

"I deal with the quote, unquote, criminally insane. I am married to the world of psychiatry."

"Well taken."

Diane was set on proving that none of the defendants who sat across from her was as they described it, "insane."

Elizabeth continued to browse the unfamiliar office. She studied the desk and the contents upon it. With her eyes attentive on the desk, she leisurely swept over a manila folder. Screech! She braked. Cautiously, she dragged her eyes back into the reverse direction. They froze on the words written on the label of the manila folder. The words "Elizabeth Webster," never appeared more pronounced.

"Hello Elizabeth," Dr. Klauss greeted her as she emerged from another office within the one they had occupied. Her warm and genuine smile along with her light and even toned voice instantly created a calming effect upon Elizabeth, regardless of her confused state of mind. Dr. Klauss, like Elizabeth was manicured, poised and gentle. She was in her 50's, though with her tight and wrinkle free skin, it was difficult to tell. She had curly shoulder length brunette hair and soft green eyes.

Elizabeth searched the room to find any indication that Dr. Klauss was Jewish as she Elizabeth didn't wish to assume, simply by name. She concluded that Dr. Klauss was simply because she was Caucasian. A Caucasian woman with a Jewish

4

name was likely Jewish. Having the name Webster, however, didn't associate Elizabeth with the "African American" category into which she was placed by the social laws of the United States, irrespective of her mixed race background. Her physical features emulated her Creole mom from Louisiana rather than her dark chocolate father from whom she received her surname. Elizabeth inherited the calm, humble nature from her mother.

"Hel-lo," Elizabeth gulped.

"Please, have a seat," Dr. Klauss pointed toward the oversized vintage brown leather chair. "I hope you don't mind," she pointed to the video recorder. I like to take the sessions for my purposes in terms of writing reports, analyzing the sessions, etc."

"Thank you and I don't mind. I have nothing to hide." Elizabeth walked over to the chair, clasped her feet together, pressed her right hand onto her right buttocks and glided it to the back of her knee, ensuring that there would be no indecent exposure as she quietly sat.

Dr. Klauss took note of Elizabeth's merged, tightly gripped hands, accompanied by her aligned back and upward shoulders. The look in Elizabeth's eyes gave away the truth she tried to hide with her smile.

"It's okay to be scared Elizabeth."

"I'm not scared Dr. Klauss. I am confused. I think there has been a mistake. I am not the Elizabeth Webster you believe me to be."

"Why do you say that?" Dr. Klauss picked up the manila folder and sat across from Elizabeth facing her.

"You have a file in your office with the name Elizabeth

Webster on it. I am assuming that you only house files of patients. I am now in your office and my name is in fact Elizabeth Webster, so it's safe to assume that you believe that I am your patient."

A silent moment accompanied by a soft stare from Dr. Klauss, resulted in a fidgeted Elizabeth.

"How did you get here Elizabeth?" Dr. Klauss stayed fixed on her patient.

"I was escorted here by a couple of male nurses, or you may call them orderlies."

"From where did they bring you?" She asked in that light, even toned, and soothed voice.

Elizabeth folded her arms. Her once aligned body was no more and her dry textured eyes were now heavily moist and pink.

"That's what I am trying to tell you," she squeaked the words as tears flowed. "I have been mistaken for someone else. I don't know how I got here and I don't know why I wasn't released when I clarified to the nurses as to who I was. There has clearly been a grave mistake and no one will oblige me or even entertain the slightest notion that I am an innocent victim and I am being held in what appears to be a psychiatric ward against my will and knowledge as to why I am here."

Dr. Klauss handed her a box of tissue that was nearby. It had come in handy on many occasions and on this one, it was needed more than ever.

"You were in the G Building. That's what we call our psychiatric center here at Kings County Medical Center in Brooklyn. I requested for a couple of the orderlies to have you get dressed and escort you here to my office four blocks around the corner, as opposed to me coming to you. I needed for this

session to be in this environment."

"Dr. Klauss..." Elizabeth leaned forward, extended both arms while the hands were in chopped position. Her desperate cry caused her voice to tremble. "I can call my friend Diane and...she can clear this whole matter up for you. Please....I don't have any forms of ID on me...but I can assure you if you allow me to make a phone call, we can all put this matter to rest and I won't even sue Kings County for false imprisonment or you for that matter. We will just let this whole unfortunate incident go... please... please..."

"Diane Roberts?" Dr. Klauss asked casually.

"Yes." Elizabeth gleamed and returned to a poised position. "Yes, Diane Roberts, the ADA, who I believe you know as you have testified for the State as per her request."

Dr. Klauss gave Elizabeth a warm embrace with her smile. She opened the folder and removed a form.

"Do you know what this is?" She reached across and handed it to Elizabeth, who hurriedly grasped it.

As Elizabeth studied the familiar form, she was once again in a slumped position, and her bottom jaw involuntarily dropped forcing her mouth to open.

"It's a copy of my Power of Attorney, that I granted to Diane over my finances, real estate and health issues, should I be deemed incompetent to make such informed decisions." She felt defeated. "Why do you have it and where is Diane?" She briskly asked.

"Diane will be here whenever you need her to be and..."

"I need her to be." Elizabeth interrupted sternly.

"Okay," the doctor motioned as if she was pressing

down on something invisible. *"But, please understand that it was Diane who checked you in, after the judge decided over a brief hearing that you were in fact incompetent at the time to make sound decisions regarding your mental health and overall well-being."*

Elizabeth sighed in disbelief, *"you actually believe what you are saying, and I am the one that's in a mental institution?"*

"I received a frantic phone call at home from Diane over a week ago, urging that I come down to the trauma center here at the hospital immediately. She said she was unable to get into all of the details, but she wouldn't have called if it wasn't urgent. Diane was stuttering the entire time and remained completely unfocused. I managed however to grasp something of what she was saying." The doctor noticed how captivated her audience was, how she yearned for answers. Her heart broke for her patient. *"According to Diane, she received a blocked call from a woman who stated that she was just calling the last number in the history listing of the cell phone; the cell phone of the lady who was naked in an alley closed to Blake and Liberty in East New York. She told Diane that she wasn't calling 911 because she refused to get involved, so Diane can come if she wanted but she was leaving..."*

"And so Diane went there and supposedly got me and took me here..." Elizabeth interjected.

"When I got here Elizabeth," Dr. Klauss regained control, *"the situation was worse than I had expected. I knew from Diane's voice that this thing was life altering. A rape kit was already conducted. It was confirmed, as expected that you were brutally raped, and..."*

"Dr. Klauss," Elizabeth leaned forward and spoke sternly and steadily, "I was never in an alley in East New York and I was never raped. You need to release me and you need to release me now."

"I am afraid I can't do that Elizabeth." She opened the folder again and brought forth a copy of Elizabeth's diagnosis, which were the grounds for which Diane exercised the Power of Attorney.

"Take it." Dr. Klauss extended her hand.

"No." Elizabeth folded her arms and leaned back in the chair.

"Very well." Elizabeth was going to learn the truth regardless of her willingness to do so. The psychiatrist placed the form back in the folder. "Can you tell me where you were last night and the last thing you recalled doing?"

Elizabeth did not respond. It was clear to the doctor that her patient was approaching the zone of being "non-cooperative."

"As a kindergarten teacher, you must have experienced many non-cooperative moments and here you are on the other side," the psychiatrist smiled. Her patient didn't. "Okay Elizabeth, we will get just straight to the point, as we are all very busy and I am sure you have things to which you must attend."

"Yes, I do." Her lips were barely ajar.

"When I first laid eyes on you," Dr. Klauss reached in her folder again and pulled a picture, "this was the person that I met."

Elizabeth sprinted and took hold of the picture. She popped her head forward, her mouth and eyes widened. The woman appeared to be in her late 20's. She bore a caramel complexion and carried a lean figure. Her five-foot four body was toned, flawless and even had a shimmer. Her hair, golden bronze, however, was in a braided pony tail. She wore tight, red leather pants, and a black sleeveless vest that exposed her belly. Her fire engine red lips formed their permanent place on the cigarette that dangled from her mouth. She leaned forward over the small plastic chair on which she sat. The back of the chair faced her and her parted legs over the chair exhibited no discomfort on her part. Elizabeth stared at the picture that also showed a devilish grin on the woman's face as she grabbed for the buttocks of another woman. Elizabeth was discombobulated.

"Who is this..." she bounced out of the chair, "this person?" She snapped. "And what the hell is going on? Who is this?" She then looked up at Dr. Klauss. "Who-is-this?" She threw the picture at the doctor. "That-is-not-me," she patted her chest.

"No Elizabeth," Dr. Klauss stood and walked toward her. "That's not you. That's Sally. The other personality that lives within you."

TWO

Darius Kramer sat across from his supervisor's desk in an office at the Drug Enforcement Administration in Long Island, New York. He had requested a transfer four years ago from the Washington D.C. field office to either the division in Kingston, Jamaica, or that of New York City. The Kingston division was his first choice as he was determined that frequent escapes to paradise-like settings would be the perfect antidote for the hell of an existence DEA agents often undergo. His obsession to experience the serenity of the Marta Brae River in Trelawny, Jamaica, had taken center fold. Even at his age, he longed for such escape.

"It's a nice day in New York today to piss off a CPOT, isn't it?" His supervisor for the New York field office located in Long Island smiled.

Not surprising to anyone in the Administration, one of Darius' transfer requests was granted without a second thought. *New York could have used the help, they probably thought*. At the time of the agent's request, at 25 years of age, he had already dismantled the operations of four CPOTs leading to various arrests and convictions. The CPOT--Consolidated Priority Organization Target list included the Administration's Most Wanted. They were the most dangerous narcotics traffickers. Some in The Practical Applications Unit (TRDP) of the Administration, which was responsible for undercover training, would have liked to credit this agent's success to the additional two courses beyond basic undercover training--Contemporary Issues in the Undercover Process and the Risk Management which had been reserved for Special Agents engaging in advanced training. However, they knew better. *Some things are innate and need only to be polished to perfection.* They knew that this agent had come to them with a particular set of mental and physical skills unlike any that they have seen. His membership in the National Rifle Association (NRA) at age 18 gave him the opportunity to train and earned his Advanced Certificate in Marksmanship. He could have shot the eraser off a pencil if he so chose. There was nothing that the Firearms Training Unit of the Administration could have taught him. Prior to the escalation of his application to the second round, a random visit to the martial arts dojo indicated on his application as the agent's affiliation, caused the recruiters to notice a red and white sectioned area toward the lower end of the applicant's Black Belt. This signaled that the applicant was a 2nd degree Black Belt in the art of Brazilian Jujitsu. There was nothing new that their Tactical Training and Survival Unit could have taught him. His facial profile and body language matched the needs of his prospective employer. The applicant's deep set lazy eyes revealed his nature—observant, private, secretive, cautious, deep thinker and could say the opposite of what was thinking, without so much of a flinch. The closeness of his eyes, according to psychologists, revealed the detail oriented nature of this applicant, and his obsessive nature to never abandon a problem until it was no more.

"What is it about this Sambino guy that has even you the great Darius Kramer aging?" Revere asked the year old 29 agent who sat across from him, as he opened Sambino's file from the CPOT designated folder on his computer.

Revere was Caucasian, about 5ft, 7 with pale blue eyes, and carried a round body weighing about 180 pounds. He was 20 years his agent's senior and the bald spot that has taken center stage confirmed it.

"He's the Lucky Luciano of our time," Darius sprawled in the chair massaging the stress ball in his right hand.

Closing this case had gone one year beyond the goal Agent Kramer had set for himself. As far as he was concerned, too much of his time had been taken up with nonsense, as that was the adjective he had used to replace Sambino's name.

"He's that love of a lifetime, the one we must have or else what is the purpose of life," Darius cocked his head to the left eying the massage ball as he added pressure to it. Achieving a goal in record time, set by Agent Kramer, was his trademark. Having earned his law degree at 21 years of age wasn't worthy of a celebration for him. *Anyone can earn a law degree at 21, it's not astrophysics.* Few things came as a challenge for this agent whose IQ was deemed superior at the age of seven. Sambino was among those few things. He had been having a love affair with law enforcement for some years and Darius was

assigned to end it. It had been three years since his assignment
had begun.

"It's just more difficult than we had thought to figure him
out, but we will get him, don't you worry." Revere attempted to
assure Darius.

Darius pierced his eyes on his grip of the ball. "He has a
god-like complex with the power of intimidation and violence as
his wing guards. His greed for power is his ultimate weakness.
His callousness toward all those in his path will inadvertently
be his downfall." Darius watched his finger intensely as he
loosened his grip. "It's not difficult to figure him out. I had the
pleasure of doing so the moment my eyes met his."

Darius was often deemed an odd child by his mother as
he spent most of his time comparing and contrasting through
listening and keen observation, the words and action choices of
those around him. Even at a young age, Darius was drawn to
the science of human behavior. *Mom, the grown-ups don't act
much differently from the children.* His obsession with human
behavior not only led to the attainment of a Master's Degree in
Psychology at the age of 18, but he had become his own protégé.
He guarded his emotions. He was vigilant as to his thoughts,
movements and feelings. *The complexity of our feelings champ,
is evidence of the human component that makes us who we are.
It's okay to feel. It's okay to cry, to hurt, to even miss someone
when he is gone. It's okay because we know it's temporary as*

each life is temporary. Those temporary feelings his father spoke of on his deathbed to Darius when he was 11 had yet to be short-lived.

Death had a way of changing the rules. The pursuit of a career in Psychiatry had shifted to a degree in Psychology and a career pursuit in law enforcement. Perhaps this was his way of dealing with a cop's life gone too soon. Darius Kramer was no longer interested in using legally prescribed narcotics to fix how one dealt with what may have gone wrong in his or her life. His only interest was to eliminate the symptom of the problem that often arose through the illegal sale and distribution of narcotics, and let GOD worry about the fixing element. He had never missed a target, as they never saw him coming; he would be damned if he missed Sambino. Darius' movements were swift, sharp and flawless. He applied his Jujutsu training in all that he did. His mother had enrolled him in class shortly after his father's passing in an effort to assist in the channeling of the energy from his pain and anger elsewhere. It didn't work. It made Darius more focused on his mission—to take down as many of them that his father wasn't able to take down, as they had killed him in the line of duty and dared to continue breathing.

"You are truly skilled at your craft Kramer," Revere stared at the pictures in Sambino's folder carefully and individually.

Darius had managed to take snapshots couple years ago of who he believed to be Sambino. He had fit the description described in the tip that the DEA had received via the "Submit a Tip," page on their website. As Sambino was supposed to be invisible, neither cameras nor telephones were allowed to be in his presence. Fortunately for the DEA agent, the flat surface camera placed as a camouflage on his tie pin worked just fine. Inside the folders were various pictures of everyone that Darius had observed coming into contact with Sambino, regardless of how insignificant they may have seemed--even a simple hello. The Japanese looking fellow he met was his favorite. Darius would study the eyes, and any hint of weakness—such as uneasiness in body language or tremor in voice, would immediately allow for such person to become Darius' prey. A picture scan would be done revealing enough information about the person for Darius to determine if he would move forward using that person for the DEA's benefit. If the decision was to move forward, Darius who was careful never to face his prey out of Sambino's presence, would have alerted his supervisor, who would have then arranged for such person to find himself in an interrogation room making a plea for his life to strangers or becoming a Confidential Informant often called CI. As the federal agents would have it, given the physical and audio evidence from which at least a case of conspiracy could be built, they made the decision for the unfortunate souls, an easy one. One of the worst things that Darius could have arranged against one in Sambino's circle was to have such persons become a CI or spy for the government. In these cases, when Darius' purpose for such informants was achieved, fearing for the lives of their families, and expressing the gratitude of the DEA for their cooperation, Darius staged a bust for their capture, hence their protection from Sambino, as opposed to death upon their family for betrayal. Dead bodies of family members delivered as an express package would prove detrimental to his case. Soon he would have had no CI's, as they all likely would have chosen to be prosecuted than to have buried dismembered body parts of their loved ones. Also, once apprehended during that stage bust, they would be kept in protected custody to avoid Sambino's far and wide stretched arms.

"Don't butter me up. This is still my last case before my long vacation otherwise known as my retirement, regardless of how good you think I am."

"Don't you worry Kramer, the Martha Brae River will still be there. It will still be flowing, I promise. It will be worth the wait," Revere teased him, having been there himself. "The Potomac River, I must say is a far cry from it," he teased.

A native of Southern Maryland, Darius longed for a boat ride down the Potomac River on a cool Sunday afternoon. Darius Kramer was going home this week and he was quite sure that his wife, Maria, was counting the days. He did not care that she hated the fact that he had to work out of state. Although he had been working in New York for a few years now, it was that job--the promotion he automatically earned after his first four years with the agency that paid the rent, all the bills, and helped her to shop. It was because of that job she elatedly remained unemployed.

She planned to stay that way. She always bragged to him that her favorite thing to do was to spend his money. He was always amazed about her callousness towards him in regard to the stress felt from being the only employed spouse. Despite her callousness, he never showed any emotion around her. He did not want to give her the satisfaction of knowing that she had even slightly hurt him. They were married four years ago, shortly before the transfer. Although it had been a heaven for Maria, for Darius, it was pure hell. She was his wife for one reason; she became pregnant with his child. He never forgot how he felt when Maria told him the news. His expression was that of remorse, not for the child but that she would be the woman who carried his child. For the life of him, he had not been able to figure out how she became pregnant. He had always used a condom with her. She took the pregnancy test and brought out the results to show him. It was a hard acceptance but acceptance nonetheless. Two days after, he married her. That same day he made an appointment to have a vasectomy. That pregnancy mistake would never happen again, not with Maria, not with anyone. At the thought of going home to a wife, he glanced at his ring finger. Kramer never wore his ring as he refused to admit to the world that he was married. He never tried to convince Maria that he had left the ring due to the hazards of his job. He did not care but he knew in a twisted way, she did. Kramer did not call her. He treated her as if she didn't exist in hopes that she would divorce him. She would be damned if she allowed anyone else to have him, though she didn't either. He refused to file for divorce because of the oath, *till death do us part*. Though, as far as Kramer was concerned, he died the day he married Maria. His mother was the only woman he had ever loved, and she prayed for the day another would join her rank.

"Sir, I have to go," Darius stood.

"Where are you going, if you don't mind me asking?"

"To work. I have to go see about a woman," Darius walked toward the door.

"A woman? Here in New York?" He asked sarcastically.

"Yep, here in New York...Brooklyn, to be more specific."

"It's kinda late to be visiting friends, don't you think?"

"I didn't say she was a friend," he smiled as he exited the office.

"Will this cost the agency!" Revere yelled to his agent who was no longer in his sight.

"Did taking down four CPOTs cost the agency?" His agent responded.

"Damn."

CHAPTER
THREE

Elizabeth was more convinced that it was Dr. Klauss who had lost her mind, and it was her who needed to be someone's patient. More importantly, she had begun to question all that she had heard about the doctor that stood before her and certainly the accolades that had so beautifully adorned the office.

"Who?" Elizabeth leaned her head to the right, walked backward and raised her hand to signal that the doctor should remain where she was.

"She emerged the night you were gang raped after you regained consciousness in the trauma unit. It was the reason for Diane's frantic phone call."

"Bullshit!" Elizabeth yelled.

"What was the last thing you remembered before realizing that you were somewhere unfamiliar? She lowered her voice. "Elizabeth, it's important that you try, please.

Elizabeth did not respond.

"I know this is difficult..."

"No you don't."

She motioned for Elizabeth to have a seat. "Yes, I do. But I need for you to try. If I am wrong, we can forget all of this and you can move on with your life. But I won't until you help me figure out this mess."

With folded arms, Elizabeth walked over, and again, clasped her feet together, pressed her right hand onto her right buttock and glided it to the back of her knee, ensuring that there would be no indecent exposure as she quietly sat. "I was at the school late and I was on my way to visit a student of mine at her home. She was just released from the hospital and so I wanted to surprise her with a teddy bear and a card that said we miss you in school."

"Where does the student live?"

"In East New York."

"That's a long way from Park Slope where you reside, and quite a difference in economic social and racial demographics, isn't it?"

"There are Blacks in Park Slope and Blacks in New York. There are folks without money in Park Slope and folks without money in East New York. I don't understand your point." Elizabeth knew the point Dr. Klauss was making. The economic and social status of those who resided in Park Slope was far steeper than those who resided in East New York. Sidewalk cafes, bookstores, boutique restaurants, dog walkers, were the norm in Park Slope.

Dilapidated stores where fried chicken, chicken wings, fried rice, fries and other extensive menu choices sold by Chinese families and thus designated as "Chinese food," lined every third block, as well as liquor stores, bodegas and NYPD officers lined the streets of East New York.

"Forgive me. Please go on." The last thing Dr. Klauss wanted to do was to upset Elizabeth as it was crucial that Elizabeth remained as opposed to Sally resurfacing. The doctor had waited days for Elizabeth to return, and she wanted to start the process of keeping Sally subdued. It was crucial that Elizabeth remembered the rape. Such a breakthrough would be the catalyst needed for her to start dealing with it as Elizabeth. This would help tremendously in keeping Sally dormant.

"It was my first time there, so I relied on my navigation system as well as a printed map."

"Where did you park? I know that it's quite treacherous for anyone living in NYC, as space in one of our most treasured commodities." The doctor smiled but Elizabeth knew she was right. Traffic and lack of parking in NYC were some of its trademarks.

"I don't know." She looked down and then up again. "I mean I don't remember. I remember a light flashed as I tried to look at street signs but ....I-I-I don't know, I don't' know."

"What is the very last thing you remember Elizabeth?"

"I was there and then two male orderlies came to get me from a psychiatric ward and now I am here with you." She bit her lips, shook her head, and repeatedly brushed her brow. "I don't even know where my car is...I don't know anything. I don't even know what day it is."

"It's May 27th. You were last in East New York on May 18th."

The doctor reached in the folder and pulled out a ticket

22

for moving violation and a picture of the car taken by NYPD cameras.

"The flash you remembered was that of the camera when you ran the red light. Also, we were able to locate your car from the security device you had purchased which enabled others to find you in case the car broke down in a remote area. We also have the license plate and the registration so that made it easy for the cops as well."

"Where's my car now?"

"It's being held as evidence. Diane had been on top of things."

"Doc, are you telling me that I have lost nine days? Nine days?"

"Elizabeth," the psychiatrist exhaled, as losing nine days was the least of Elizabeth's concerns. "I am going to show you a video of a session I had with Sally. But before I do that, there are some things I must tell you."

"I'm listening." Elizabeth folded her arms again, leaned back, crossed the right leg over the left and dangled it.

"What has happened to you is more common than you would like. Multiple Personality Disorder is a complex, bizarre and often mysterious syndrome." She leaned forward and with her index finger pointed upward. "You have two or more distinct personalities occupying the same body. And as in your case, they don't realize when the other personality is taking over."

"I would know if..."

"No, you would not. As I was saying, the most they would remember is that they don't remember, they would feel confused or feel light-headed or faintish."

"So, out of the blue, I develop multiple personalities, is what you expect me to believe."

"No Elizabeth, not out of the blue. You can't recall parking the car because you didn't. You ended up on the wrong street at the wrong time. You last remembered being in your car because that is where you were when you were knocked out by one of the assailants. The video camera showed a young woman approached the car, pretended as if she was seeking your assistance, directed you to turn down your window, and the moment you took your eyes off her, she knocked you out. When you regained consciousness, you were being raped. Like you, most individuals who suffer from multiple personalities, have experienced sexual trauma."

"And to cope, I created another personality who can deal with it?"

"Your psyche parceled out the pain, and had Sally bear what was too much for you to bear." Dr. Klauss felt the intensity from Elizabeth's look."

"So how do I know what she's bearing and what I am?" She grinned uncomfortably.

"You don't. You both have strong psychological separation from each other. You have your own memories, your own allergies, likes, dislikes, sexual orientation. You like men and Sally, for instance likes women."

"Okay, I have heard enough…" She unfolded her arms, uncrossed her legs, and pressed down on her legs with her hands and positioned herself to stand.

"Sit down."

Elizabeth sat.

"Let me finish. You even have your own handwriting and physical abilities. And, not to scare you, in some cases, your own brain wave pattern. You can have one medical condition and when Sally resurfaces, the medical condition is nowhere to be found in Sally and she may or may not have another condition."

"Are you kidding me?" A frightened Elizabeth tried to inhale oxygen.

"What I am trying to stress to you Elizabeth is that you and Sally are as different as you and I."

"Oh my God," Elizabeth whispered, as she slouched back in the chair...She grabbed the neck line of her dress and pulled it towards her face as she attempted to bury her face in it. "Oh my God...Does she know of me?" Her voice sounded faint.

"In this case, and unfortunately yes."

"Why is it unfortunate? Doesn't she like me? We are one and the same for crying out loud." She lifted her head.

"You are not one and the same, and no, she doesn't like you. In fact, she has declared you as her sworn enemy."

"What!" Elizabeth stood hunched and reached for something to brace her fall. "Sworn enemy?"

"She believed and I quote..." Dr. Klauss stood and helped her patient back to her seat. "'If she wasn't such a fool—this kind-hearted, always giving, always smiling, always helping, always trustful fool—this wouldn't have happened to us. She clearly doesn't know how to take care of us so this is why I am here, and this is why I am going to stay here. Someone has to protect us and it is clear that that bitch can't do it,' unquote."

"Am I supposed to be the bitch?" Fury smacked Elizabeth and she sprung to her feet. "This-is-my-body," she spoke with conviction as she tapped her chest with index finger. "Nobody is going to take over anything. Nobody."

"That's very good Elizabeth. Very good. Your determination to fight will help you greatly. The will of the spirit is the most powerful weapon ever given to us. To take on a fight, you need to understand the war and the rules of engagement. When someone is raped, she oftentimes blames herself, so it's not a surprise that Sally blames you."

"So, this is me blaming me. I thought we were two different people." Elizabeth paced the room. "She clearly remembers this so called rape and I don't. How can I be responsible for something I don't even recall happening to me?" She was fluttered. "Answer me Doctor. How?"

"You are not responsible." The psychiatrist remained in her position and spoke in that calm, soothed hypnotic voice. "The person who is violated is never responsible. You never asked or invited it to happen. It was just people engaging in cruel acts randomly."

"Dr. Klauss," The patient raised her right hand and showed her palm, "please...I don't need the you are not the victim speech."

"You are not."

"I know! I wasn't raped!"

"Okay Elizabeth, we will work with that story for now. Why don't we watch the video of a couple of sessions I had with Sally?" She went to the video recorder. She positioned herself sideways as she never turned her back to a patient.

"I wasn't raped. I wasn't raped." Elizabeth sunk in the oversized leather chair and gripped onto her hair at the top of her head while her body steadily began to vibrate at a faster speed. "I wasn't raped."

Then there was silence. The video was still recording. Dr. Klauss repositioned herself in her seat, facing her patient and waited. Her loud exhale broke the silence.

"What's up Doc? I missed ya. Did you miss me?" The patient who sat across her dangled her legs.

"Damn," the psychiatrist murmured to herself, as she was hoping not to see her for a while. "Hello Sally. So good to see you again." She forced a smile. Where have you been?"

"Ahhh shit." Sally commented as she inspected the clothes she was wearing. Sleeveless, knee high sunflower dress with buttons lining the center. "That bitch was here, wasn't she?" She continued to inspect the attire that was on her. "How could she wear this garbage? You see Doc, this is exactly the shit I'm talking about. How the hell does she expect us to walk around the place looking like granny?" Sally exhaled and leaned back. "The shit I gotta put up with." She threw her right leg over the chair's right arm, exposing her underwear. She slouched back. She eyed Dr. Klauss. "You got a cigarette Doc? I could use the hit."

Pow pow pow! The sounds of gunshots brought Elizabeth back to the alley from that dreadful day. She turned around and ran back towards the dumpster. She had accepted the reality thanks to the taped sessions, where she witnessed the emerging of Sally, including the one she had just remembered. She lent herself to treatment for years. It had been few years since she had experienced amnesia. The sudden return of amnesia meant one thing. When she arrived at the dumpster, she reached for the opening of her bag. She prayed that her cellular phone was still there, and it was. Elizabeth dialed.

CHAPTER
FOUR

"Listen you little piece of shit, I will shove my foot right up your ass so fast and then have your balls for breakfast. You're fucking with the wrong cop. Now I am not asking you! I'm telling you to get your ass down here with my goddamn information and don't fuck this one up Samurai! I'm serious; your ass is one fuck up away from Sing Sing!"

"I thought cops were supposed to be nice, lieutenant," Samurai smiled. "I don't think the captain would take this news very well at all. I don't think he would appreciate his lieutenant behaving, how do you put it in this case? Ahhhhh…discourteous, unprofessional, and disrespectful. Isn't your behavior against your code, all that the great NYPD stands for? I mean…"

"Listen you maggot, you got 20 minutes to bring your ass to the precinct, otherwise, you're mine!"

As Samurai heard the clashing of the phone receiver onto its base from the other end, he smiled. He knew that the lieutenant could not have touched him with a 10-foot pole. Samurai was the Confidential Informant, a private citizen who secretly worked for the cops. He gathered and provided them with information that assisted them in their case against Sambino, the infamous and elusive drug dealer. Samurai was also the Brooklyn's District Attorney's main witness in a murder case. Like Lt. Smith, the prosecutor to that case, Carlitta Davis had little patience for Samurai. He was the only one who had detailed information about the murder of Cassandra Willis. In exchange for assisting the cops and for his testimony, the District Attorney agreed to grant him immunity from his drug-related charges. Samurai never quite grasped how is it that cops were aware that he was even in Sambino's circle, and he feared it may be only a matter of time before the feds would be on him too. As appetizing as the offer was that he took, Samurai still preferred to go to jail. He felt that he would have had a chance of survival, especially because he would have gained respect from his fellow inmates for not snitching. Despite how miserable an existence jail would have been, it would have been better than the harsh death he would have faced as soon as he left the witness stand and walked away a free man. No one testified against the infamous Sambino and walked free. Samurai knew that. He did not want Sambino to make an example out of him. The witness protection program was at least a slim possibility at a decent life. Despite his reluctance, Samurai headed to the precinct to report on the little he knew regarding Sambino.

"Hey you!" Samurai yelled at a nearby cabbie and ran to the cab. As the car stopped, he jumped in the back seat. "Franklin and DeKalb, please. Take…"

"I know you're not trying to tell me how to do my job."

"I'm not trying to tell you how to do your job man I'm just…"

"Trying to tell me how to get there. I know. That's telling me how to do my job. I've been driving cabs for eight years now and I know my way around Brooklyn. I don't need no goddamn directions."

"Well excuse the fuck outta me. You know what your problem is? Your problem is you've been driving cabs for eight years." The car screeched.

"Get out."

"What!"

"Get the fuck out, you fucking asshole."

"Hey," Samurai exited the cab, "if you hate your life so much, make use of the Brooklyn Bridge and jump, mother fucker, jump."

"That would be five bucks asshole!"

"Bitch, you drove two fucking blocks, then tell me to get the fuck out and you want my five bucks? Fuck you."

Samurai proceeded to the front of the car, turned to the driver and gave him the middle finger.

"Hit me motherfucker," Samurai said. "Hit me. That's what I thought." He crossed the street in an attempt to catch another cab. He had 12 minutes to get to the precinct. It was not that he cared if he was late, he just did not feel like hearing Lt. Smith's mouth and that was all he had, mouth.

"You piece a shit!" The cab driver screamed out from across the street.

Samurai smiled, shook his head and hailed the approaching cab. This time he gave only the address, "as quickly as you can please."

The cab pulled up at the precinct as Samurai instructed.

Samurai gave the cabbie a 10-dollar bill, thanked him and exited the cab. He was well dressed in straight black plaid cotton pants, a black cotton two-button blazer, and a medium grey short sleeve collared cotton shirt that was tucked inside his pants. The zinc buckle illuminated the smooth leather belt that fit perfectly in the pants. Although his shiny polished loafer shoes were also black, the hand stitched thread was conspicuous. His skin was smooth and slightly tanned, and he was about five feet ten. His straight black hair was slicked back. His Italian watch carried a stainless steel bracelet and face, with three additional time zones depicted within it. For cologne, the scent was subtle and masculine. Although night had fallen, he was wearing oversized shades that hid the Japanese eyes he inherited from his mother. Samurai lived on the Upper West Side across from Central Park in Manhattan. He was the older of two boys of an affluent family. For some reason, Samurai liked to live on the edge. His brother always told him it was because he was bored with life that he chose the life he now lives. Samurai agreed. He walked into the precinct with confidence and arrogance. He informed the officer at the front desk that Lt. Smith was expecting him. The officer directed him to have a seat. He was waiting for at least 20 minutes. *That asshole Smith has me waiting out here on purpose just to piss me off. That mother fucker knows I'm out here and he's just gloating at the fact that I'm waiting for his ass.* As Samurai waited, a cop hauled a young man inside the waiting area.

"Yo!" Samurai yelled. "Whatever it is, don't say a word man, just be cool."

The cop looked at Samurai and addressed the other

officer at the desk. "Who the hell is that?"

"Lt. Smith's people," the other officer answered paying Samurai no mind. The cop began talking to the young man he had hauled inside.

"Hey!" Samurai continued. "You don't have to answer any questions man. Tell him to read you your rights, demand to see one of those things, I think they call dem lawyers, and then tell him to kiss your ass."

"Shut your mouth," the officer who was at the desk now walked toward Samurai.

"Yo, if he is not pressing charges, tell him I say to kiss your ass."

Samurai loved taunting cops. He was rich. Both his parents were respected attorneys, especially because of their handsome contribution toward the war against drugs in Bedford Stuyvesant, Brooklyn. Samurai knew his rights. The cop was approaching him when a man approximately six feet tall, medium build came out.

"Don't even waste your time on him, he's a jackass," Lt. Smith said.

"Is this impropriety from the NYPD that I'm seeing? Noooooooo." Samurai's lips widened. "Good night Lt. Smith," Samurai stood. "You look well."

"Shut up." Lt. Smith headed upstairs to his office. When they arrived, he directed Samurai to a seat. Lt. Smith's salt and pepper short cut hair went well with his rugged facial look. His chiseled chin and low cut mustache complemented his beardless medium brown long face. Although he was in his late 40's, his lean, six feet built stature made him appear younger. His sex appeal was evident given that he communicated more with the eyes than with words. His gun in his shoulder holster was in plain view as he was not wearing a jacket or blazer over his button down long sleeve striped shirt.

"Listen up," Lt. Smith addressed Samurai. "It's a busy night. I'm already in a bad mood from the acquittal of a drug dealer based on tech-ni-ca-lity. And I don't know why I was surprised, given this note. He took out the note and read it, *"You will lose based on tech-ni-ca-lity. Sambino."* Clearly, we tried to trace this and it's a dead end, so the last thing I need is a smartass criminal in my face. Now — sit down."

"Lieutenant, where are your manners? You are supposed to ask me if I would like some coffee, juice perhaps, for crying out loud, at least share the donut. I know you got some donuts up in here." Samurai noticed that the Lieutenant was not smiling. "Oh come on, that was very funny."

"What's funny is the jail cell you'll be looking at if you don't start talking."

"The humor of the N-Y-P-D." Samurai leaned back in the chair with both hands clasped behind his head. Smith stared at him with a smile nowhere in sight. Samurai leaned forward, removed his hands from his head and placed them on the table. "There's a shipment coming in next week."

"And?"

"It's coming in next Friday, bags of cocaine disguised as flour."

"Alright, go on."

"The shipment is going to that mini market on the corner of DeKalb Avenue and Pulaski Street."

"Bed-Stuy," Smith said softly and clenched his teeth as he looked down to the floor. He looked up and stared seriously at Samurai.

"He will then send someone to go to the maestro in charge there to buy flour." These words caused the lieutenant face to crinkle. "The maestro," Samurai continued, "you know, the guy in charge, the owner of the store, Señor Vasquez." Samurai spoke to the lieutenant in a manner slow enough to suggest the lieutenant was mentally challenged. The lieutenant was not amused. "Señor Vasquez is involved in the operation reluctantly. He either assists with a smile or his mini-market will be robbed accidentally on a daily basis or all his customers will be coincidentally harassed. Either way, his mini-market will tragically go out of business. Or worse, he may accidentally lose his life, if nothing else to ensure that he doesn't talk."

"Elaborate. Who is this *he* that sends someone to do his dirty work?" Samurai leaned back with a smile on his face as he stared at the lieutenant.

"You know, you are a funny man lieutenant."

"Am I?"

"Yeah, you are. Where is that donut, juice, something? I would go for cocaine myself but I know that it's illegal and all. Besides, if you give me some right here from your private stash then we'll know you're taking it for sure, because you have got to be high if you think I'm going to give you that information…."

Lt. Smith flew across the desk, grabbed Samurai and threw him against the wall.

"Before you threaten me officer, please note that though I am half-Japanese, I have a black belt in Korean Tae Kwan Doe.

I am allowing you to physically abuse me so I can sue your ass and the police department for, how do they put it? Yeah, assault and battery, police misconduct, whatever my parents can think of." Samurai eyes danced.

"Don't think for one second that I won't bust you Sammy," the lieutenant went face to face with Samurai.

"Oh come on," Samurai took the officer's hand off him and got out of his way. "You and I know better than that. To bust me, you need probable cause, which you'll never find, because I only have information, I'm not the information. Listen, the deal was I give you info on the guys who are making the crack directly and then selling it to the dealers who give it to their guys on the street. That's a major bust. You can put some undercover cops as the dealers who buy the crack and give it to the guys to sell on your street corners. That's access to three levels of drug dealing. If they don't get the cocaine, they can't make the crack," he paused, "and it can't trickle down to your," he paused again, "how do you say it? That's right – your people."

Anger clothed Smith. "Trust me wise ass when I say this, your days are numbered..."

"Are we finished here?" Samurai admired his manicured nails.

"No, we are not. Who are these guys that are going to buy the cocaine?"

"They work for Mad Dog. Legal name, Pierre Washington, place of residence 200 Bainbridge Road in Bedford Stuyvesant. He owns the entire Brownstone so there's no issue of harassing other tenants. His business, where he makes the crack, is located in his basement and on his first floor. The second and third floors make up his residence. As for the guys, they vary so you will have to stake out and see who's doing what. They vary from male to female, child to adult. Sometimes, one of his men will pull a kid over and pay him ten dollars to go in the store and ask for Vasquez. He'll say the password of the day and Vasquez will know what to give the kid. They usually purchase it during opening hours so it's less suspicious. They also purchase it over an extended period, maybe a month or weeks, because you can't purchase all that flour at once without people asking questions. Vasquez makes sure he is in the store on those days."

"Why flour, the dogs can sniff through that. And who the hell uses flour?"

"It's not flour when the distributor gets it, especially when the distributor is in Flushing, 10 minutes away. When it leaves the distributor to Vasquez, it's flour. It has to be something that sells in his shop. This time around it's flour. Next time, it will be something else. It's usually a spontaneous decision to avoid the routine." Samurai's cell phone alarmed. It reminded him of the phone call he needed to make.

"What's this distributor you are talking about?"

Samurai took a deep breath, closed his eyes for a few seconds, reopened them, leaned back in his chair, clasped his hands and stared at the lieutenant.

"Yes, that's right mother fucker," the Lt. said, "break it down to me like I am a two year old."

"The cocaine is taken to a manufacturer warehouse which is where the stash house conveniently is located. Who takes it there, I don't know. When it's taken there, I don't know. How it gets there, I don't know. All I know is that it is taken to one particular manufacturer. It is packed amongst some of the manufacturer's product, which makes it almost impossible to detect the drugs. When the distributor gets it, it is repackaged into one of the products that Vasquez gets from them. Whatever product that is, that is what Pierre's people purchase from Vasquez and then take it to Pierre's drug warehouse, his place of residence. It is then processed down to crack, at least some of it, sold to the dealers one step down the hierarchy, who then give it their boys to sell on your street corners."

"How does Vasquez know how the cocaine will be packaged by the distributor?"

"He is given a phone call with the information and instructions the week of its arrival."

"From whom?"

"I don't know. Now, if it's not too much to ask, may I leave now, lieutenant?"

"Yeah, get out. Don't leave the country or the state. I'll be contacting you."

"Yes sir," he saluted. As he left the room, he addressed the incoming officer. "Make sure the lieutenant learns some manners and has some kind of refreshment ready to offer his guests," Samurai smiled. He went down the stairs, said good night to the officers in the front and exited the building. When he was several blocks away from the precinct, he made a phone call.

"Yeah, the bust is going down, so we'll be able to move in on his territory." The other person cleared his throat. Samurai knew to hang up the phone. Samurai's thoughts went to Lt. Smith. He had made it his duty to study Lt. Smith. He knew after this last session that the lieutenant most likely stayed in his office, sat at his desk, and chewed on his toothpick. Samurai knew the lieutenant was trying to figure out how to discover whatever it was that Samurai was not saying. Samurai enjoyed the fact that the lieutenant never really could figure out how Samurai knew all the information that led to the drug busts. He certainly didn't know how he knew so much about this one either, especially when it came to key players, where Samurai was usually clueless. He was aware of Lt. Smith's mistrust. From Samurai's background research on the lieutenant, he discovered that he had a degree in psychology and criminology and he was committed to bringing change in his community by being directly involved, hence, the police officer position. Bedford Stuyvesant was there for him when his family needed a home and he would be there for Bedford Stuyvesant when it needed him. The lieutenant believed he had some kind of control over the madness that existed in his community. He believed in getting to the root of the problem so he could stop it from surfacing. He was convinced that if he understood the psychology of the people who lived in his neighborhood and the psychology of the people who assisted in "suppressing" them, then he would be a step ahead of the madness. Drugs were supposedly the madness and so Lt. Smith's area of expertise was narcotics. Samurai smiled at the "savior" in Lt. Smith. What the lieutenant didn't know was that he had another madness he had yet to truly experience, a charismatic, wealthy young tyrant named Samurai.

CHAPTER

FIVE

Diane's vibrating phone caused her purse to dance on the coffee table in front of her. She looked at her watch. It was eleven at night. With hesitance, she opened her purse. She noticed the name on the caller ID. Diane paced the room, her body swaying.

"No Liz, I am not in the office. I am actually at Michael's place for the night spending quality time. I promise that I will try to spend less quality time with Michael, and more with you... starting next year," Diane said sarcastically.

"I woke up a couple of minutes ago behind a dumpster, naked. I was lying on the ground. I am yet again, in a strange place with no recollection of getting here."

Diane listened to the familiar story. It took only a few seconds to explode.

"God damn it Liz, not again!" Her flying hand knocked the nearby vase to the floor. She stooped and lowered her head. The greatness of her pain impeded a high pitch voice from prevailing. "This shit is ridiculous." She searched desperately for the words. "Liz... maybe... she took you there. You know Sally, maybe... she had dealings over there and..."

"You mean dealings like a hooker. I checked over the area for any evidence to prove that Sally was here, but there is nothing."

"Maybe you missed something Liz..."

"Diane, there are no cigarettes. There is no red lipstick or any lipstick. There are no loose bills and that is how Sally likes her bills. I am in the heart of a Red Light District, and I am telling you that this is definitely Sally. She is known for leaving me in Red Light Districts. So, where are her things? Let me see something, anything."

"How on God's Earth do you investigate the scene in the same manner as a detective would have as opposed to someone who is emotionally entangled in the situation? As always, I remain flabbergasted by your calmness and nonchalant attitude..."

"I don't see why she can't go to an escort service like every other normal decent person. Is that too much to ask? I am sick and tired of her constantly putting my life in danger."

"Yeah, the escort service is a little bit cleaner and safer... Hold on. We can't just discuss this calmly. This is a serious situation, and..."

"D, I'll talk to you later. I have to go home and clean up and get some sleep."

"Liz, try and figure out what it is that she wants, why is she back and..."

"Say hi to Michael for me."

Before Diane knew it, Elizabeth had already hung up the

phone. Diane was always amazed by the strength of her friend. Maybe to Elizabeth, Sally was just another part of her everyday routine. Diane had always warned Elizabeth that if she didn't kill Sally, Sally would kill her. Diane also knew that Elizabeth was always the savior instead of the killer.

Michael's entry into the living room interrupted Diane's thoughts. She watched as he noticed the broken vase, and ignored it. He took off his shirt and threw it on the sofa. The six-foot one, lazy dark brown eyes, rugged facial hair, Caesar haircut, chiseled face, plump lips, firm body and buttocks, chocolate complexion man walked over to the bar next to the kitchen, grabbed a glass and slowly mixed some vodka with some of his coffee liqueur.

"What's going on Diane?"

"Sally has decided to return to cause havoc in Liz's life again."

"That's fucked up. I tell you there's nothing like this drink right here." Michael walked back to the living room and sipped his favorite drink. He loosened his pants button and sat down on the sofa.

"That's all you have to say?" Disgust swept Diane's face.

As far as Michael was concerned, any response at all was an improvement toward coming face to face with the humanity that always managed to have escaped him. A response showed some sort of care, even if it was a lack thereof. Born in Bedford Stuyvesant, Brooklyn, to a pimp and a prostitute, with five other children's mouths to feed, Michael had to grasp fairly quickly, skills of surviving life on the streets, especially when such life had with it the power to increase his family's "wealth."

Determined to assist in supplementing the food stamps and other governmental assistance that his family relied upon, he began hustling at the age of eight. He worked as an errand boy for junkies and other of societies' *undesirables* by earning 50 cents for every food, cigarette or liquor purchased. He kept an eye on the pimps and drug dealers' rides and alerted them of any wrong doing for a moderate fee of two dollars. He served as security detail for the ladies of the night, by standing outside of the doors of the apartments where they were performing service. Should he hear the secret password from the ladies indicating danger, his job was to alert the pimps so the situation could be handled. That task would cost his employer about $10. Due to the reputation of dependability and trustworthiness that Michael had earned, the scope of his duties extended to engaging in the purchasing and transporting of cocaine from nearby dealers to the pimps. It was essential that the working girls remained "coked up" in order for them to work their 16 -18 hour shifts. Michael at times easily earned at least twenty five dollars in a day's work. At that young age, he knew he valued money, and he knew he valued a freedom that could have only come with money. He saw the prison in which his family lived—the prison of can't be doing that, or can't be possessing that because of lack of funds. He saw how people feared his employers, and he liked that. He needed that. *"Respect must be earned, Shorty. It's better to have them fear you than love you. After all we hurt the ones we love, right?"* One of his employers at that some point counseled him. He noticed that those who engaged in fear were the ones who labor for his employers' benefit. They appeared weaker as if always seeking permission to breathe, to exist. He noticed that he was different. He stood out, as he was fearless. The image of helplessness invoked disgust in the eight-year-old, and he vowed never to appear weak before anyone. Never to be like his father, who became a pimp and who traded what little ambition he had for heroin, which had established a relationship with his veins. A callous attitude grew toward those who possessed that trait. A callous attitude grew toward those that reminded him of his father. The man whose body he noticed in the gutter foaming at the mouth, and with tears in his eyes, but conviction in his soul, ten year old Michael, stepped on over and kept on walking. *Dumb motha fucker.*

"Michael, I am talking to you," Diane tried to disregard his rudeness when he tuned her out.

"That's all I have to say."

"Well thanks for nothing Michael. As always we can count on you for your compassion."

"You are welcome."

"Why the hell are you so cold? Where the hell is your humanity? She's your friend..."

"She's your friend who I know, and she's weak. Sally coming back means that Liz has lost the fight and I don't care for losers. Damn, I love this drink."

"You are such an asshole." Hastily, she walked towards the exit of the living room, passing the sofa. Almost immediately, she felt Michael's leg extended. She tripped. She crinkled her face as she stood. "What the hell are you doing?"

"Let's have sex." Michael twirled his glass, as he appreciated his drink.

"Are you out of your mind? How the hell can you think

44

of sex in a time like this? I just told you that Sally is back and…"

"And what?" Michael placed his glass of drink on the coffee table, stood up and faced Diane. "Why should Sally stop me from getting my freak on with my girl? I'm sure Sally got her freak on tonight with her girl."

"You bastard!" Diane leapt towards Michael and threw her palm towards his right cheek. He caught her wrist.

"You don't want to do that sweetheart," he pushed her away from him. "Don't get too comfortable, D. You are slipping."

"What the hell happened to you? You used to be a human being at one time." Diane stared him up and down. She stared at the stoned face man who in an instant appeared to have been gone.

By the age of ten, Michael had earned the nickname Stony, as he never carried a smile. He didn't find that there was much to smile about. He was on a mission to be elevated to the "respect" level and he couldn't do that smiling. He had managed to develop key traits of a businessman rather quickly. *I'm never in a business to lose.* He would take some of the monies he had earned and invested it for 100% profit.

"Listen up," he stood in front of his fifth grade class. The candy vending machine broke and it's gonna remain broke, so I'm the new candy vending machine. Whatever you need, I have, and if I don't have it, then you will get what I have." Stony made it a point to break the machine in an effort to kill his competition and he will continue to do so until he deemed otherwise. *Always remove the competition. Monopoly was the way to go.*

"Well how much for that candy right there?" A little girl pointed toward some candy in a purple wrapper.

"One dollar."

"One dollar? It's 50 cents in the store."

"So go to the fucking store and get it then."

That sales pitch proved effective as no kid wanted to wait until the end of school to get what must be had immediately. Stony's determination and uncompromising business deals followed him to high school. Time was money, but important as it was the most valued possession, as it was designed never to repeat itself.

"How old are you?" 15 year old Michael approached his 10th grade math teacher after class, who was erasing the board. She looked like an older teenager.

"Now Michael, I don't think that's any of your business, do you?" She dusted the chalk off her hands and turned to him with folded arms.

"Why you defensive, I'm only asking you your age."

"I'm not defensive…"

"You folding your arms, you defensive, but whatever… do you. Listen, I'm thinking, you finished college about 22, 25 or so, and you probably earning about 27 or 30k a year give or take as this clearly is your first teaching job."

"What the hell is that supposed to mean?" She now held each of her side with the respective hand.

"I'm not trying to insult you or anything…I'm just saying it's fucked up how you spent all these years studying, to end up making what you make to deal with fuck-ups like me who don't give a shit about what you are trying to teach us, and I say trying

46

because you do a piss poor job at it…"

"Excuse me?" She leaned back to the right with a crinkled face.

"You are excused. You are a math teacher. You ought to know that the numbers you earn don't add up to freedom."

"What?" She pouted forward.

"I'm just saying that your pathetic life has become my inspiration."

With his teacher being an added inspiration, Michael set out to make no less than 30k a month and soon no less than 30k a week. He knew the platform from which he would begin his reign. *Like father like fucking son*, he thought to himself. That day, he sat on the stoop of his steps. He hadn't done so since he was about eight. He used to sit with his mom and watched her as she begged for pennies knowing that she would have likely received dimes, nickels and even bills instead. It propelled him to his first job, working for society's "undesirables." From his stoop, he watched the prostitutes, one in particularly named Mary Jane. She was about eight years his senior, but that has never stopped Stony from achieving his aim. He noticed that she was working increasingly less, and that most of her time was spent at her pimp, Clemmie's side, in his car, as his prized trophy. He was noticeably about 40 years her senior. She was the crowned jewel in his stable as his customers often vowed a particular "high" after receiving services from her, and so he increasingly wanted her for himself. Clemmie named her Mary Jane—the natural high. Stony knew to begin a stable of his own, he needed a product like Mary, and he needed the competition gone. He strolled over to Clemmie's car where Mary Jane was massaging his hands. Stony noticed the car's custom made white leather interior. He walked up to the car, and without giving Clemmie a second look, and with his right hand thrust in his front pocket and his legs apart with his trademark stone look, he spoke the words to Mary that would become the foundation for his mini empire.

"That's a waste of motha fucking time for somebody with your talent," Stony said unapologetically. Clemmie swiftly turned around and sliced his left forehand with a razor. Stony let him have that one as he knew that pimp would never have another opportunity to harm him. Before Mary Jane knew it, Stony had a stable of one. From Mary, other girls followed. It wasn't too hard for her to convince the other girls, as like Mary Jane, Clemmie demonstrated his "love" to them by beating them once in a while, leaving longer lasting makeup. Stony's stable led to three apartments, with three bedrooms and basements for his girls to live. He promised them protection and safe keeping, or consequence to those aided in breaching his promise to his girls.

Clemmie learned of what had taken place and decided to make an example out of her. No one was going to leave him and live. Word reached Stony. He went to Clemmie's home, hid in the garden adjacent to the driveway and waited for him to pull up in front of his home. It was customary for Clemmie after he parked to throw his head back and relax a little. The car pulled up and he parked. As he threw his head back, Stony caught it and pulled it with his right hand. He swung his body to the left and faced Mary Jane's former pimp with an automatic 32 caliber.

"You fucked with my business and you fucked with my

money and you fucked with my time. Her time was my time and that's a prized possession I can never regain. Now you get to relax forever motha fucker." Clemmie's brain painted the white leather interior red. His girls walked free from harm. At the age of 15, Michael aka Stony had committed the first of many murders on his way to freedom.

"I feel sorry for you Michael," Diane continued to look him up and down and turned to walk away.

"I didn't know prosecutors had feelings. But okay, I will bite."

"Go to hell Michael."

"I will. That I guarantee you, but before I do that, I need for you to get Otis off."

"My job is to represent the People of the State of New York, not to let criminals roam free."

Michael swung Diane to face him, grabbed her neck and pulled her towards him. "You will do what the fuck I want you to do. And right now you are going to work Otis' case to his benefit. Don't forgot how you became a prosecutor. Need I remind you how law school was possible?"

"I am not doing this right now. What are going to do? Kill me?" She refused to give him the satisfaction of fear. He released his grip and then his hands.

"That's why I like you Diane. You gangster." He stepped back. "Fearless," he smiled. He stripped off her clothes with his eyes. "My kind of girl."

The muscles in Diane's face tightened. Her nose squirmed upward and she squinted her eyes and pouted. Her chest tightened. Her heart began to beat at a fast pace. She was convinced she hated him. He was tolerable once before, but lately, for reasons unknown to him, he was now intolerable to her. She wished she could make him walk away from their relationship, and then things would be perfect. If only she could free herself.

"I think I will spend the night at my own place tonight," Diane said. Michael said nothing. She watched as he sat back down in the sofa. He put his foot up on the ottoman, grabbed the remote control, turned on the TV and sipped on his drink. Diane proceeded to the bedroom and gathered some of her things to leave. In less than five minutes she was at the door.

"What? No good night kiss?" Michael remained fixated on the TV.

"Not tonight." She closed the door behind her with the broken vase still shattered on the floor. She stopped and panicked. She definitely had been daring to Stony lately, and for the life of her, she could not figure out why he had been putting up with it. She brushed it off. Maybe he hadn't noticed, she told herself. It would be hours before she saw or heard from Michael again. She smiled at the thought of it. She decided to enjoy the rest of the night, at least what was left of it.

CHAPTER
SIX

"Hey you!" A driver screamed as he continued to honk the horn trying to get Diane's attention. "Hey, lady, move it! People got places they need to be!"

Diane did not even realize that the red light had turned green. She was still lost in the moments of last night. She didn't make it home. She had had another one of her sessions with her unnamed friend. His sole purpose was to help her to become comfortable with her sexuality, to help her lose her inhibitions because that's what friends were for--to give a helping hand. After all, he was convinced that he was put on this earth, if for nothing else, thanks to be a very good friend to her.

"Get off the goddamn road!" The driver sped and aligned his car next to hers and pointed his middle finger on his left hand. He then sped up in front of her.

Diane, get a hold of yourself.

She tried not to go 31 miles per hour where the speed limit read 30. She was still in heat from last night and quite elated from the fact that she had finally found the one person it seemed, who was able to transform her into this woman who did things she didn't even imagine in her fantasies. She had finally learned the meaning of ecstasy. The vibrating cell phone interrupted her thoughts.

"Hi hon, what's up?" Diane's face lit. She was even more elated to hear from Elizabeth given last night's situation.

"Nothing much, just calling to see if you and Michael wanted to join Roberto and I tonight. He's throwing another party at his place." Elizabeth yawned.

"Where are you and how many parties is he going to throw? I don't know Liz, I mean I am tired and…" Diane tried hard to find an excuse. She hated Roberto's parties because for some reason or the other, she always felt as if the guests were being watched, but she could never prove it.

"I just need someone to talk to so the time will pass quickly. You know Roberto spends most of his time probing his guests, and that in itself takes all night as he considers it rude not to personally entertain everyone individually."

"Don't you find that strange?"

"Not particularly. Roberto has always been intense in a warm and welcoming way. He let others in and so in his mind, he probably views it as normal to engage in plenty of small talk."

"To each his own I guess. Maybe that's the immigrant in him." Diane joked.

Roberto Garcia was from Managua, Nicaragua. His soft but firm appearance was one of his most attractive qualities. He too was approximately six foot one with a lean body firm as steel. His dark brown curly hair somehow complemented his smoothed honey glazed skin. He too was manicured as is expected of any socialite. The innocent smile he wore lit the eyes of even gentlemen in his presence, much less the ladies. Chivalry and pleasantry were considered current events as opposed to things of the past as far as Roberto was concerned. His accent had a little twang to it given that he was educated abroad as most of the elite in Nicaragua usually were. Roberto, like many of America's visitors, was an investor in this land of opportunity. He had an import and export business that he had established a few years ago, and of course with the financial backing of established friends, it was doing quite well. These parties, inevitably, were simply other ways for Roberto to expand his business by discovering who may be in need of his services and to ensure that the clients of those he served were also satisfied. He was a modern day businessman who believed business and pleasure were as intertwined as the woven thread in any fabric.

"Or maybe it has nothing to do with him being an immigrant Diane, but rather because he's been here, he has picked up some of our friendly habits."

"Roberto engaged in lots of small talk Liz…he reads you like a book…you think that's common in our culture?"

"Yep. In this country Diane, our culture is to look each other in the eye when we communicate. Anything short of that is deemed untrained."

"Yeah well in Brooklyn, looking at someone too long can get you killed."

"Well lucky for us, Ms. Prosecutor, who has lost all faith

in mankind, this party is not on the streets."

"With all the who's who of crooks that will be there, it might as well be."

"Michael's past doesn't necessarily make him a crook today and that doesn't mean those on the VIP list will be either."

"All I know Liz, is that birds of a feather flock together and I am going to pay particular attention to the guest list and then look in the papers or watch the news the following weeks. Guarantee we will see a color photo of someone who was at that party but this time he will be headed to another party to be held at Sing Sing." Diane laughed.

"Or she."

"Whatever," Diane was no longer amused. "We will be there. Not that we have a

choice. He and Michael are bosom buddies."

"That they are, and so are you and I. You'll have a great time, you'll see. And no one will be watching you. It's all in your mind. Just like whatever it was that made you turn ghostly when I first introduced you to him."

Diane remembered that she stopped dead in her tracks, when she met Roberto. *There's no way...it's him. He's real after all. She had told Michael of the out of body experience she had when she noticed this man looking at her from a park bench, but she hadn't experienced that sunken feeling before, so she hurried away. In her mind, she thought it was an angelic being of some sort, but as time has revealed, he was just a man.* She happily changed the topic. "Listen Liz, about Sally...if you want to meet up with me and talk, I can cancel my..."

"No, D, thanks though, I gotta run. I gotta get home and

take care of something. I really can't answer any questions now so I'll catch up with you later."

"Alright Liz, later."

"Later."

Diane knew that she and Elizabeth could have always counted on each other. They'd been friends since college, and they were going to die that way. They were the kind of friends that could have called each other and said nothing on the phone but breathed, and each would have instantly known that something was wrong. Most of the time, they had a good guess at it. Unknown to Elizabeth, Diane shared that relationship with another. She looked at her phone to see who was causing it to vibrate this time. She took a deep breath, swallowed hard, drove over to the side of the road, put the car in park, turned it off, put her head back against the seat, closed her eyes, and put the phone to her ear.

"Hello." Each conversation with her unnamed friend transformed her into this person only he was able to create. All she knew was that she became lighter than a feather, and she soared to the highest peak whenever she thought of him, much less heard the sound of his voice. Whenever he gave her lessons, the fire from their passion burned so deeply, Diane always stayed in heat until the next session.

"Hi," he whispered back softly. "Can you talk?"

They had an understanding. If she was with company, she would have remained silent or made some unrelated statement so he knew to get off the phone instantly.

"All day long if you desire." There was a long pause. She wanted to say something but the words couldn't find themselves in the open.

"What's the matter Diane?"

"Nothing."

"What's the matter?"

It was moments such as this that she wished he didn't know her so well. They were so in tune with each other, it was criminal. They had become close confidants. They were there for each other if there was news to be shared, or if someone needed a listening ear. They were as comfortable with each other as they were with themselves, if not even more comfortable. With each other, they did no wrong; they passed no judgment. Each time she left his house, she remembered that she used to play and laugh that heavily at one point in her life. She remembered it happened when she was 10 years old.

"I had another argument with Michael and it just crossed my mind briefly, that's all. So, how are you?"

"I am the same as you left me last night. Great. What was the argument about?"

"Sex," she painfully lied, "among other things."

"I'm listening."

"He thinks I'm different and I tell him he's different, stuff like that."

"Is he?"

"Yes. In order to enjoy myself with him, I have to bring my imagination to life."

"Does he suffer from the same thing you do?" The friend was rather curious.

"No, he doesn't need to imagine anything. Hello, have you seen me lately?" Diane laughed, as she remarked on her highly complimented body.

"Yes, as a matter of fact, I have," he signaled a grin. "Has he tried touching you in places that make you crawl like a spider?"

"Oh, so now you are an expert on the female body."

"No, just yours," he said in such a sexy tone. She almost jumped out of her seat.

"Shut up," she giggled like a kid. "Anyways," she continued, "I should not be discussing my intimate moments with my man with you. You don't discuss your intimate moments with your lady with me."

"That's because I don't have a lady. I'm in a non-committed relationship and she knows that. I have expressed to her in no uncertain terms, that we are just kicking it. If someone comes along for her, hey she goes; if someone comes along for me, hey I go. We will give each other advanced notice. Otherwise, what he does, she does, what I do, I do."

"But, you know she only sees you, and what the hell do you mean advanced notice? What is she, a job which requires two week notice before quitting? You'll give her time to find somebody else?"

"I am ignoring that statement, and I have been seeing only her till you started treating me like your little five dollar whore."

"Two dollar and I'm not seeing you. You are just helping me explore my sexuality, so I can decipher..."

"What it is you like or don't like. Yes, I forgot. But you and I know that you lose your inhibitions with me simply because I am the forbidden fruit. Most importantly, Diane, I have become the forbidden fruit because something has happened to either you or Michael in the relationship that has caused you to seek the apple no longer from within."

"Well that's not really true, I…"

"Yeah it is," he paused. "Diane," he called almost as if in a whisper.

"What," she answered nervously. She felt that whatever he would say next she wouldn't be able to handle.

"Michael is not your problem. You are. He is not the reason why I am fulfilling a void in your life. You have chosen this route to mask your problems which will one day create for me much drama than I cared to have, but that's a consequence with which I have chosen to live. You on the other hand, need to deal with whatever demons are haunting you. Demons don't leave because you wear a mask."

Diane remained quiet as she continued to listen to her friend. Diane sensed that her friend knew there was something that she was not saying. Whatever it was went much deeper than the reasons she gave. With her personality, she would have bounced the relationship a long time ago. Something didn't seem right and she knew her friend would have played along. She admired that he didn't really mind if she didn't go to him totally, as long as she was happy even if it was with someone else.

"Are you afraid to leave Michael?"

"I am afraid of no one."

"I didn't ask if you were afraid of him. I asked if you were afraid to leave him. You are behaving like someone who is emotionally abused, whether it is self-inflicted or otherwise."

"Don't psychoanalyze me. I resent that statement,"

Diane tried to command some respect.

"You can resent it all you want, that's the great thing about this country, you can do many things."

"I love him."

"Let me save you the time for coming up with some over polished reasons as to why you have allowed yourself to stay in a relationship where there is clearly no sign of happiness, not now, not in the remote future it seems."

"I'mmmm hap-py," she struggled.

"That's why when you were moaning last night and you looked down, it was my eyes you met and not his?"

"I'm not having this conversation."

"Of course you're not. It's too real. It reminds you of your harsh reality. I'm telling you this as your friend."

"Yeah, the friend who told me he has never had another connection with another woman the way he has with me. The friend who knows every intimate detail of my body." Diane's voice steadily grew.

"Don't get it twisted, I am a man. I can fuck you today and love you all over and the next minute, tell you to get the fuck out and mean it. Why? I have mastered the ability to separate my emotions to know that one has nothing to do with the other. I have never felt the way I do about you for anyone before. Shit, that day when you bumped into me, our eyes locked. I knew you were mine. Fuck who you think your man was or was going to be, I knew at some point, whether it was the lifetime before, this one, or the next, you were mine or will be mine, even if it was for one moment."

Diane was instantly soaked between her legs. Everything

about this man turned her on. His attitude, his aggression, and his non-apologetic personality. *She* was taken back to the last time they had lunch at her favorite Italian restaurant on Montague Street in Brooklyn. *The restaurant was dimly lit and sparsely occupied. Diane perused through the menu as her friend attended to his email via his phone.*

"In all the places we've been, what's your favorite meal?" She asked casually.
His fingers tapped away on the mini keypad, as he kept his eyes fixed on the screen of his phone.

"How about when I laid you down and plastered your body with honey and devoured you?"

"Please stop…" Diane felt the warm rush shoot up her body.

"How about when you sipped on the wine, and I swallowed it from your mouth?"

"For the love of God…" Diane pressed her hand against her chest and smiled awkwardly at the waitress who was approaching. She felt as she was going to burst.

He finished his email and closed his phone. He placed it on the table. He leaned back and reached for his wine. "Counselor, you shouldn't ask questions for which you do not want the answers."

Diane exhaled.

She gathered herself and returned to the conversation at hand. She tried to think of a response that would let him know that he was not in control. It didn't work. She has never gotten one up over on him. She just wasn't quick enough. He was quiet most of the time observing and listening. She could not get anything past him. Diane was silent.

"Look Diane, I know it seems like I'm biased because it's hard to conceive that I can make love to you and then objectively tell you that you need to leave your relationship for your sanity, but I know when something doesn't smell right and this has garbage all over it." Diane succumbed in silence. He was right. "And I am officially leaving this alone."

She loved talking to her friend. He always gave her clarity though she never did anything with it. He always told her what she already knew but still needed to hear. She never admitted to him that their friendship gave her strength. She saw him as a *"necessary evil"* in her life. When they were alone, she was simply a woman, one who was loved and adored. She longed to be that woman constantly. At times, he simply stared at her. She then dropped whatever it was that she was doing, walked over, got on her knees and without saying a word, made him thank God he was a man. He had that kind of spell over her. She was everything she wanted to be when she was with him. She was convinced that her true self existed only with him. He was that push she needed to love herself. How could something that felt so right be so wrong?

Diane gladly changed the topic. "I have to go to another party tonight and I am simply not in the mood."

"Am I seeing you before or after?"

"Who said you are seeing me at all?" She blushed.

"So am I seeing you before or after?"

"I'll be at your place around five," she tried to figure how much time she really had to get all her errands done.

"Tell your friends I said hello."

"Oh, so you are a comedian now?" She giggled.

"Good bye Diane."

"Goodbye."

CHAPTER
SEVEN

Agent Kramer had to attend to one small detail before meeting up with that certain woman. Roberto Garcia was having another of his parties tonight and everything must be in top shape. Much progress had been gained since Roberto arrived on the scene and Agent Kramer was not going to let his guard down at this stage of the game. Taking no precautions, he checked to ensure that the consumer's market state-of-the-art bug detector was still unable to uncover the covert wiretapping he had put in place. It would take a Technical Surveillance Counter Measure Specialist to overtly sweep and scan the premises for any detection of the high level intelligence type of covert eavesdropping used by DEAs and the Federal Bureau of Investigation, the FBIs, in order to uncover what Darius had put in place.

A soft wiretap was in place. With the cooperation of the local cable provider, modification to the software used to run Roberto's telephone service system and his internet was made. The fabulous parties Roberto held would make up for the small inconvenience of going through a secured Wi-Fi for all cell phones usage. The security company which also discreetly provided indoor and outdoor video footage of Roberto's premises also obliged Agent Kramer with that small modification to the software request he had made. In addition to the soft wire-tapping, and wireless video bugs placed in vases, paintings, furniture, ceiling fans, electronic devices and whatever else Darius could think of, basic hard wiretap was securely in placed. Every window and door seal was intercepted. With this, he was able to rest easy knowing that the DEA's presence at the upcoming party would be undetectable to the untrained eye and would require more than a second glance by the trained. It was very unlikely that anyone would conduct a sweep at Roberto Garcia's dwelling, especially at a party.

For his security, Roberto had everyone and their belongings, before entering his apartment, scanned. He took no chances regarding possible danger to himself given his net worth of 450 million. Every guest that had attended any of Roberto's parties was invited and it is commonly known that uninvited guests were rarely seen again. There was one VIP in particular tonight that had Darius' attention--Sambino. Although he would be a guest, he would pay particular attention to Roberto's place as he did any place he attended. If anything was out of order, or was slightly shifted, he would question it, even if it was to himself. And although Sambino threw no party at his place nor invited anyone to his place to ensure the very same thing that has taken place at Roberto's address wouldn't take place at his, he was cautious nonetheless, as he trusted no one. With that, Agent Kramer ensured that all paintings, etc., were just as Sambino last saw them. Roberto's place was immaculate, that of a true gentleman.

Darius looked at his watch. He was expecting a certain woman and so he had to disappear to make him himself ready. In his daily goings and comings as an undercover agent, he had managed to meet someone. He was going to miss her severely. As tragic the circumstances were when he met her, it would be more tragic when he bid her farewell. He knew that even the serenity of the Martha Brae River would not be able to distract him from thoughts of her. Of all the cases, he has done, he was careful not to release his guard in any way.

"Every man has an Achilles Darius," his father once told him. "Be careful yours don't cost you more than you can bear."

"And what do you suppose mine will be, dad?"

"You are only ten, and I can tell that yours will be what has been for most men, a woman."

"A woman?" Darius asked as that was out of left field for him.

"Yes, a woman. When you meet her, the one whose spirit aligns with yours, you will know. Regardless of whether the circumstance is good or bad, you will know. You will know as she will leave you breathless."

His dad was right. Not too long from now, she would leave him breathless alright. For Darius' sake, he hoped his father was speaking of multiple "the one," as he knew a heart wrenching goodbye was inevitable. But the inevitable was not yet here, so he smiled in the moments of now. He smiled at the thought of seeing her again. As twisted as the plots in his life has become, she was the temporary escape from it. There must be a first in everything he thought. A first love, first regret, first failure. She had undoubtedly become his first love—at least that was his only explanation to the giddiness he endured at the thought of seeing her, much less making love to her. In a strange way, he was complete with her. He knew in his heart of hearts, she would be his Trojan Horse in this case. She had become a small distraction that could lead to his ultimate downfall—his first failure.

CHAPTER
EIGHT

Elizabeth could not have waited to get home. She ran inside of her apartment as if her life depended upon it. The person was going to have to wait because there was no way she was going to answer that phone. She went to her top dresser drawer, hastily shuffled her undergarments and lingerie around to find that box that would have sealed her fate in a couple of minutes. She grabbed it, ran to the bathroom, and locked the door. She hastily removed the foil wrapper from the kit and took off the over cap. Elizabeth pulled down her skirt and underwear. As per the kit's instruction, she positioned the absorbent tip underneath her genitals. She watched as her urine saturated it. She placed the test stick on the nearby sink, cleaned herself and anxiously waited outside the bathroom for a few minutes, pacing impatiently by the bathroom door. With unsteady hands, she grasped the knob, turned it and pushed the door opened. She covered her face with both palms and peeped at the test stick through her fingers.

"What the hell do these two straight lines mean?"

Elizabeth stood there confused as to what to believe. She wasn't too bright in the common sense area. After still being confused, she did the test again and the same thing happened. She didn't know if she should have laughed or cried. She was on her way to becoming a mother. Naturally she thought only of Diane. She ran to the phone, dialed her number but received only the voicemail. "D, this is urgent, call immediately upon receipt of this message." Now what? Diane was unavailable. She thought of calling the man responsible, Roberto. How would she break the news to him? Where would she break the news to him? The party, of course. What would she wear? Oh all these things ran through her head. She went to her room and lay down. All this was too much too fast. She stared at the ceiling in hopes that she would see the writing on the wall, literally.

A buzzing sound awakened Elizabeth, and caused her to jump. Was that her phone or her doorbell? After a thought or so, she recognized that it was her phone. She reached across to the nightstand and fumbled for the phone.

"Hey D," she laid back and placed the phone to her ear, while she used the other hand to rub her eyes.

"Did I just wake you?"

"Yep," Elizabeth yawned. She heard a tapping noise from Diane's end of the phone. "Where are you D?" There was silence on the other end of the phone.

"D, where are you and what is that noise?" Elizabeth asked loudly enough to get Diane's attention.

"Sorry Liz, I was a bit distracted. I am in my office."

"Distracted about a case? And that noise isn't you tapping

on your desk by chance is it? Because that would mean that you are nervous and really you shouldn't let a case get to you like this. I mean the mere fact that you are a lawyer means that you are already assured a seat in hell, so get used to it, no need fretting now." Elizabeth smiled. She was proud of her ability to be cynical.

"The asshole nature of Michael I see is rubbing off on you. And, yes, I am tapping on my desk. The most difficult case of my career is literally killing me, and I will not violate the oath I took years ago and share the information of the case with you."

"Why were you distracted?" Elizabeth asked concerned.

"I had reached out to some folks a while back regarding a situation that I desperately needed and still need to be handled."

"And?"

"And I haven't seen any signs of it being handled. I thought I was specific, I mean I even told them of the scar... I was thinking that maybe they were handling the matter and there was no need to …."

"You are babbling Diane. What scar and is it a matter of life or death?"

"Yes, and I'm sorry I can't say anymore."

"I can respect that." Elizabeth sighed. "Did you get my message?" Again, there was no response.

"D!"

"What!"

"What the hell is happening? Can you focus please?"

"I am sorry. Do you think Rebecca is alright? Maybe I should give her a call. Anyways, no I did not get your message. What did it say?"

"Your baby sister, Rebecca is fine Diane and my message said for you to call me pronto. Never mind that, I need to talk to you about something."

"Is it going to be seconds or hours?"

"Years."

"Then we're gonna have to postpone this little chat honey because it is now 4:00 and I am expecting Jim any minute now, and then I still have another meeting at five before I meet up with you guys at 7:00. You don't mind waiting, do you?"

"No, I couldn't do it on the phone anyway. How's that case with Jim?"

"Okay," Diane paused. "You alright, Liz?"

"Yeah, thanks."

"Good. I will see you later then."

"D."

"What?

"Putting aside your case loads, you don't have any secrets from me, do you?"

Diane breathed in and out loudly. "No Liz, of course not." She was quiet. "Don't be ridiculous, I have no worlds to which you are not privy."

"You know what is so interesting about that answer?"

"What?"

"The word worlds. That in itself is very interesting. I never even thought of other worlds to which I may not be privy. I was thinking of secrets in the world that I know of."

"Stop the psycho-analysis. I have had enough for one day."

"Are these worlds of yours going to collide, Diane?"

"Honey, I will talk to you later. I have an appointment for which I cannot be late. And I have to look over this case file quickly before Jim gets here."

"I am sorry I am not as good of a friend that you feel you cannot confide in me about everything."

"I don't know what you are talking about. I will see you later, love you. Bye." Elizabeth heard the click on the other end.

"Bye," she said to the silence.

CHAPTER
NINE

The human component of Darius--the flesh, didn't care at this moment of his father's warning. This new love of his was like a drug and for the first time, he understood addiction, and appreciated all too well all the intellectual arguments against it. First love, first failure, but there was just no way, it could top his first regret, his wife Maria.

It was two months after his wedding day to be exact. Kramer's phone rang. It was Maria's gynecologist.

"Hello."

"Hello, may I please speak to Mr. Darius Kramer?"

"This is he."

"Are you the husband of Maria Kramer?"

"Yes. What's her problem now?"

"Your wife left your name as a contact in case of an emergency, and I can't seem to reach her, so I thought it was appropriate to contact you."

Kramer knew Maria only gave his contact to highlight

she had a husband. He had made it clear that he wanted nothing to do with her, so he could have cared less about an emergency. She had made it clear to him that she didn't care what he wanted.

"Mr. Kramer, as you know, because your wife terminated the pregnancy…"

"What! What did you say?" He remembered he was a trained government agent and he had just failed course one, never reveal what you didn't know. It was too late.
"What did you say?" Kramer asked calmly, as he tightened his fist. The only thing on his mind was murder.

"Ahhhhh," she said slowly. "Mr. Kramer, I am going to go, I apologize. I thought you knew and…"

"Have a nice day doctor." There was silence. He was an instrument that Maria had played. It finally made sense to him that Maria was determined all along to get pregnant by him with or without his permission. It was common knowledge that he never believed in unprotected sex. The memories of Maria where she insisted that he ejaculated in her mouth every time she gave him oral sex now made sense. He always inquired as to why she liked that, and she always responded that it was more pleasure for her. Like a gentleman, he aimed to please his ladies. As usual, he watched her go into the bathroom after sex and then moments later, she always had to leave. He never questioned her as to what she did in there or where she was going. His answer was now clear. He needed confirmation. Kramer recalled how he called his office and asked for the extension of his friend and colleague, Peter and the things that transpired after that phone call.

"This is Peter Viezzer, how may I help you?"

"Meet me at our usual spot," Kramer said hastily.

"Okay, give me…"

"No. I wouldn't ask if it wasn't urgent."

"I am on my way."

Kramer paced back and forth like a mad man. He didn't see Peter when he arrived.

"Kramer," Peter said softly as he tried to get his attention. He pulled his arm. Failing, he yelled.

"Kramer! Darius! What's wrong?"

"I want that bitch dead Peter. Peter, I want her ass to disappear so that not even GOD won't be able to find her."

"Kramer," Peter whispered softly as he felt sympathy for his friend.

"Yeah, yeah, yeah, save the let's talk as friends bullshit. It will be alright when the bitch is no longer breathing." Kramer noticed how Peter became quiet and troubled by the words he had just said. Kramer was such a cool, calm, level headed guy. In fact, this was the first time anyone could have said Darius Kramer was seen angry.

"This is what we are going to do. We're going to roll up on her somehow," he stopped himself. He took a deep breath and faced Peter and said calmly. "Meet me at my home in two hours. Don't be late."

"Kramer."

"Don't worry, Peter, I won't harm a hair on her body. I just need to talk to her and I need someone around to make sure I don't do anything stupid." He knew Peter would go for that instead of what he had planned.

"Alright…two hours."

DEADLY INSTINCTS

They parted. Kramer called Maria on the phone.

"Hi baby," she said jovially, though she knew he hated that.

"Maria, we need to talk. Can you meet me home in an hour?"

"What's this about?" She sounded concerned because Kramer never needed to talk.

"Well I figure, we got off on the wrong foot when we got married and I'm sick of us simply coexisting when we are a married couple. Look, I just think we should try something different. I mean what happened has happened and we did take a vow after all that says for better or for worse. What do you say? You're in?" He knew she would have accepted the idea. He was never moved by the fact that all she ever wanted was for him to love her and accept her and be nice to her. He was a lady's man. He could have looked at a woman and whatever thoughts she had of a man, whether good or bad, were instantly great. He made clear to Maria and everyone else his ethics and how much he valued children. His weak spot would have been his child. He would have done anything for the best interest of his child, even if that meant being with a woman for whom he had no feelings. He regretted exposing his weak spot to Maria.

"I am in," she jumped. "Besides, I'm already home, so I'll just stay put."

"Good."

"I love you Darius."

"I know." He hung up the phone.

Half an hour later, Kramer walked through the door. Maria rushed to him and hugged him as if she hadn't seen him for

75

years. He hugged her back painfully. He removed her body from his as nicely as possible. He noticed that she was wearing one of her sexiest outfits, and one of her most expensive perfumes. He also noticed that she had fixed her hair and applied makeup. He chose not to comment. He walked over to the kitchen. He poured himself some juice to drink.

"What, no beer, honey?" She asked.

"No. I decided since we're pregnant, I should be as supportive as possible and if you can't drink alcohol, it's not fair that I should."

Maria swallowed hard. "Ahhh, baby, that's so sweet." At this point, Kramer realized that because she was no longer pregnant, coincidentally, in about a week or so, she would tell him some story about a miscarriage and how she would need all the emotional support from her husband. Little did she know, he was a step ahead of her.

"So, how are you feeling Maria?"

"A little tired, nausea all the time, you know how it is."

"No, I don't. I am a man." He faked a smile and waited for the moment when he would smile over her grave.

"Of course. Well I am beginning to feel some pain in my uterus. I don't know what's going on but I'll go see the doctor."

"You do that." He looked at his watch and time was going slow.

"Maria," he continued, "every visit from now on I want to go with you. I need to be more involved. I have neglected you in your time of need and it's eating me alive."

"No Darius, don't be silly. I'm fine, really. Besides, if there is any concern then I'll let you know."

"Every woman wants her man to accompany her to the doctor when she's pregnant. She thinks it's cute and he is being sensitive. And here you are telling me not to come. Is there something I should know?"

"You are right. Come if you wish." He knew she was thinking there would be no visits anyway because of the planned miscarriage the following week. That was her style.

"I'll be right back." He walked toward the bedroom.

He kissed her on her forehead as he passed her by. She was elated. Minutes later, he walked back out. Maria approached him with her brightest smile. She reached out to hug him. He grabbed her right arm and swung her around, with her back against his chest, and then with his left hand, he placed the cloth soaked with chloroform over her nose. Her lifeless body swindled to the floor. He then dragged her up onto one of the chairs that sat around the table and tied her to it. He went to get his secret stash of truth serum from his locked trunk in the bedroom. This always seemed to work for him during his undercover duties when it was that time for the truth to make itself known. He now waited for Peter. When Peter arrived, he was awe struck by what he saw. Kramer told him to get over it. Kramer was about to do what he did best--get the truth one way or the other. He slapped Maria across the face to wake her. That worked well because it was about 40 minutes since he knocked her out with the chloroform. She was horrified when she realized what happened. Kramer walked over to her, knelt down next to her arm, tied her left bicep with an elastic band and waited for a good vein to surface.

"Darius, what are you doing? What's going on?" She

was frightened.

"You'll tell me in just a minute," he shuffled through the stash of truth serum. He pulled the needle out. He grabbed the syringe. He walked over to the kitchen and got a large spoon, and walked back to her. He grabbed a chair, dragged it directly in front of her, turned it around so the back of the chair was facing Maria. He sat down on the chair that he placed between his legs, as he also faced Maria.

"Whatever questions I'm about to ask you, I'm asking you once. If I even sense that you are lying, even if my sense is wrong," he then leaned over to his stash and pulled out some brown powder. It was heroin. "I will heat this shit up in the spoon and then I'll light up your ass with heroin." He then stared her directly in the eyes and spoke to her slowly. "And when I'm finished, nothing will be left but your body and a suicide note."

Maria had never been so scared and Darius had never been more serious. "Why is he here?" She asked nervously.

"Oh, he is an expert on telling if someone is lying. I need a second opinion, because as you can tell, this is a highly emotional situation and I may not be thinking clearly right now. A second opinion is good, don't you think?" Fury engulfed Darius. Peter was extremely nervous. Maria pissed on herself.

"Are you pregnant?" Darius introduced flame under the heroin filled spoon.

"No," Maria cried, as she trembled with fear and closed her eyes. She now realized that she had played a deadly game.

"Were you pregnant?"

"Yes," she sniffled.

"What happened to the baby?"

"Darius, please, let's just talk about this," she cried.

"This is talking honey. Now, answer the fucking question."

After crying for a bit, she answered, "I had an abortion."

"Why?" He asked as pain ripped through his body. She had killed the only reason they were still married. He wanted to kill her instantly.

"I never planned on having it. It was done intentionally to get you to marry me and I know you are against divorce so no matter what you wouldn't leave. You know I hate kids." This time, she cried uncontrollably.

"Did you put a hole in the condom?" He was callous.

"No."

"No?"

She dried her tears and gained strength. An arrogant smile replaced her fear and remorse. "I used to place the sperm from my mouth into a container I got from the clinic where my friend works. I would always leave after sex, and it was easy because you never cared enough to ask where I was going or why I was leaving. I kept going to the clinic and after enough attempts, the artificial insemination process was successful. I knew you would never get anyone pregnant because of the non-wife status, but not everyone is me." She was thoroughly enjoying this moment. Darius stared at her in disbelief as she continued to rip him to pieces.

"Why, Maria?"

"Do I need a reason to want the irresistible, unattainable Darius Kramer? *I need for you to know and understand something, this is not a monogamous relationship, and I am seeing other people. If this is an issue for you and I do understand, please leave now instead of making my life complicated later on or calling me out of my name later on.'* " She mocked him. "Yes, we loved your raw honesty. You gave us no disrespect, no lies, no games, we could have either dealt with it or not, either way no hard feelings. You were the bachelor of the century. The problem was you didn't really want anyone. We really were just playthings no matter how graceful you tried to look. You were no better than the other players who were not honest." Darius had a perplexed look on his face. Maria continued.

"You were not ready for marriage and you had not found anyone you believed was worthy to be your precious other half. None of us was up on your out of reach pedestal. We were just low enough for a good time. That was your story in not so many words and you were sticking to it. You damn well had your cake and ate it too. You got high off the fact that all these women love you and damn well worshipped you. You were going to milk us dry and then use your bullshit raw honesty as your 'you chose to be with me despite the facts.'"

"You fucking psycho."

"Ya well, psycho or not, I was going to have the last laugh. I knew you didn't believe in divorce so there would be no marrying yet. Children however warrant marriage and I knew that. I don't see you on your high horse now, do I?" Maria gloated at the sight of Darius's agony.

Darius was now stoic. Peter walked over, and slowly took the lighter and the spoon with the heroin in it away from Darius. Darius did not even recognize what Peter had just done; in fact, he forgot that Peter was even there, he was so fixated on

Maria.

"Kramer," Peter called to him, and shook him in an effort to get his attention.

Darius didn't know if he should have felt sorry for Maria because she definitely was sick in her head or if he should have hated her now more than ever because she meticulously planned how to ruin his life. He could have simply gotten rid of the body he thought. He could have dismembered her, spread her across some desert or better yet, fed her to some wild animals, and nobody would have ever known. He was torn. He reached for his gun that he always carried on him. As quickly as he snatched out his gun, he put it to Maria's head. "You crazy fuck."

"Kramer, no!" Kramer felt an impact upon him the same time the gun was fired. Maria screamed. Both men were on the ground. Peter was on top. He had managed to deflect the bullet away from Maria's head when he jumped on Kramer. It hit Darius for the first time in his life, someone was about to control his destiny and if he killed her, somehow she would still win. The bullet hit no one. Darius was grateful. He slowly got up, told Peter to untie her. Maria smiled. In a daze, Kramer walked out and left them both there. That was the last time he saw or spoke to his wife. He requested a transfer the same day.

One of her friends had run into Darius in New York, so she knew he was in New York. He had set up a joint account where he deposited funds so that all of her financial and basic necessities were still being met. He married her; it was his responsibility to provide for her, whether or not he wanted to do so. His dad was right…women.

As quickly as Maria came in his mind, she left. He

refused to allow her to occupy space in his mind. All too soon, the only thing that would be on his mind would be the sounds of love making. He looked around Roberto's apartment again. All was set for the party. He felt the beating in his heart. All was set for his.

CHAPTER
TEN

Diane sat at her desk and slouched in her soft leather chair. She thought that given the stress of an Assistant District Attorney, she needed all the comforts possible. She reached for the nearby tray of files and pulled one in particular, *THE STATEOF NEW YORK VS. OTIS RAYMOND. This mother fucker is about to have his day in hell. He thought he was going to walk this earth free after the shit he did to me. I don't give a fuck about how much of a little brother he is like to Michael. Both he and Michael can go fuck themselves.* She browsed through the criminal complaint she wrote. One count of possession with intent to sell or distribute cocaine, one count of conspiracy to sell cocaine, and two counts of keeping and maintaining a motor vehicle for the sale of a controlled substance. Though these realities were the norm for Diane, there was one thing about this case that wasn't. Her office phone rang.

"Yes. Send him in, thank you."

Jim Gordon, the defense attorney for Otis Raymond walked into Diane's office. It was customary for Assistant District Attorneys and Defense Attorneys to meet in order to possibly strike a deal about their cases. Jim was particularly optimistic about his case, as he knew Diane had reasons to believe that his client was in fact not guilty. He did not know that Diane had his client framed. Otis was going to suffer for having taken a valuable possession from Diane. Unfortunately for Otis, he had no idea about the woman that he had scorned. Diane watched as Jim giddily positioned himself in the chair across from her. He was a white male, and although only five feet eight inches in height, weighed 340 pounds. His appearance was drab. His protruding belly blocked Diane from seeing his belt. It was as if his handkerchief was falling out of his right pants pocket. Diane noticed its dampness. Due to his persistent sweating, Jim carried a handkerchief. As per their agreement, they never shook hands. Diane became tired of washing her hands after she shook his. His brown crop of hair seemed out of place with the rest of his appearance. His soft green eyes, however, were kind and warm.

"Thanks for coming in Jim, I appreciate it."

"Sure, Diane. We are not just colleagues, but friends. We go way back to college days." His eyes danced.

"How are your wife Betty Sue and the kids?"

"Good, everybody is fine. How is Rebecca?" He swallowed nervously at his own question as she was Diane's little sister.

"Fine." She watched him as he jerked his body and looked away. "Being that everybody is good, let's get down to business, shall we?"

"Certainly. My client is not demanding an apology. He understands that this was a natural mistake. He is simply requesting to be released as soon as possible and returned to his life."

"Jim, that's not going to happen."

He pressed down on both arms of his chair and helped himself up forward.

"Why not?" He was frazzled.

"How about you lose your case?"

"Why the hell would I do that when there is no case?"

"Say you and your client."

"And you Diane, You have proof!" He stood. "This is a case of mistaken identity. Why on God's earth would you try to ruin this kid's life? He didn't even do it, but more importantly, this smells like a set up. You can't do this!" He slammed on her desk. "You have an obligation to protect the people of the State of New York and to see that justice prevails when possible. Damn you! He is a good kid. Damn you!"

Diane knew that Jim was naïve about his client. "And I'm sure he will continue to be a good kid. You will be glad you did this. Get your sweaty hands off my desk." She looked at the file and then looked back at Jim. "This mother fucker you represent has made a mockery of the judicial system, but most importantly, he has made a mockery out of me."

"It's not his fault that the cops didn't follow procedures in gathering the evidence against him in the past. Beating the shit out of someone for a confession is not necessarily constitutional."

Diane recalled how she had arranged for Otis' constitutional rights to be violated as a mechanism to get his prior case dismissed. He never knew how it happened but was always grateful despite the busted lips. She knew it pained Michael that Otis has chosen the life he was living, but Michael had come to accept it and looked the other way. He always did whatever he could to help Otis, even to the detriment of Diane's career. For Diane, those days were now over.

"Jim, your client, is a notorious drug dealer."

"That cannot be proven."

"From what I hear, he works for Sambino, in the accounting part of the business."

"That's hearsay and you know it."

"So is the information that I have that can set him free."

Diane twirled a pen between her fingers. "Otis Raymond has taken something very dear from me, and being that I can't get it back, I will take something very dear from him."

"What the hell could he have taken from you that is worth his life!"

"Never you mind that Jim."

"Dia...."

"Shhhhhhhhhhh..." She spun her chair, pressed the power button on the TV
and VCR that she commonly used in Court to exhibit video tape evidence. The TV screen lit. Diane did not have to tell him to sit. His body dropped in the chair. He slowly and carefully closed his eyes as if he were rehearsing for a scene. He opened them and Diane watched as shame covered him. He hung his head.

"Diane..."

"Shhh.... It gets better." She increased the volume.

Jim heard the moaning of both him and the super model type body young lady. He was lying nude on a bed in what appeared to be a motel room. The young lady's tan smooth silky body gyrated on his penis with her back facing him.

"Betty Sue sure looks different, wouldn't you say Jim? She looks a lot like my little sister and from the date of the recording, it looks like Betty Sue changed her outer appearance last week to match Rebecca's. You don't want me to become the angry sister who discovered that her baby sister was taking advantage of by a family friend. Now would you?"

"She's hardly a baby being 25 and all. What do you want?" Jim frowned.

"Lose that mother fucker's case, or lose the one you have at home."

"We are supposed to be friends for crying out loud."

"We are friends. This is why I have made you such a ludicrous offer. As for your client, call it justice cashing in for all the illegal shit we didn't get him on." She leaned back and rocked in her leather chair.

"Are you that desperate to win because people have taken notice of your whimsical losses? It's as if you have been intentionally losing some of your cases."

"Never you mind that. I won't lose this one. I am transferring the case to another ADA. Bring the new ADA a plea bargain or fuck up your defense. Either way it's a conviction. I don't give a fuck."

"He didn't do it Diane."

"My role in this case cannot be discovered Jim. I need say nothing else."

"For Christ's sake, have a heart," he pled.

"This has nothing to do with Christ. He doesn't live here. Now do we have a deal?"

"What happens if he fights it? He has witnesses."

"And I have written statements from all of them with the same story, all different from his. Besides, immunity will let anyone squeal like a bitch." She smirked. "Seems to me that your client is being crucified for your sins. Now that's Christ-like."

"You f..." He braced and humbled himself. "Please Diane, for old time sake."

"No. You have 10 seconds. I don't get a yes, and Betty Sue gets this tape and your client gets to hear "don't drop the soap.""

"You fucking bitch."

"Ten, nine, eight, seven, six, five, four, three..."

"Yes," Jim softly and reluctantly whispered as he hung his head. "This is a violation of all kinds of lawyers' code of ethics..."

"Save it for the first year law students over at Brooklyn Law." Diane observed Jim's teary angry eyes. "It's business. You are a lawyer. Your job is to represent your client to the best of your ability, which includes getting him the best deal. The evidence reflects he is guilty. The law doesn't give a fuck about what's real or not. You and I know the only thing that matters is what you can or cannot prove. If I were you, I would go for a plea and save the court's time. You never know, the judge may be grateful and kind at sentencing." She turned her sight to her nearby calendar. Instantly and in a nonchalant manner, she switched her tone. "How about dinner next week at your place? Let's see..." she turned the pages. "Michael and I will be available on..."

The door slammed. She looked up and Jim was gone.

She felt bad for him but that feeling would leave quickly, as the end was justified. She closed her calendar and leaned back in her soft leather chair and spun. What would Elizabeth think if she knew what it was that Otis Raymond had taken from Diane? What would Michael do to her if he knew she had made it her duty to bring this case against Otis and arranged for his conviction? They could never find out. She looked at her desk clock. It was time to meet her friend.

CHAPTER
ELEVEN

Diane pressed her friend's doorbell.

"Yes."

"Open the door," she could hardly contain herself.

"Say please," he joked.

"No," she teased him.

He buzzed the door open. *No* was her favorite word. Her intention was to be difficult with him, if nothing else, just for fun. It made her feel that she was running the show. Of course they both knew better. As she approached his door, he was already standing there. Damn, she thought, if this man looked any better God himself would have come down and bragged over his creation. His button down shirt was open and his white undershirt covered his beautifully defined honey glazed chest. His belt was unbuckled and simply hung from the pants of his tailored suit. He leaned his six foot-one lean muscle defined body against the door and stared at her from his dark brown lazy eyes, as she approached him. As she came closer, Diane became nervous despite her comfort with him. As she passed him by, she reached out for his left hand, and pulled him. He closed the door behind them. She pushed him against the door and started to undress him without saying a word.

"Well hello counselor. How are you doing?"

Diane ignored him and he continued his one-sided conversation.

"Well my day was not too bad. Thanks for asking, how was yours?"

She knelt down, tugged at the zipper of his pants, and completed undressing the lower part of his body. Without hesitation, she surrounded his penis with her moist mouth, and massaged it up and down. Occasionally, she used her tongue and licked his penis from the baseline to the head, concentrating more on its tip. He pressed his teeth on his bottom lips as he threw his head backwards. As his penis swelled, so did the palpating sensation in his chest. He had to comply. After she was done, she slowly stood and nibbled her way to his lips.

Diane looked at him and pulled his lips toward hers. As they became lost into each other, tears filled her eyes. She did not believe the magic they shared. There was no way this could be wrong. She wanted to whisper the unthinkable, "I love you," but she was afraid this would lead to the end of their relationship. You know men, she thought, you say those words, and they say the automatic response, "bye-bye."

He had told her once that she was everything he wanted – gorgeous, gentle, kind, educated, soft spoken, lady in public, whore in bed, playmate and someone who cooked and cleaned but damn, she belonged to another. She knew she was his friend and he was not going to jeopardize that by telling her how much he loved her.

He gently moved her away from his lips. He started to undress her without taking his eyes away from hers. When he was done, he gently laid her down onto the floor with heated passion burning through his eyes as her body quivered in anticipation of her inner most desire. With his tongue, he passionately caressed her neck and continued down until he was between her legs. There, he buried his head, causing her to raise her thighs and thrust her pelvis upwards. She gently stroked his soft low cut brown curly hair. Diane gasped and moaned as she surrendered to him. He continued to suckle on her private lips and then moved on down to her thighs, her calves and very succulently, her toes. He raised his face to hers and simply stared into her eyes. She swallowed nervously. She occasionally opened her mouth to gasp for air. He parted her legs with his and slowly glided inside of her. His eyes were still locked into hers. There was no need to speak. Unable to control herself, Diane clutched onto him, and unintentionally sunk her nails into his skin. She moaned like a hog. She was a slave to insurmountable pleasure. As their bodies could have only taken so much heat, they eventually released themselves. When the ride was over, she was breathless. As they waited for their body temperatures to decrease, they talked.

"I have to meet up with some people at 7:00. I gotta go do the shower thing and the get ready thing." She stood up and went to the bathroom. He smiled, and joined her as she went into the shower.

"Have I told you that you have the most beautiful body I have ever seen?" He watched as the water slid down her full C cup round breast. As she turned, he couldn't help but to admire her firm plump buttocks. Her body extended approximately five feet seven. From her frontal view, he saw the toned muscles, which went perfectly with her visible biceps and triceps. Her thighs were firmly shaped. Her face caught his attention. Her high cheeks bones and dark brown almond shaped eyes that she inherited from her Indian ancestry, combined with her full lips and midnight black hair, created a striking beauty. Her skin color was like tanned olive. Her eyes shimmered as she gave a deadly seductive grin.

"Baby, you think everything about me is the most this and the most that."

"Have I told you that you are very modest?" He asked. They laughed and played.

Diane noticed the time. "I gotta go."

She kissed him passionately as if it was the last time she was going to see him for a long time.

In a rush, she hurried away. He noticed that she had left her black panties and they had agreed to leave no evidence behind. He dashed for the door but it was too late. She was gone and in his hands were black panties belonging to the woman of another.

CHAPTER

TWELVE

Based on the turn-out, the ambiance, free liquor and the DEA's invisible presence, Roberto Garcia's party was set to be a smashing success. He called it the White Party as such was the required attire. It would add to the dim lit ambiance creating a lighter energy allowing folks to let their guards down even more. Latin Jazz was the choice of entertainment for the party. The ladies who assisted Roberto in offering Dom Perignon Vintage Champagne to his distinguished guests were Brazilians, with a non-abrasive quiet seductive energy—light enough for the women to appreciate, and just enough for the men to be distracted from whatever else was happening beyond the immediate purview of the Brazilian. The aroma of the gardenia fragrance lit the air. It was just about seven and the wireless video camera discreetly placed in Roberto's Cartier watch displayed Diane, Elizabeth and of course, his new best pal, Michael, in the front lobby of the apartment building, located on Montague Street in Brooklyn Heights. It is said to house the most expensive apartments in Brooklyn, and can only be occupied by the owner—never to be rented. This way the occupants were ensured to among the most desirable. Roberto smiled when he signed the contract. He smiled at the irony of human definition of "desirables." The Brazilians were in place as he welcomed his first set of guests.

"Bem-Vindo," one of the ladies gestured, "do come in."

Elizabeth and Diane were taken back both by the sex appeal and unexpected gracious welcome that had come upon them. They simply stood there.

"Why thank you, don't mind if I do." Michael stepped past the ladies after realizing that they had decided to remain awestruck. "You will have to excuse them," he said to the one who rendered them bem-vindo, "they are not used to seeing earthly angels, but you can take me to heaven any day."

"You are so fucking disrespectful," Diane interjected."

"They are also ill-mannered," Michael added.

Roberto hung his head and then lifted his eyes toward Diane. He managed a smile. *Michael will be Michael.* Diane smiled in agreement as if she knew his thoughts.

"Sir, your phone," the gracious lady extended her hand with a smile, ignoring the tension that was in the midst.

It was habitual for Roberto to single handedly put in the security code for Wi-Fi access on each of his guest's cell phones. As he put in the code, each guest was offered a glass of the vintage champagne so that there wouldn't be a dull moment. A captivated audience was one of Roberto's specialties, and he ensured that all of his guests were sufficiently attended to as he captured their night.

"Babe, you don't think the Brazilians were enough, you had to subject us to flamingo dancers as well," Elizabeth eyes widened as she handed Roberto her glass of the vintage.

"Well what can I say, beautiful," he smiled, "we aim to please."

"The men yes, and maybe if Sally was here…."

"Who?"

"Aww nothing. Nothing at all. I am talking nonsense and getting my thoughts confused."

"Nice to know I can still have that effect upon you," he gently pulled her toward him. *Who the fuck is Sally he thought?*

"You are a gentleman, Roberto, and gentlemen reserve such intimate affection in private settings," she shook her index finger at him indicating, bad Roberto, bad. "I will be right back. I have to use the little girl's room."

He stared at her buttocks as she glided away. "Que bonita." As Elizabeth disappeared from his sight, his eyes took hold of his most important VIP, Sambino. The moment they first met couple years ago, only seemed like yesterday.

When Roberto's guards welcomed Sambino, it was obvious that he liked what he saw. The Brazilian women, sangria—wine and fruit juice, mamosa—champagne and orange juice and the likes of others. The sweet sounds of reggae music to which one slow danced saturated the twilight evening on Roberto's yacht. Roberto took particular notice as to how Sambino didn't react when he and his companion's phone and other articles were swept for bugs or wire.

"The Hamptons never looked so beautiful," Roberto recognized Sambino's scar as he approached and handed him an empty champagne glass. "I figure a man such as yourself would need to see the champagne flowing from the soon to be opened bottle, rather than one that has already being poured for you."

Sambino smiled. "What can I say, I had a poor upbringing—never learned to trust." Both men laughed as Roberto bust opened the champagne.

"To trust," he poured.

"To trust," Sambino accepted and they drank.

"It was kind of you to accept the offer from my lady friend to join us for dinner. From what I understand, you trust no one, hence hardly socialize. I feel privileged."

"And I still don't," Sambino smiled. "But I figure, if you were man enough to have her attention, you were man enough to meet me. Besides, all I hear is praises about you, and being that I aspire to be the best, changing my circle is a must."

Roberto fixed his eyes on Sambino's with a genuine smile, "you are exactly as I expected you to be—a man of intensity and definitely one who watches the company he keeps, and that my friend is a good thing. You know what they say… birds of a feather flock together."

"And looking at how you live, I am definitely going to be a part of your flock." They had a good laugh.

"To good flock," Roberto raised his drink again.

"How about a Black Russian as my drink?" Sambino tried to get the attention of one of the passing Brazilians.

Dominant personality fits with his arrogance, Roberto thought and gestured for one of the Brazilians.

"What's up with the bug checking?" Sambino interrogated Roberto with his eyes fixed on his.

"Can't take any chances," Roberto indicated that the

lifestyle he led was a risky one. He needed say no more as Sambino understood that code all too well. Roberto knew it crossed Sambino's mind as to whether Elizabeth was aware of his risky business.

Nevertheless, Sambino has now found something he longed for—someone with whom he can associate that shared a common interest. Roberto knew he had fit Sambino's profile of a friend. He was self-sufficient, authoritative and was not about the rat-race society had demanded of its citizens. Engaging in the routine 9-5 work day in order to survive was definitely not Roberto. He was eager to learn a thing or two from this new found friend.

"What about you?" Roberto asked casually putting his drink down to avoid eye contact so Sambino could feel more at ease, more relaxed.

"Like your guys sweep me, my phone and other articles of mine for bugs or wire, every day I have my place sweep for bugs. Can't take any chances," he smiled.

"Expensive habit."

"No more expensive," Sambino looked around, "than say…the Brazilians." They had a good laugh. From the Brazilians came the topic of women. A friendship was formed, something that was rare to both men. Over the years, things were told to each other, Sambino made an effort to introduce Roberto to a regular life—with friends and more interaction with everyday normalcy, like riding in Prospect Park. They conducted business in the presence of each other and though a trust was formed, neither man observed the other with the product.

Diane caught hold of Michael paying keen attention to his surroundings as if he hadn't visited Roberto's place on numerous occasions. It was no surprise to Diane that Michael quickly befriended Roberto when he learnt of his power and money. Fearless, classy, but humble, Roberto was, and those were attractive qualities to Michael, like moth to a flame. Why and how did Roberto allow for Michael to get so close to him, was beyond Diane and the least of Michael's concern. He was in with the big guys now and of course knowing Michael, his aim would be to remove the competition. Diane held her belly as if she had lost a child at the thought of that something happening to the man that Elizabeth had introduced to her, as her proof that some women do get lucky. Elizabeth was right—some women do get lucky.

"Enjoying the party," Roberto walked over and handed Diane a glass of champagne.

"It's lovely as usual, though there is something I meant to ask you the last time and it slipped my mind," her spirit instantaneously was lifted when her host appeared.

"What's that?" Roberto asked rather curiously.

"The cell phones…"

"What about them?" He sipped his champagne."

"Why don't you just tell us all the password for the Wi-Fi, and then if you are worried about hackers, then just have the password change for every party?"

"That would be a lot of changing of passwords, don't you think?"

"I guess," Diane said unconvincingly.

"To each his own, I suppose," Roberto's eyes danced.

"That's funny you said that… I said the same words to Liz today when I was talking about you." She appeared more amazed than suspicious. She rocked her body happily as she took a drink of her champagne.

"Great minds think alike, or should I say, it's just lovers dancing to the same tune." Roberto waited for Diane's champagne to accidentally get into her trachea causing her to cough, due to her sudden reaction of what he had just said, which shocked her. He sipped as he watched the ghostly look appeared on her face.

"Are you insane?" She frantically whispered as she coughed and stopped, coughed and stopped. "Not here," she urged him.

"You forgot your black panties in your haste. It's in the bathroom where you left it not too long ago."

CHAPTER
THIRTEEN

The party was over. The pier was not even ten minutes away by walking and so the two couples decided to go for a walk to the pier. Elizabeth insisted on getting something to eat. The multitude of cafes that lined Montague Street only strengthened her cause.

"Is it too hard to ask that we go get something to eat?"

"Is it me or was it someone that looked just like you that ate constantly at the party?" Roberto was amazed at how it was remotely possible that Elizabeth was hungry again, and exactly where was the food going as she was a lean figure.

"Guys, do you mind if Liz and I walk behind you?" Diane asked. "I need to talk to her about something." Diane tried to hide the concerned look on her face.

"Sure, we will see you down at the pier." Michael responded.

"Great." The men walked in front and laughed and giggled. The ladies walked a few feet behind with nothing but worry on their faces.

"Alright Liz, you only eat like this when you are nervous, so what the hell is going on?"

"I'm pregnant." Elizabeth was abrupt. She remained serious and stoic as she held her head high and looked directly ahead and kept on walking. Diane on the other hand began to literally trip over herself. It's as if she had forgotten how to walk.

"What!" Diane whispered as she pulled Elizabeth aside.

Diane's world crashed instantly. She was so afraid to hear who the father was though she believed she had a pretty good idea. She had to muster enough strength to put her emotions aside and be there totally for her friend. Now, more than ever, she had to protect her and Roberto's secret love affair.

"Ahhhh," Diane cleared her throat as pain and disappointment slapped her around. She looked down to the ground. "Is it Roberto's?"

"Of course, it's Roberto's, who else?"

"Well honey, I don't mean to be insensitive, but how do you know that it isn't Sally who is pregnant, as opposed to you?"

"Does it matter? Me pregnant, Sally pregnant, it's the same body, the same person..."

"It's not the same person. We don't know who Sally has been with, and for all we know, especially after last night, she could have had you pregnant for anyone Liz..."

"I am not pregnant for anyone but Roberto. Sally doesn't like men, remember."

"For someone who doesn't like men, she sure loves the red light district."

"Well from what I recall, it is females who hang out on the corners of red light districts, so she would love it just fine."

"Liz…"

"Diane!" She took a moment. "I am in control now, not Sally. The last time I checked, she was suppressed and she is going to stay that way."

"The last time I checked, you found yourself in Sally's favorite part of town with no recollection of getting there, so she can't be that suppressed."

"D, this conversation is over. Roberto is the father and that is final."

Diane took a deep breath. "Does he know?" Diane closed her eyes. She waited as the pain struck hard.

"No, he doesn't know."

"Why?" Diane asked as her eyes remained fixed to the ground. She wanted to roll in a corner and simply die. She did not believe all of this was happening. She could not have helped but believe that it was Roberto's especially when Elizabeth seemed so sure.

"I just found out today and I didn't get a chance to see him or talk to him in private," Elizabeth said softly.

Diane tried hard to stop the tears from flowing and tried hard not to choke. She breathed slowly. "Ahhhhhh, sooooo, is it congratulations or is it a what are we going to do situation?" Diane faced her toughest challenge, which was to remain strong.

"I guess it is congratulations, D." Elizabeth did not flinch.

"So, you're having it." Diane barely said those words, as she slightly kicked her foot outward to release some of the anger. The reality ripped her in different pieces. She stopped suddenly, looked up to the sky and managed to smile. It was a smile that said just kill me now. As she continued to walk, she stopped and bent over with her hands on her knees.

"D, you alright?" Elizabeth rushed to Diane's side.

"I'm just trying to breathe. I've been having shortness of breath lately," Diane lied to her friend again.

"Guys!" Elizabeth yelled to Michael and Roberto ahead. They turned around and Roberto ran to Diane's side as he tried to pull her up. She snatched her hand away from him.

"I'm fine."

Robert didn't understand the sudden hostility. "Did I miss something here?"

"I'm sorry," Elizabeth said, "she's just dealing with some news."

"What news?"

"Honey, just have a seat over here," Elizabeth said to Diane, as she directed her over to the nearby bench. As they sat, Elizabeth took Diane's face in her hands.

"D, I'm going to be okay. Please don't worry. Okay D?" Elizabeth pled and Diane nodded her head.

"Michael, can you come over here and take over please? I need to talk to Roberto." Elizabeth reached out to Michael.

"Sure," Michael walked over and sat next to Diane.

"You don't look too well Diane. Everything alright?" Michael asked disinterested.

"Fine."

"Good. I spoke to Otis today. He mentioned that due to unforeseen circumstances, he has to make a plea."

"How unfortunate. I kinda like the guy."

"Yea well, liking him is not the issue. You were supposed to be the ADA on this case."

"It's not that simple Michael. I can't just dictate to my boss what I want and don't want. There are politics involved, shit like that. He looks up to you for God's sake. Pretend like you give a shit about him, and lecture to Otis about the company he keeps and his visible surroundings. Then his identity won't be mistaken." She hated speaking to Michael. "And what about my career, Michael, does that shit even mean anything to you?"

"No."

"Well it should. So why did you go through the trouble of financing law school?"

"You know why. It was one of my three ends of the bargain. Now get this. If Otis Raymond goes down, so do you. And your precious career won't matter."

"Is that right?"

He faced her. "Very much so counselor, and don't you fucking forget it." He turned away from Diane. He felt that she was vexed and probably wanted to put a dagger through him. "Is the reason for your sour face the same reason why Liz needs to speak to Roberto?"

Diane closed her eyes and turned her face away.

"Wanna talk about it?" Michael asked callously.

"Liz is pregnant."

"Wow," Michael said calmly as he looked up and out to the street, "a baby among us."

They sat in silence.

CHAPTER
FOURTEEN

Elizabeth and Roberto walked to get privacy. They were well away from Diane and Michael as they had reached the pier. They sat down and Elizabeth nervously rocked back and forth taking in the view of South Street Seaport. Roberto waited patiently.

"Alright," Elizabeth turned around and faced him. "Roberto, I'm just going to say this because I don't know how to make it any easier, so here it goes. I'm pregnant."

Roberto pushed his head forward, his eyes popped open. "Pregnant?" He was more amazed than worried. Roberto forgot momentarily that he was her lover and not just a friend.

"I know. It seems like only yesterday that you came to my class as a guest speaker warning my kids of the dangers of drugs...you came out of nowhere it seems, heaven sent to be exact, and now here we are."

"Yep, here we are," Roberto spoke in a dismissive voice as that was of no interest to him. "How far along are you?" He asked as that was far more interesting.

"I don't know. I mean I just took the test today, so all of this is still shocking to me. We were always careful so I just don't see how this could have happened."

Robert picked up a small stone and rolled it around and around in his hand. He leaned back against the bench and continued rolling the stone in his hand. "Wow Liz, this is some heavy shit." Elizabeth nodded her head in response and held it down. She placed her face in her hands, bent forward and placed her hands on her knees. "I tell ya Liz, life is funny. You can plan it and make sure that every "T" is crossed and "I" is dotted and then life comes around laughing at your ass, saying oh, you think you are in control of things ahh." Robert sighed. "Look at y'all for example, careful as can be and still you end up pregnant."

Elizabeth slowly turned to face him; her face crinkled as evidence of her confusion. Before Roberto could ask whose baby she was carrying, Elizabeth interrupted him. "Ya'll?" She snatched Roberto's arm as to have him face her. "Ya'll?" she asked again. Roberto had a puzzled look on his face. "Don't play with me, this is not funny." She continued being shaken up by Roberto's reaction.

"What do you want me to say? Liz, I mean…. Hold on," Robert smiled nervously.

"Liz, you don't believe it's mine, do you? I mean, is that why we came for this walk, is because…" he suddenly stopped. *That's why Diane was mad at me. She thought Liz was pregnant for me.* He now remembered that he was in this situation as her lover and not as a friend. How on God's earth was he going to tell her that she was not carrying his child. She was already at a low point and the last thing she needed now was baby daddy drama. Robert kept his head low and started to think.

"Roberto, I've been sleeping with only you," Elizabeth said convincingly, now with a shaken voice as tears now drowned her eyes.

"Roberto!" She yelled at him, which brought him back to the reality at hand.

He looked at her with sadness in his eyes. He saw her pain and she would have felt more of it tonight.

"I'm sorry, Liz. I promise, if nothing else, we'll get to the bottom of this."

"What the hell is that supposed to mean? You are not trying to deny this child, are you?" She cried.

"I'm not denying anything. I'm sorry." He took her hand and hugged her. He had just lied to her but he needed her to remain calm until he could have gotten her to the house with Diane. One way or the other, tonight, friendships were going to be tested.

"Let's go Liz." He pulled her up and they started to walk back to Michael and Diane.

"Roberto," she was about to engage in conversation.

"Shhhhhhhh. Let's just enjoy the quiet night and the full moon," he said calmly. He held her on the way back. His heart ached for her. His heart ached for him.

"You guys alright?" Michael asked as he stood up to greet them.

"Liz and I are going to go." Roberto responded. He walked over to Michael and they gripped each other's hands. Roberto then went and hugged Diane.

"I am so sorry D," he whispered in her ear. As he pulled

away from her, she turned away from him. She refused to look him in the eye.

"Are you guys okay?" Roberto asked.

"Yeah man we are alright," Michael said. "You go handle your business man."

Roberto took another glance at Diane.

"Goodnight D," Robert said as he hoped that she would have looked his way.

Diane said nothing nor did she acknowledge him. Instead she turned to Michael.

"Michael, if you don't mind, I really wish to be alone, so I'll find my way home."

"D, I don't feel comfortable…. Are you going to be alright?" Michael said with no sincerity, "I mean you weren't feeling well and…"

"Nothing a couple of shots of rum can't cure, Michael. Thanks so much for your concern," she responded sarcastically. With that, she hugged Elizabeth and walked off.

After Roberto saw Elizabeth safely home, he asked if it would be okay with her if he left; he needed to be alone to grasp all of what was happening. He made it very clear to her that he would be there for her. He knew she was going to need as many friends as possible. There was no mystery as to where he was heading. He got in the car and sped to Diane's. He knew everything was about to come crashing down but it was best to take it head on than to procrastinate. He would do something that an undercover agent is prohibited to do. Besides, this was his last case before retiring from the DEA. What were they going to do, fire him?

"You are only ten, and I can tell that yours will be what has been for most men, a woman," he heard his father's warning. *The sooner the damage, the sooner the recovery, he justified it. Stay focus Darius, he warned himself, focus. Put your emotions in check. It's a case, not your life. Where is the fucking Martha Brae River when you need it?* With that, he went up to Diane's door and rang the bell. Darius suspected that she had already had her first shot of Hennessey and was on her way to being among the intoxicated.

"Go away," she responded to the doorbell.

"D, it's me, Roberto. Please open the door." He tried to compose himself. "All these fucking names are getting to me," he mumbled to himself.

"Go away!"

"Diane, I – am – not – leaving. So you might as well open the door right now." Diane didn't respond.

"Baby please," he said softly with his head against the door. She cried and opened the door.

"I hate you. I really hate you." She bawled.

Darius was tired of being sad. He noticed that under her right arm was a bottle of rum. With that same arm, she held a shot glass with settled liquor at the bottom. He quickly covered his nose and turned his face as the scent of alcohol from her pores hit him directly. Her hair was out of place. Most of it was separated from the hair clip that had held it in together.

"We have to talk, and we can't talk here." Robert gestured for them to leave.

"Why the hell not?"

"Because your place is bugged."

"What? Bugged? Roberto, what are you talking about? You know what, don't answer that. I'm drunk so things are not making sense right now." She put down the bottle of rum and shot glass and looked for her keys. "You're right, let's get outta here." They walked to the nearby street and sat down on one of the benches. Diane folded her arms across her chest, crossed her legs, and tightened her face. She was determined not to speak in order to avoid saying something she would regret later.

Darius on the other hand was more forthcoming with his thoughts. *How the fuck is she pregnant and how the hell did I miss...?* He clasped his hands and placed them on his head. He leaned his head back and closed his eyes. For Elizabeth to be pregnant and for her to truly believe that he was the father only meant one thing, someone was on to him or the tables had been turned against him. He had to act fast. He now had to go straight for the kill, even if that meant his happy days with Diane would come to an abrupt end, which they had already. This was deliberately done to throw him off guard.

"Diane," he removed his hands from his head and faced her. "There are things I'm going to tell you that will make Liz's pregnancy seem like Santa Claus on Christmas day. Your world is going to turn inside out, and this is the first dose of it. You are going to hate me because you're in love with me. But in spite of all that, you cannot utter a word of what I'm going to tell you. I'm also going to use this opportunity to tell you something that I've never felt much less utter before, and I don't know if life will grant me the honor of saying it again."

"Look at me," he demanded softly.

As much as she wanted to disobey, she couldn't. He

always had that commanding presence. She turned to look at him.

"Diane. I'm in love with you, and when your world comes crashing down, don't forget that." He said it so casually as if he had said it over a million times. "I can't get into much right now because I have to go. The next few days or weeks, you may not see me or hear from me. You were not a part of my mission; you were only the fucking best incidental effect of it." He held her face in his hands, wishing he could have used a magic wand to make all the pain and confusion in her disappear, especially because of the bombshell that was going to blast right now.

"I am not the father of Liz's baby."

Diane instantly gave him the look of death. "Don't you dare. Don't disrespect her like that."

"I know this is going to be difficult for you to hear and to deal with afterwards. God knows it has been difficult for me."

"What the hell are you talking about?"

"I am talking about how it is impossible for me to get Liz pregnant or anyone else for that matter."

"Uh? Come again."

"D, I know that's not my baby."

"How the hell can you be so sure Roberto? I mean…"

"Darius, my name is Darius. I know because four years ago, I had a vasectomy."

CHAPTER
FIFTEEN

Samurai's patience was dwindling. He was definitely getting sick and tired of dealing with cops in order to achieve his ultimate goal. Frankly, he just wanted to kill all his enemies, the adversaries and the authorities that tried to make his life unnecessarily difficult. He was definitely getting tired of everyone and his partner was next on the list. Samurai's phone rang. He looked at the Caller ID. The number was unrecognizable, so he knew instantly who was calling.

"Let me guess, you have a superb reason as to why you were unreachable tonight."

"I don't answer to you, not now, not ever," his partner spoke coldly. "Right away, same place, we've got a situation."

Before Samurai could comment, he heard his partner slam the phone. "Enjoy slamming the phone mother fucker," Samurai said as he pulled out a cigar. "Those days too shall come to an end." He lit his cigar and walked to the well-secured garage where he parked his latest model black sports car. He paid the attendant and drove to meet his partner.

His partner was sitting on one of the benches in the Brooklyn Korean War Veteran Plaza when Samurai arrived. Samurai sat on the other bench behind his partner so their backs were to each other. Samurai pulled out another cigar and lit it.

"Don't light that here," his partner said.

"I don't answer to you, not now, not ever," Samurai lit the cigar and drew his first puff.

"I take it that Vasquez got the supply without anything going down."

"Yeah, it went down without a hitch, I saw to that." Samurai put the cigar to his mouth.

"When I get my money from Maddog, he and Vasquez will get eliminated."

"What the hell for?" Samurai asked angrily as he caught himself turning around and turned back. "That's a bit much, isn't it, especially when Vasquez is in this thing, oh so willingly?"

"He has to be eliminated. The evidence must be destroyed."

"Is everyone involved with you somehow evidence?"

"Yes." His partner meant it with every breath he took.

"So what are you going to do, eliminate everyone?"

"The thought did cross my mind."

"So that means I am evidence too."

"Yes you are."

"Let's move on to a sweeter topic, shall we?" Samurai asked clearly disturbed, as he tried to control his emotions. He wished he could kill his partner right away. "What's this situation that you were talking about on the phone?" Samurai wanted to clear his mind.

114

"Undercover named Darius Kramer, DEA . I just found this out a few months back, so I created a situation to fuck up his mind...hard for the mother fucker to be focused now."

"Or it could make him more focused than ever. How'd you find out anyway?"

"He got careless."

"How so?"

"We went out for a drink, to catch up on old times because we've been so busy, we really hadn't had much time to sit and chat. The bartender was Richie as usual. I gave Richie enough mickie to put in whatever that mother fucker was going to order that night. Richie did just that and when the mother fucker was knocked the fuck out, that's when I went through his shit. Mother fucker was stupid enough to bring his DEA ID with him. I wanted to kill him instantly, but that shit hit me so hard, it was as if I was knocked the fuck out. I was losing my mind the whole time, trying to trace my steps as to what the hell I had let slip or how the hell I had allowed this mother fucker to get so close to me in the first place. I mean, I checked this mother fucker out and he was clean as a whistle, and that's because the person I checked out doesn't exist. My mind is still boggled by that shit, every time I see that fuck face, I want to shoot him right between the eyes."

"What made you want to check him out again all of a sudden?"

"We were having lunch one day, and some lady ran up to him and was truly excited to see him, practically knocked him over as she tried to hug him. She then asked how Maria was doing, and he, of course, acted like he didn't know her and said he was sorry but she had him mixed up with someone else. She kept saying *"Darius it's me, Jennifer. I was at your wedding for crying out loud, one of the two witnesses and the only two guests for that matter."* You could tell she couldn't figure out why he didn't know who she was, but eventually she said, okay and walked away. She kept looking back as she walked away, until she was out of sight. When the mother fucker looked at me, I was red and I'm a black man. He tried to play it off, but at that moment, I'm sure we both thought, it's either kill or be killed. We both were now on the same page. I found out he was not who he said and he was busted. I found out that he knew I was not who I said, and I was busted. He was no longer alone in this game. The problem was though we knew it, we weren't sure if we were correct or just being paranoid, so we kept on playing the game. I had private investigators on his ass. I come to find out he's fucking this bitch, who is someone else's girl, so I decided to start the killing. I wanted to start with the closest thing to him."

"What did you do?" Samurai asked, afraid of how an innocent person was yet again at his partner's mercy.

"I set it up so his bitch gets pregnant and so the side bitch, who is closest to his heart, would leave."

"How the hell did you get his bitch pregnant? You did it yourself?"

"Hell no!" A look of disgust covered his face. "I paid someone to take care of that shit."

"Do I want to know?"

"I paid one of my peoples one hundred a session. He would do it when she's most likely to get knocked up and at times he would do it for the hell of it. Either way I don't give a fuck as long as the job gets done."

"A session?" Samurai asked suddenly being nauseous.

"Yeah, a session, each time he fucks her."

"You mean rape her. You pay someone at least one thousand bucks for God knows how long to rape her until she gets pregnant?" Samurai wanted to snap his partner's neck. Instantly, he wanted a drink to escape this madness. Samurai hated the thought of continuing this conversation but he did nonetheless.

"Let me guess, she wasn't conscious when he did it. She probably has no idea still that she ever got popped." Samurai was disgusted at the thought of it.

"You are right on that. Because whenever she woke up most of the times, she would be in the same place where she was — in her apartment. Sometimes she may find herself other places but there exists circumstances that take care of that inquiry."

"Such as what?"

"None of your fucking business."

How the hell you knew she wasn't on birth control?"

"I had her place checked out repeatedly when she wasn't home, not only that, I know her personally."

"You had someone break into her house for a couple of months to see around what time she is on her menstrual cycle, so you know the best time to have that asshole attack her? What kind of a sick shit is that man? I mean fuck, what the hell has this girl ever done to you? I mean, what happens if he gave her some shit, AIDS for example? The mother fucker was probably in jail and who knows how long, because I know you used one of your convicted rapists."

"That's not my problem. That motherfucker is going down. And as far as I'm concerned, anyone is an opportunity to get to him, anyone he has any kind of relationship with, any fucking one."

"I am just curious. How...uhh...how did he uhh...did he knock her out?"

"1 milligram of Alprazolam, each time. He would shoot it in her system after shooting her with a stun gun and watch her fall out, then take her wherever and do whatever. She never knew what was coming because it was always unexpected."

Samurai turned back around, put his right elbow on his right thigh, leaned over and used his right fingers to caress his forehead. He was having a headache. His partner was the source of it. This son of a bitch was capable of anything, Samurai thought to himself. He could not believe his partner would destroy lives, if he had to, just to get to one person. *I'm gonna have to kill this mother fucker, otherwise, when all is said and done, who says he won't try to kill me. Samurai continued to think to himself.*

"I'm afraid to ask but how do you know she is pregnant?"

"Because we were all together tonight and when she and Darius walked away to chat, the other girl told me."

"The other one that belongs to someone else I gather?"

"Yeah, the one that used to belong to me. But don't worry, soon enough, her ass won't belong to anyone. Watch your back Sammy, trust no one, I don't know how many infiltrators there are among us." He stood. "And to think he found out my true identity the night we met on his yacht. The mother fucker I'm sure ran my prints from the glasses I held. Found out all he needed to know from my regular life to infiltrate those people. And who knows what that fucking whore spilled to him in between her fucking orgasms. Fucking women. Aww! How could I have been outdone?" He was tormented.

Samurai sighed, as all of this was heavy. *This DEA guy was real good. How safe am I then? If he got to my partner, who is to say he hasn't got me, and those in my life. Shit...shit.* "Where are you going?" Samurai asked, but was ignored. "I know, you don't answer to me, not now, not ever."

"Hey," Samurai called out again, "what are we going to do with the DEA?"

"We are going to carry out stage two against the man I once considered a friend."

"What's that?" He was fearful of the answer.

"The word you meant to use is who. And, her name is Diane." Michael walked away. Samurai closed his eyes and took a deep breath. Blood was going to be shed.

Samurai decided to walk to Manhattan that night from Brooklyn. After meeting with Michael, he wanted time to himself. Once he got there, he probably would rent a hotel room. He wasn't in the mood to go home. It would have been a long walk to wherever he was going, but he needed that. Too much was happening and he hadn't had a chance to digest anything. He had another partner that Michael didn't know about. This partner wanted them to move in right away so Michael's operation could be suddenly derailed. Michael's sudden vulnerability due to this distraction would have made it easier for him to be eliminated. On the other hand, Samurai now discovered that there was a

DEA agent assigned to Michael. Samurai's former plan was now more difficult. Michael was more careful and less trusting of anyone than ever. Samurai was feeling stressed.

For the first time in his life, he found himself in unfamiliar territory. There was no turning back now, and zero margin for error. To preserve his own life, others would have to die. If it was Michael, so be it. If he had found out that Samurai had a remote thought of betraying him, he would have served Samurai his own balls for dinner. If the other partner found out that Samurai tried to back out of their partnership, he would have made sure that Michael accidentally found out about Samurai's other partnership. Either way, Michael would have had Samurai's balls among other body parts served to him for dinner. Samurai knew this because Michael had revealed to him an episode when Michael dismembered the body of a young lady's father as a favor to her. He recalled how Michael reminisced about placing the body parts at the beautifully set table with the finest china, best wine, and aroma candles in elaborate candleholders. He also played his favorite classical piece. In addition to the extraction of the man's limbs, Michael ordered someone to brutally sodomize the young lady's father. Samurai remembered the blank facial expression on Michael when he told him that he then sat and bet on whether the next round of Russian roulette would have been the one to take the young lady's father off the planet. That was done to a man who had done nothing to Michael. Samurai learned that the man had molested his daughters repeatedly. Since he liked to exert power over the weak, it was only fitting that he got a taste of his own medicine.

Again, Samurai reminded himself that this was done as a favor to someone. He thought of the manner in which Michael had gotten a woman pregnant, all as a strategy to get to someone else. What the hell would Michael have done to him? Shivers ran through his body at the thought of it. He decided to take a cab to the Waldorf Astoria. He did not have the concentration to drive and his knees were too weak for him to walk. That witness protection program became more and more attractive.

SIXTEEN

The news that Darius had just inflicted upon Diane made the English language suddenly incomprehensible to her. All this time, the DEA had gotten back to her. They had gotten back to her a couple years ago. Their answer was the man she had grown to love, or was he? Was this independent of her tip to them? Couldn't be. Too coincidental. Oh my goodness, everything had spun out of control. What did she do? She had requested help, and help had arrived, but in such an unexpected package.

"What! What! I don't understand a word that you are saying!" Confusion had used her as a toss doll and she was still being thrown. Darius put his hands on her face.

"I know I'm being unfair to ask you to accept all of this at once. Shit, I don't even expect you to accept any of this. But what I need for you to do, is to not utter a word of this to anyone because my undercover status is already blown and the more people who know, the worse it is for everyone. D, am I clear?"

She nodded her head to indicate yes.

"No one," he stressed again.

Tears flooded her eyes. "Roberto, ahhhh, I'm sorry. I'm sorry." She removed his hands from her face and held it. "Darius? That's it, right?"

Darius felt as if he had betrayed her. They were making love some hours ago as best friends and lovers, and now she was holding the hand of a stranger. Her body language asked how the hell any of this could have happened.

"Yeah, that's it," he smiled and stroked her hair.

"That's a pretty name."

"Thanks." He appreciated the compliment.

"How do you even know that Michael is the person that you are looking for? I mean how can you be so sure of his identity?" Her eyes were desperate for an answer.

"The tip you sent to the DEA described him perfectly, especially the scar on his left hand. Then I ran his prints from the glasses and beer bottles from which he drank on the yacht."

Darius was able to confirm who he was and had his computer at work encrypted as the one at home was off limits. Darius knew that wouldn't be wise.

Diane jumped up, "I thought that was anonymous. How did you know that I, Diane Roberts sent it?" She was frightened.

"Are you serious? The computer you used…like all other computers that are connected to the internet has an IP address, short for Internet Protocol, and it gives the physical location of the computer which narrows it down to one of the 50 states," he tried to make light of the situation, but he saw that she didn't feel anyways light. He noticed that she was even more tensed than ever.

"You sent it from the library on 42nd Street," Darius continued, "and of course from our face recognition software, we ran your picture that was captured on the computer's camera, and then we discovered all we needed to know about you. I mean if you wanted to hide..."

"Wear a mask is what you are saying..."

"No Diane, but you gotta be smarter than that. That was a dead give-away, com'on."

"Damn..." she expressed disappointment. "There's just nothing sacred, is there? No privacy whatsoever." Her body became subdued.

"Not since the Patriot Act, no," he smiled uncomfortably.

"What do you mean you have discovered all there is to know about me?" She was troubled, and commanded an answer in such a tone as if her life depended upon it.

It wasn't her fear that concerned Darius. It was her body language, that unspoken communication to which he had taken notice with people since he was a little boy—centered eyes-focused, gazing up-thinking, gazing down-shame/lies, gazing to the side-guilt. Gesture, posture, and facial expression communicate countless subtle and complex meanings. It tells a person's true feelings. It dictated how Darius received Diane's words. He was taken back at what he saw now that he was observing her. She paced back and fro, and mumbled unrecognizable words as if talking to herself in a whisper. *I'll be damned,* Darius thought to himself.

"What are you not telling me...?" The expert body reader asked.

"Nothing," Diane swiftly uttered. "I'm not hiding anything," she looked him in the eyes.

Interesting. She just lied to me twice. "Glad to know

that." *The plot has just thickened, just like that. What the hell am I missing? What is she hiding? Why would she send the tip? No need to even ask her as she would lie and with every lie thus far was a dagger.*

"Why are you telling me all of this again?" Diane recognized her behavior and forced herself to behave "normal."

"Because the shit has hit the fan," and he bowed his head, as it hurt him now to say this, "I love you." He knew she believed him and he smiled at her blush. "It's more important to me for you to know that Liz is not pregnant by me than for you to believe the lie, especially when I realize that you believing the lie, is more dangerous for you." *Focus Darius.*

"How so?"

"Because knowing the truth will give you a head start in saving your life"

"From what? From whom?"

"From the person who saw to it that Liz got pregnant, Michael."

Diane looked at him as if he had two heads. "Michael, ahh…. I can assure you that he has nothing to do with Liz's pregnancy."

"No you can't."

She snatched herself away from him. "Are you saying that Liz is pregnant by Michael?" She stood up.

"No, I'm not saying that." He stood up also. "I don't know who she is pregnant by, but I can tell you this, he knows."

"You don't know what the hell you are talking about! You don't know!" She hit him in the chest, "you don't know!"

"Diane, you don't know the man you've claimed to love

over the years."

"Believe me when I say this, I-actually-do."

"No, Diane, you don't." There was silence. She turned away from him and he continued to plead with her. "Baby, if you did, you would have never risked being with me."

Darius didn't understand that Diane risked being with him, despite what would happen to her if Michael found out.

"Oh, and let me guess, you just know him so well."

"Yeah, I do. I know him better than I'd like to."

"Maybe I risk being with you despite what would happen to me should Michael find out."

"I find that hard to believe."

"You would. Is Michael your suspect, your whatever you call him?"

"He's my perpetrator, yes. I've been assigned to him for as long as I have known you guys."

"Shut your face. You shut your face right now! Are you telling me that we've been living a lie for over three years!"

"No. We, you and I, we weren't a lie."

"Oh please. That's why I didn't even know your name?" She put up her right palm and dismissed him. She turned her back to him. "I hope you are satisfied with the great job you've done to upset my life. My friend is pregnant by God knows who. The man I love is a fraud, and my boyfriend is about to be on America's Most Wanted list! You don't know how much I want to vomit by the thought of all this chaos!"

"He is not about to be D, he is on it, hence my assignment." Darius approached her and held her gently until she calmed down. Let me walk you back home, I gotta go do something right away."

"What do you have to do, or is that top secret because of your job?"

"I have to go see Liz immediately."

"I'm going with you, and that's not a question."

They walked back to Diane's apartment where they then took Darius' car and drove to Elizabeth's.

CHAPTER
SEVENTEEN

They were both quiet during the entire ride to Elizabeth's place. As they walked up to her apartment, Diane became nervous. Darius rang the bell.

"Hey guys, come in," Elizabeth opened the door. She walked towards her sofa to have a seat. Darius and Diane walked in behind her. They decided not to sit down.

"Sit down guys," she casually suggested to them, and they politely refused. Moments later, after she recognized the uncomfortable silence in the room, she tried to break the tension. "What? What is it?"

"Liz," Darius approached her as he cleared his throat. He was just so thrown with all of this. He was now more determined to take Michael down. Michael's plan was to distract him, Darius was so certain of that, but Michael underestimated who Darius really was. He was more concerned for Elizabeth and he would have dealt with the loss of Diane if he had to, but Michael, Michael's days of reign were very much numbered. This time, it was personal. If nothing else, he would avenge Elizabeth's misfortune. Darius was more focused than ever.

"Liz, I'm going to cut to the chase and Diane will have to fill you in with the rest." Darius changed his mind and sat next to her and faced her.

"You are not pregnant by me."

Elizabeth motioned to jump up to protest but Darius reached out with his left hand and gently pushed her back down.

"We don't have much time because we have to get someone to confirm what I suspect. We have to find out if you were drugged with some sort of sedatives, which would explain why you don't recall being with anyone else but me. And being that those things don't usually stay in the body for a long time, maybe two days, we have to move quickly."

She was flabbergasted by what Darius had just said. By the look in her eyes, Darius and Diane knew that Elizabeth's state was worse than Diane's.

"Liz…" Darius continued.

"No!" This time Elizabeth pushed Darius's hands off her. "Roberto, you've said enough, I want you to get the hell out." She got up and walked to the door and opened it. "Get out." She demanded of Darius, but he instead walked to the door and slammed it shut.

"You are going to hear this whether or not you like it. I'm sorry that I'm about to wreck your world." He pulled out a black leather badge, and showed it to her. In the middle was a gold crescent in the shape of an eagle. In the middle of that a blue circle was the inscription, *Department of Justice*, and below that *Drug Enforcement Administration*. The name Darius Kramer was printed on it.

"My name is Darius Kramer, and I am not who you think I am, but that's neither here nor there. What you need to know is that I can't get anyone pregnant, not because we always used protection but because I had a vasectomy four years ago. I can't get into it right now, but we need to find out whose DNA matches the baby you are carrying. We also need to have you checked for any recent sperm that may have deposited in you and have that examined for a DNA match with the baby. If nothing else works it gets us closer to a definite on the father."

"You are crazy if you think I am going to have an amniocentesis to satisfy your delusions." Elizabeth was convinced that the Roberto she knew was crazy. "I am not risking anything to harm my baby, especially taking out fluid from my baby's sack just so you can test it to find out DNA information. You can go to hell and by the way I won't need you or your damn money to help raise my child."

"Of course Liz, I'm sorry. I didn't mean to suggest that we pose any threat to the baby. But, we need to at least try to see if there is any sperm in you so we can get the DNA and then compare it to the baby after birth." He bowed his head. He didn't want to say it. "Liz, we need to do a rape kit…and if there is any left-over sperm in you…" he cleared his throat, "then we would have likely discovered a rapist."

"Have you lost your mind Roberto!" She screamed.

"Either way Liz, this is going to happen. We're getting any possible sperm in you, so you might as well make it easy on yourself. We know that person may not be the child's father as you are already pregnant, but I have a feeling it will lead to somewhere. At least it's process of elimination."

She realized that he believed what he was saying. She looked at Diane with tears in her eyes. Diane walked towards her.

"None of this makes sense Liz, but he is telling the truth. I am still in shock myself."

"Both of you are crazy. You are clearly on drugs. And how the hell are you going to believe him Diane?" Darius saw that this was getting nowhere.

"This is going to hurt me more than it hurts you," he mumbled to himself. "Excuse me, I have to go and get something from the car." He went to the car, opened the trunk and reached for his bag with his secret stash. From there, he pulled out one of the pieces of cloth from the bag, reached for the chloroform and wet the cloth with some of it. He hurried back to the apartment. Diane opened the door, and Darius walked up to Elizabeth from behind. He held her and quickly put the soaked chloroform cloth over her nose as she resisted. She was instantly lifeless in his arms.

"Grab her keys Diane." They walked toward the car as he carried Elizabeth and placed her gently on the back seat. Diane sat next to her.

"Where are we going?" Diane asked as she tried to identify the number that appeared on his vibrating phone that rested on the cup holder. She couldn't.

"My last resort. Excuse me; I have to answer the phone. "Darius engaged in a conversation with a person on the other end of the phone. "Yes, we are heading there now. Hurry and meet me there."

"Who was that?" Diane demanded.

"You'll find out soon enough." Silence accompanied them.

From his rearview mirror, Darius observed that Diane was fixated by her surroundings. The Brooklyn Queens Expressway led them into the Brooklyn Battery Tunnel, which brought them to the West Side Highway in Manhattan. Darius exited onto 54th street and took 10th Avenue uptown to 62nd Street. Diane slouched in the seat and leaned her head back and to the right. She had taken herself back in time. And then Darius saw it. Fordham Law School was on the right near the corner of Columbus Avenue. Darius reflected upon Diane's profile with the DEA's office, having being linked with Michael. Her stress of having to endure the political consequences for having lost few too many of what seemed to have been open and shut drug cases at the Brooklyn District Attorney's Office. All of that was a long cry from her days as a student at Fordham Law. Diane smiled at the cultural attaché she once called home. The Julliard School of Performing Arts, The Metropolitan Opera, The New York Philharmonic, and The New York City Ballet all shared one thing in common — Lincoln Center was their home. The Center was ordained with elaborate fountains with some having encircled Roman inspired sculptures that sat on six feet squared stone structured pillars. She was once again dazzled by the sight of guitars, even at night, strapped across shoulders and trumpets and violins as hand luggage. Wine was the popular drink as she pierced into the stolen moments of friends, lovers, and business partners who left no seats empty, as cafés extended themselves to the exterior. The scenery changed from strips of glass-faced boutiques, banks, Fortune 500 companies to 19th century terracotta tile and brick structures having the façade of Victorian architecture. One such grandeur site was the old Alfred Waterhouse building later renamed the American Museum of Natural History. Diane admired the elaborate gardens, full of visitors and the plush greenery of Central Park across the street. Not too long after, Darius directed the car in the garage of one of those terracotta tiled Victorian architect structure. As Darius parked the car, Diane noticed that all the vehicles in the garage were priced at no less than $70,000, and they were newer models. They had no scratches, no dents, and no bumper stickers. Their shiny coatings sealed the notion that they were well maintained. They exited the black, hand stitched leather interior of the Escalade.

"Welcome to Central Park West counselor," Darius said to Diane.

"Rob... I mean Darius, what are we doing here?"

Darius didn't answer her. He was too busy trying to get Elizabeth to the elevator and then upstairs without much intrusion. He managed to do just that. He opened the door to apartment 7A.

Diane was marveled when she entered the apartment. To her left, the kitchen countertop, back splash and floor were, marble. The microwave was one of two drawers depicted on the black and silver stove that had a black tinted glass surface with no burners as it was electrical. The other drawer was the oven. To actually cook a simple meal involved programmed features. It took her a moment to realize that the room across from her was a library. Its walls were painted with antique leather faux paint with the Library Mahogany base and Saddle Brown glaze. The vintage chair was beautifully conspicuous. The wooden ladder leaned against stacks of Charles Dickens, Shakespeare, Richard Wright, William Faulkner, Claude McKay, Langston Hughes, and others who reached toward the cathedral ceiling. The apartment was more spacious and possessed more personality than many suburban houses she had visited. She made her way into the living room. The dazzling Japanese inspired waterfall caused her to question whether or not the water was silently and smoothly crawling down the vertical flatbed that had camouflaged itself with the semi-gloss tan walls. Something relatively cost effective caught Diane's attention. She tripped over herself as she tried to walk and have her eyes fixated on it. Darius looked to see what had caught her attention. A picture of her lying in Darius' lap caught her attention. It was a picture he had taken at his place on Montague Street with the automatic camera.

"What is this picture doing here?" She picked up the picture. She then noticed some of Darius' clothes on the sofa and his favorite shoes thrown down on the living room floor.

"Darius! Where are we?"

"My other apartment."

"Other apartment?" She was bewildered.

"Yes." He realized she remained as she was, bewildered.

He went to the phone and called Peter Viesser. "I'm here Peter."

"We are on our way Darius."

Minutes later, they arrived. At the buzzing of the intercom, Diane heard the doorman.

"Mr. Hosten, there's a Mr. Viesser and Ms. Stein here to

see you."

"Thank you, Mr. Sams. Please send them up right away."
Darius spoke politely and with a more sophisticated accent.

Diane simply stared at him and shook her head.

"Yes, I am aware that was just another of your pseudonyms
and I don't wish to even entertain it."

"Good. I'm glad we are all on the same page."

At the sound of the doorbell, Darius went to the door and
opened it.

"What took you so long?"

"You know, you really need to get a butler," Peter joked.

"Peter, Julie, this is Diane Webster and Elizabeth
Roberts." Darius pointed to Elizabeth who was laid out on the
sofa.

"Peter, I must go, so you take over. They are not to
leave the apartment from now on, for their own safety." Darius
had already brought Peter and Julie up to date on what was
happening. He turned his attention to Diane.

"May I see you for a second?" Darius walked into one of
the bedrooms. She accompanied him. He closed the door behind
them.

"D, I have to go, but I will be back."

"Please be careful Ro…"

"You know, I'm the same man," he affixed his body
to hers. "I am the same man D," he whispered as he put his
forehead on hers. She cried.

"This is all so much," she sniffled.

All night Darius just wanted to hold her and never let go.
He knew she just needed a good cry. He held her head up and

placed his lips on hers. After kissing for a while, Darius pulled back. "D, I have to go, don't ask, please." She nodded her head. They hugged really tight and then Darius escorted her to the living room.

"Peter, call me." He exited the apartment.

EIGHTEEN

Elizabeth woke up to find Peter, Julie and Diane staring at her. She also recognized that she was in unfamiliar territory.

"Hi Elizabeth. I am Dr. Stein and this is Peter Viesser. We work with Mr. Kramer. Ahhhh....., he explained to us that you needed us to remove some specimen from you, so we may run some tests and come up with a DNA match as to your assaulter. "Tears flooded Elizabeth's eyes and soul. There was no need protesting anymore. She was curious. Diane's presence confirmed that she was in no danger. Her friend would have made sure of that. Elizabeth did something she had never done before. She consented to doing something though none of it made sense.

"Diane, is it okay? Is it okay for me to do this?" She needed confirmation.

"Yes," Diane cried. She rushed over to her and held her. They both cried.

"We'll get through this Liz, we will. "Elizabeth gently moved Diane away, stood up and addressed Julie.

"Let us get this over with, if nothing else to prove

that there is only one man's sperm in me." She was suddenly uncertain, yet sure at the same time.

"Let's go in the bedroom," Julie said.

As Elizabeth passed the coffee table, she saw Diane quickly block a picture that was on it. She dismissed what she saw as unimportant. Everything was already out of sequence, so Diane's action didn't even seem odd. As they entered the bedroom, Elizabeth saw that Julie wished she didn't have to do this. It was evident that Julie tried to remove her emotions from the situation. Julie directed Elizabeth to the bed, and she prepared herself to extract any bit of sperm to be found. She also performed a rape kit. After Julie was finished, she excused herself. Elizabeth remained on the bed. She just wanted to disappear. She decided to walk around and pry a little to find out who was this Darius guy. She didn't wish to be disturbed. She informed Julie and Diane that she was going to lie down and that she would appreciate no interruptions. They agreed. She started to pace around the room. After she searched through everything, she found nothing. She threw herself on the bed. She lifted the pillow to fluff it. She noticed something under it. She put the pillow to one side and reached for this thing. She took a closer look and dropped it immediately. She threw herself back quickly, fell to the floor and started to crawl backwards. She shook her head. *No, this can't be.* It was a picture of Darius. This time Darius was in a young lady's lap. His left hand was on her head as if he had brought her head down so their lips would have met and they did. His right hand was on her left breast and they were both smiling, clearly a very intimate picture of lovers. It was a very intimate picture of Darius and Diane.

Samurai had decided that he was restless. He had to see his other partner. He needed to discuss what was to be done about Michael. The sooner they took him down, the better. He got up, picked up the keys and walked toward the elevator. As he got to the lobby, he thought again and wondered if he had the energy to go see his other partner. The thought of Michael boosted his energy. He exited the hotel and hailed a cab. He was going to see his partner who lived relatively close by New York City according to yellow taxicab standards. That was too close for comfort, Samurai thought. He gave the cabbie the address and decided that he would rest his mind until he got there. In a time too short for Samurai, he heard the cabbie.

"Sir, we are here." Samurai handed him $20 and didn't wait for the change.

Samurai went up to his partner's building, and greeted to the doorman. He then walked up to the attendant at the desk.

"I'm here to see Mr. Hosten, apartment 7A, please.

CHAPTER

NINETEEN

Lt. Smith sat attentively in his office. His phone rang and he immediately knew who it was. It was his wife calling to ask him if he had forgotten his way home again. It was three in the morning after all and Lt. Smith could not have convinced his wife that anyone had a practical reason to be working 23 out of the 24 hours in the day.

"Baby, yes I am very much aware that it is three in the morning," he picked up the phone.

"Don't baby me, and I don't want to hear oh it's this case that you're working on or that case. What about your case here at home? You know - me, your wife, remember me?" She was not trying to be understanding.

"I know," Smith rubbed his head. "I'm packing up to leave now."

"Why bother? All you are going to do is come home, shower and leave again." She became quiet. "Are you having an affair?"

"Oh yeah, It's called Samurai, and Cassandra Willis, and

Sambino and drug dealers. Yeah I am having an affair, with my job." The slamming sound of the phone on the other end actually hurt his ear.

"Well nice talking to you too." He hung up the phone. He got up, shoved some papers in his bag, walked out of his office, closed the door behind him and headed for the stairs.

"See you guys in a few," he said to the rest of the staff. She was right. All he was going to do was get ready and leave again. He had no reason to take work home. With that thought, he headed back to his office, put the bag with files in his desk and locked his desk. He headed back downstairs. As he reached outside to walk to the direction of his car, he noticed a man being very conspicuous. He was standing across the street. The lieutenant walked to his car and the man walked in the same direction. He crossed the street right before the lieutenant reached his car. As the lieutenant approached his car, the man tapped his coat pocket and pretended as if he was searching for something on him. He did not look at Smith.

"Lieutenant, Internal Affairs is going to be on your ass regarding one of your own. It's going to be much sooner than you can squint. You have to get Samurai back in your office tomorrow and get to the bottom of this Cassandra Willis murder. It will answer many questions you want to ask me right now but won't get the chance. Don't look as if you're noticing me. You could lose your life, and that is not a threat from me, it's actually to save your life."

Before Lt. Smith could have asked or said anything, Darius was gone. Lt. Smith headed back to his office. He would have called his wife when he got back and she would have argued about it whenever he reached home.

Elizabeth was on the floor in a corner. She tucked her knees under her chin. She wrapped her arms around her legs as if she was pulling them into her body. She rocked back and forth. It seemed as if her tears were endless. With no sound coming anywhere from her, Elizabeth tried to breathe. She tried to figure out what the hell had happened between when she woke up this morning and now. *At what point exactly did the world decide that I could have gone to fuck myself?* She had enough for one night. She was pregnant. She instantly decided that she would not remain that way. Strangers were trying to convince her that the man who had sex with her was not the father, but in fact another stranger who she had yet to know existed. To push the dagger in a bit deeper, her lover was playing the birds and the bees with her former best friend. She stood, brushed off her buttocks, stared at the door and headed to it. She held on to the lock, mustered enough strength, opened it and walked outside.

"Liz, honey, are you alright?" Diane ran to her being genuinely concerned. "I thought you were going to take a nap or something, you know – try to get your mind off some of this. I don't even know what to call it." Diane twirled her hand in front of her mouth signaling for the words to come forth, "Nightmare." Diane stood directly in front of Elizabeth. She reached out and held Elizabeth's arms. "Liz, it looks as if you just saw a ghost, baby you alright?" She shook Elizabeth gently. "Honey?"

Julie apologized to Diane as she interrupted her. "Liz, I gave Peter the specimen to take to the lab to run some tests so we can try to get a DNA match," Julie said. "It may be some time."

142

Elizabeth didn't budge. She just stood there and looked at Diane. Her eyes were dazed as if she needed a quick fix. She spoke slowly and carefully as if she had just learned the language.

"Julius Caesar had always been your favorite play. It's ironic how you don't like Brutus. I mean, he should be your favorite character. After all, you are one and the same."

"What are you talking about Liz?"

"It wasn't enough just to have Michael right?" Elizabeth continued to speak in a slow and calm manner. "You just had to have Roberto too, whatever his name is."

Diane's face and body dropped instantly. "I know we were supposed to be best friends Diane and best friends share everything, but some things I thought were implied that best friends don't share."

Diane was soaked in shame, regrets, pain and disappointment. Her facial expression asked the questions; how did Elizabeth find out? What did Darius have in that room that Elizabeth had seen? Diane hung her head with only her tears to comfort her. She couldn't look up and was beaten by remorse.

"You are the only sister I've ever known," Elizabeth continued, "but I guess I was born alone so it's only fitting that I die alone, being that I no longer have a sister."

Diane screamed out in pain; the agony was unbearable. "Liz, pleeeeeeeeeease! Pleeeeeeeeease! Don't do this!"

From the content of their conversations, it was obvious that Julie figured out what was happening. Elizabeth turned to Julie. "Thank you for your help, but identifying the father won't be necessary."

Diane was traumatized. Elizabeth then turned to Diane.

"I hope you never remotely feel what I'm feeling D, because let me tell you, it hurts like a bitch."

Diane cried harder as she bent over and held her belly in an effort to alleviate the pain. Elizabeth walked towards the door.

"You can't leave Liz," Julie said. Elizabeth looked at her and smiled.

"It was nice meeting you." With that being said, she closed the door behind her and waited for the elevator.

⌒⌒⌒⌒

"I'm sorry sir, Mr. Hosten is not at home, and he left specific instructions not to allow anyone else in his apartment," the desk attendant said to Samurai.

"Do you know if he'll be right back?"

"No sir, I'm afraid I don't." Seconds later, Elizabeth exited the elevator and headed for the front door. Samurai noticed her and was immediately attracted to her. Her smooth caramel complexion, hazel eyes and golden bronze hair seemed dull to the gloom that clothed her right now.

"Are you alright?" Samurai asked Elizabeth as she passed by.

"Yes, I'm fine, thank you." Her cheeks slightly elevated and tears simultaneously flooded her eyes. She walked steadily out the front door.

Samurai thanked the desk attendant and also headed out the front door. He looked to his left and noticed Elizabeth's beautiful body gliding down the block. He shook his body and muttered "holy mother of God" as a sign of approval of her beauty. She was as striking as the women that often times surrounded Mr. Hosten.

"I will have your phone sir," Samurai remembered the talking beauty that greeted him when he first met Mr. Hosten in his apartment upstairs. Mr. Hosten's name was no stranger to the Blazer's household, as Samurai's parents were respectable business attorneys and have vested heavily in Bedford Stuyvesant, and apparently so did Mr. Hosten. He wondered what his parents would say should they discover that he has met the notorious Mr. Hosten, much less being his partner. His parents have never met him nor did they care to do so, as they would never want to be seen with a man such as Mr. Hosten. He thought of how they would be disappointed at such a move on Samurai's part.

"It's just protocol sir," the talking beauty continued, "We have to do a sweep on your phone as well as you to ensure that you are not bugged."

"Understand." Samurai was relaxed. Unknown to him, for everyone who released their phones to these undercover DEA agents, their phones were never returned to them the same. They never seemed to notice the microscopic bug that had been set in place. The DEA, like it had done to the others, had entered the private sector of Samurai's life.

"Why Samurai...such a pleasure to meet you in person." Mr. Hosten was younger than Samurai had ever imagined a supplier would be. He knew though it was him as the code name in their email was 'Bread," and such was the code texted to Samurai. Only two sets of people knew the code, and as far as Samurai knew, the supplier was the other.

"I don't mean to be stereotypical, given that I am half black, but I pegged you for latino, given the fact that the goods come from Nicaragua, but Mr. Hosten is not a Spanish name… though you are a native of Nicaragua."

"I was born in Managua. This is my business name, for obvious reasons—helps to protect my true identity. Surely you can understand. "

"Of course. In this business, you can't be too careful. My parents speak a lot about you given the fact that Bedford Stuyvesant is one of your territories and they invest so much there. "

"Yes, that is ironic, isn't it? We share a similar interest; Bedford Stuyvesant," his eyes squinted. "Sammy. May I call you Sammy?" He raised his eyebrows.

"Please…"

"I see that you are doing great things for the business, and I just wanted to say thank you in person for your hard work."

"Of course," Samurai wavered. "We aim to please." He was so excited that someone at that level would take notice of him and reached out to him to engage in a joint venture as a silent partner. He had outdone himself this time.

"I know that you have allowed someone else to partake in your business, and I am rather concerned."

"Why is that?" Samurai was perplexed.

"From what I hear and can see, he's a bit arrogant, pig headed, no other opinion but his goes…and that can be dangerous and bad for business, don't you think?"

"Absolutely, I couldn't agree with you more." Finally someone was on his page. "Have you met him?" Samurai was

146

at attention. "He has a scar on his left hand, can't miss it."

"No, I'm afraid I haven't. I'm cautious as to whom I allow in my circles, but I have eyes and ears on the street. It's important that he never finds out that we have met...you know jealousy about meeting the boss, stuff like that."

"Yeah, I can see that with his personality."

"Yeah and, who is he anyways? All orders for the product come through you and are delivered to you, and then you distribute it accordingly, right?" Samurai notice that Mr. Hosten just saw his eyes wandered. "Well that's how we understand it on our end," Mr. Hosten continued, as we don't trust just any one with our product in fear of contamination."

"I can assure you your product is sold as you sent it," Samurai tried to reassure his supplier.

"That's what I thought," he offered Samurai a cigar. "It's said that this Sambino guy quadrupled your money...but is it really your money, when there's such a significant split? Imagine if he wasn't in the picture," he gave Sammy a moment to think. "Imagine with me as your investor--how far you would really go, calling all the shots, getting all the respect and definitely much more of the loot."

"But we are making good loot. Sambino is useful."

"But for how long? He's getting sloppy. Creating logos for everything he touches, and messing with the Court System getting people off. How long before the feds take over your stomping ground? Now you will be left will cleaning up his mess." He saw that Samurai was thinking. "Look, he is not like you and I. He's not used to money, power or respect, so he will stop at nothing to get it..."

"And that's the worst kind of virus, the one that can't be stopped." Samurai finished for Mr. Hosten.

"A man of my own heart." Mr. Hosten drew a puff.

"I am in." Samurai stood. "How will we get rid of him, and won't he talk?"

"A guy like him never talks. He would die first as he's the type that doesn't believe in burning bridges, especially to those who have been good to him in terms of making him loot. He did it once, he can do it again, under better luck next time," Mr. Hosten's eyes danced.

"Let's make it happen," Samurai was elated. Finally, he would be running all the shots.

"Great, so we will stay in contact via this cell phone," he handed a phone, "as it is a secured line.

"What's wrong with my phone?"

"I don't know, and I won't take chances. You speak to me only on this phone. Otherwise, we won't speak at all. No one gets this number, am I understood?" Mr. Hosten was authoritative. Oh Samurai, one more thing-- I can't stress enough that it is imperative that your parents being who they are don't become aware of our meeting. The last thing we thing we need is to out fires and then you won't get the chance to prove to yourself what I know—that you can do this.

"Of course."

"Great, so we will stay in contact as to how we will move forward with a change of plans for Sambino."

Those plans couldn't be fully implemented fast enough for Samurai. He headed the opposite direction from Elizabeth, with his mind on Mr. Hosten and Michael. His father had warned him of Michael—that Samurai needed to watch the company he kept. Samurai never forgot how Michael chased down the limousine one afternoon, and kept hitting it until his father directed the chauffeur to stop. His parents had conducted business at a medical clinic and a legal office.

"How can we help you?" Samurai's father, Mr. Blazer, rolled down the window, annoyed.

"Just want to say they thank you for the great work you doing are here; it's truly remarkable," Michael was short of breath.

"Thank you young man," Mr. Blazer responded and rolled up the window while summoning the chauffeur to drive. "That's the man I saw you with earlier today Samurai. You are playing around with him. The mere fact that he felt he could do what he just did is a mistake."

Most thought Michael's actions strange, but Samurai dismissed it by saying that his friend didn't get around much and what else one can expect from someone living where he lived. He watched his father's eyes.

"Precisely, that was out of character for someone who lives here," Mr. Blazer was evidently concerned, and now so was Samurai.

CHAPTER
TWENTY

Prosecutor Carlitta Davis paced across her living room floor, with both hands on her hips. This murder of Cassandra Willis was driving her crazy. The evidence she gathered to eventually take down Sambino had too many holes. She didn't trust her main witness. She sensed something disastrous might happen with the case. She feared it would happen in court. The last thing she needed was to be caught off guard. How could she prepare a case when she didn't trust the evidence? How could she even be sure that Samurai could really produce this Sambino guy? Getting Sambino was the only reason why Samurai wasn't getting life; shit the damn chair, if New York had actually used it. Why the assistance to the authorities all of a sudden? What was in it for this guy? I mean no one even knew about Cassandra until Samurai blurted it out one day in exchange for them to get Sambino, the drug lord who had been escaping them all. Samurai's drug related charges were so insignificant, it probably wouldn't even hold up, so why reveal such a massive piece of information when it wasn't asked. Why intentionally put yourself under a microscope?

"Tell me again what happened?" Carlitta recalled her interrogation of Samurai.

"I told you, I shot her, wham, right between the eyes. Would you like for me to show you?" He smirked.

"And why did you shoot her again?" She was not amused.

"I already told you."

"Well, tell me again," Carlitta leaned over the table and put her face up to his, trying to intimidate him.

"If you are not going to kiss me," Samurai joked, *"I suggest you get out of my face because I now have no reason to tolerate your tuna breath."*

"You-are-going-down, Samurai," Carlitta moved away from his face.

"I'll plead necessity as a defense," he started to light a cigar but the cop in the room snatched it from him.

"How so? Enlighten me."

"It's simple Ms. ADA. I had to kill so not to be killed. Sambino had a gun to my head, and I had one at Cassandra's, as instructed. Either he pulled the trigger or I pulled the trigger. Either way someone was pulling the trigger that night." The entire time, Samurai was smiling. They both knew that defense would not have worked.

"You rotten ..."

"No...no...no...no," Samurai shook his head and waved his finger. *"Watch it counselor, you don't want to get sued for defamation of character,"* his facial features danced.

The sound of her pager distracted her. It was Lt. Smith. He had left a text message for her to head down to the precinct first thing in the morning. Something urgent regarding the Cassandra Willis case had just surfaced. Sleep was the furthest thing from her mind. She called Lt. Smith right away.

"I'm on my way Smith."

"You do know what time it is, don't you?"

"As I said, I am on my way." Carlitta didn't have to spend any time getting ready since she had never changed from her jeans and T-shirt that she had worn on the day before. She put on her sneakers, grabbed her keys and dashed to her car. She could have not reached the precinct fast enough. As Carlitta pulled up to the precinct, a drive that normally took 30 minutes seemed like it had taken five.

"Good morning, Ms. Davis," the officer at the front desk greeted her as she ran upstairs to Lt. Smith's office.

"What do we have?" She was practically out of breath as she quickly dropped her bottom in the chair.

"I had a visitor not too long ago." Lt. Smith slouched back in his chair. He rested his chin on his right knuckles and used his right index finger and tapped on his right cheek. "This Cassandra Willis case goes deeper in the rabbit hole than we think. I was advised that it would be in our best interest to get to the bottom of the rabbit hole as quickly as possible and it seems as if our lives could be in danger on the way down."

"Informant or someone on the inside?"

"Ms. Davis, I couldn't tell you. I have never seen him before. But I can tell you this; I have a feeling that I am going to see him again."

"Why didn't you hold him? Everyone knows if someone has information on a crime, you hold him and question him, as long as it doesn't exceed 24 hours."

"Really? I had no idea." Smith got up and walked over to the window. He stared into the early morning. "I need everything on Willis. I need her hospital of birth, childhood everything, favorite cookie, work, FBI file, whatever."

"What about Samurai, Lieutenant?"

"I don't trust him as far as I can throw him. I want an undercover on him."

"You want my main witness followed?"

"Hell yeah, stalked if necessary, either way, bottom of the rabbit hole, here we come."

He took Cassandra's file from the pile on his desk and put it in front of him.

"Cassandra, I am Lt. Smith. And the million dollar question is--who the hell are you?"

"Do we know anything more about this Sambino guy besides hearsay? I mean how do we know that he really exists for crying out loud? Isn't it odd that no one has really seen him, just heard that he has sent word, actually threats if things are not his way?"

"And we have all seen the consequences of people not doing what he says, counselor. In fact, he does the exact same thing he says he will do."

"Okay, so we know he has a reputation on the streets. Everyone fears him and from what we've heard from people themselves, he is not to be messed with."

"Yeah, what's mind boggling is that Samurai says that Sambino is one of us. He does not live in a mansion on the hill. He works a regular job, lives a regular life and you could be having coffee with him and not know it's him."

"Why would he live like a regular Joe?"

"It's harder to find a chameleon and he can keep his eyes on things himself, I guess."

"How long have you guys been looking for him?"

"Since he first came on the scene, some years now. He goes so far as to have his name on the crack vial or whatever these drugs come in. It's like his name is a trademark or logo, or even yet a walking commercial. It's even on the victims he killed, 'Sambino was here.'"

Carlitta closed her eyes and shook her head in disgust to the likes of Sambino. She quickly changed the topic.

"So, we start with the Bureau of Vital Records and how far back are we going for this Cassandra Willis?"

"All the way to the beginning of the previous century," Smith was serious.

"You are kidding right?" Carlitta asked and looked at him as if he had just lost his mind. "So, you want to go back as far as 100 years old?" She thought that Smith had lost his mind due to a lack of sleep.

"We are leaving no stones unturned, Davis, no stones unturned," he continued to stare through the window. "We'll also check Social Security, Homeland Security and the IRS." He answered before she could have asked her question. "Yes, the Internal Revenue Service."

"How do we even know that this Cassandra person is real? And even if she is real, how do we really know she died the way he said and why her? What's her connection in all of this?"

"We know she's real because the Good Samaritan I saw

not too long ago at my car confirmed that."

"Who's to say he's real?"

"My gut feeling." Smith eyes were still fixated on whatever it was outside. Carlitta sighed. Smith needed not to say anymore, she understood all too perfectly. "I am sick of this shit, this entire case. Go home and get some sleep, Davis."

"Where are you going?"

"Home, to my wife, to not get sleep," he smiled.

"I'll walk you out lieutenant." They headed out the door and down the stairs to face the sun and yet another day.

CHAPTER
TWENY ONE

As Michael aka Stony sat in his living room all night, rage ripped through him. He sat in disbelief at the notion that he had found himself in this position. He was left with no choice but to just kill them all, one by one. His thoughts went to Otis having entered a plea. Michael reassured him that it was far from over and that he wasn't alone. He guaranteed that someone would pay for this especially if he Michael went down as well. As he put his head back on the couch, his head faced the ceiling. He closed his eyes to escape his current thoughts. It took him back to an earlier time.

It had been five years since Stony had been engaged in the "service" business. His stable of one had taken him to a stable of 25, and a lucrative business had ensued. After counting a week's revenue, Stony decided that even with the $27,000 he had made that week, it still wasn't enough. It wasn't consistent and anything short of an annual income of 2.5 million with his 20th birthday approaching was simply unacceptable. After his father's death, he had promised his mother never to venture down the road of user of illegal narcotics. That would be the least of her worries, as she would never have to ask that twice of him. To supplement his income, he kept his promise to his mother, and became a salesman of illegal narcotics instead. Unlike the path chosen by many who have earned their promotion after proving themselves in the streets as foot soldiers, or being risen to the next level lieutenant, Stony decided that he would simply begin at the boss' position, even if he had to take it.

Bed-Stuy's residents were notorious for seeing everything but knowing nothing, and not having heard anything. That code remained true as people often times passed and noticed kids apply the art of graffiti on buildings at random, but still knew nothing. It was business as usual until that art was applied to the Blazers' Drug Treatment Center. The Blazers were looked upon as saints by the residents for bringing help there as well as a business thus attracting work for the locals—custodians, security guards, receptionists, counselors and of course health care professionals. The Blazers were not going to allow the fear of trespassing, loitering and vandalism to paralyze them in investing in the community. As they were attorneys-at-law, they provided a law clinic for those seeking legal counsel. Such pro-bono work would be written off as charitable contribution to the likes of $250,000 a year, which included overhead costs such as salaries to attorneys, utility bills, etc. Landlord-tenant cases were taken, but the majority of the caseload seems to be that of criminal defense—drug possession and the intent to sell.

"How can I help you officer?" Stony answered the knock on his door.

"You wouldn't by chance know or have seen the kids who painted the Blazers' Drug Treatment Center green with graffiti, would you?"

"No."

"Of course not."

Stony looked at the youthful appearance of the officer and wondered if the NYPD was a gimmick. They actually assigned someone that young and who appeared not to be street savvy to walk these streets, out of all the streets in Brooklyn. The department clearly didn't value the safety of its officers. Stony looked up and saw the NYPD van. *Ahh...maybe they do have some smarts to them after all.* An idea of another step that will take him closer to freedom was born.

"Sorry I couldn't have been of more help officer...but perhaps you can help me," Stony had never been prouder of himself.

Later that evening, Stony decided to walk to Senor Vasquez's bodega to buy a beer and just to get some fresh air. As he had noticed many times in the past, a delivery truck was parked outside of the store getting ready to move the goods into the store. It had no company's name on it, which suggested that the goods were being brought from a particular manufacturer. Through rumor, Stony had heard that some of the goods that were being delivered to Mr. Vasquez, in an unmarked delivery truck weren't as they appeared. Tonight, they were delivering flour.

"Gentlemen," he approached them in calm demeanor. "What have we here?" He pointed to a bag of flour.

"It's flour asshole, can't you read?" One of the men

mistakenly addressed him.

"You will regret that," Stony said as he slid out his pocket knife, and pierced the bag of "flour."

"What the hell are you doing?" One of the men rushed him.

Stony's 32 caliber wasn't far behind. "Shut up," he would have shoved the gun up the man's nostrils if it was possible, but in the meantime, Stony settled for the nostrils being protruded upwards. "Never came across flour that made my tongue numb," he commented after putting the powdered knife to the tip of his tongue.

"I don't know what you are talking about," the man said as he walked and tripped backwards drenched in fear.

"Where are you coming from with this?" Stony knew the man felt the danger.

"I don't know man," he trembled as tears trickled.

"Oink, wrong answer," Stony stood still with his eyes fixed on the man before him, and in a perpendicular move, switched his right hand from the man's face to the head of the other. Click, the bullet left the gun's barrel and exited through the back of the other man's head. Stony lowered his hand, "you were saying?"

A statement without saying a word is all that it took for Stony to be introduced to the one in charge of securing the goods onto the delivery truck. After Stony commented to the other man as to how beautiful his wife and children must be, he was informed of the manufacturing company that was responsible for getting the goods to the man in charge so he could repackage and deliver. The New York Division of Corporations' records showed that the company was a foreign corporation established in the State of Nevada, but authorized to conduct business in New York. Whoever the owners were ensured a strategic move by choosing Nevada given its secrecy laws; but that was only secrecy to some. Ignorance would bring him knowledge.

"Hello…yes, good morning…my name is Michael Walker and I'm interested in establishing a corporation in your great state, and I'm in need of some information," he politely addressed the representative at the Division of Corporations in Nevada.

"I would be happy to help you sir," the bouncing voice came in from the other end of the phone.

"What did you say your name was again? I missed it the first time."

A trip to Nevada and the bouncing voice's misfortunate introduction to Mr. Walker led to the cooperation and all the information he needed. As he perused the information, he was dumbfounded, and his knees could have no longer sustained him, "I'll be damned." But, that wouldn't be for long. Stony had found his ticket to the overnight promotion to boss. Without the blood, sweat and tears, he has now earned his way to the top of a hierarchy—dealing directly with those who handle the product as opposed to going through a middle man. He had an offer that the boss at the time could not have refused.

That was eight years ago. Stony had since made his 2.5 million and more, though there were no accounts in the United States that could have attested to that, thanks to his young accountant Otis.

Michael's mind rushed to the present and the events of

the night that had taken place. Cassandra Willis rushed to his mind. He was grateful for her full cooperation as he could have never easily achieved his goal without it. It took a while to find her, but it was worth his efforts. He had done enough research on each of the anesthesiologists at Kings County Hospital, to figure out who would best serve his interest. He had to make sure that this person had the personality to be his *bitch*. This person was stable, meaning no drugs, worked hard and valued his or her life and things. He or she would have had much to lose. He needed someone with a close family unit so he could have made an example out of one of them should his victim develop a sudden backbone and threaten him to stop being his *bitch* or go to the cops. After he completed extensive research on each of them from childhood to adult, his *bitch* this time would be a female. He smiled as he recalled the moment that Cassandra's life as she knew it, ceased.

Cassandra came out of her car from the driveway and walked to her mailbox, as usual. After she had retrieved her mail, she browsed through them as she walked to her front door, opened it, entered into the living room and without looking, closed the door behind her. Michael didn't have to imagine what was happening inside her house because everything was in full view, thanks to the camera he had installed. Cassandra continued to browse through her mail. She separated the junk mail from what appeared to be important. The personal addressed letter as if from a friend grabbed her attention and she happily opened it. She smiled as she started to read.

"Cassandra, tomorrow, around six after work, go to Prospect Park across from the Grand Army Plaza Library, near the replicated Parthenon. A man around six feet one will be sitting alone on a bench. He will be wearing a red sweatshirt, worn blue jeans and a blue cap. He will be reading a newspaper, which will be in his lap. The remainder pages will be on the bench next to him. He will be looking down as if he is reading. You will not make eye contact so you won't know what he looks like. You will just happen to be passing by when you will feel the sudden urge to have a seat. You will ask him if the seat next to him has been taken. He will then know it's you. He will not respond. Move the papers over a little to him, and without looking up; you will have yourself a seat. Whether or not you choose to look busy, I don't care. What I care about is the 20-milligram dosage of the Propofol wrapped in a black plastic bag that you will leave him under the newspapers on the bench. You will be as normal as possible. Leave right away or not, I don't care. But know this, I care about the manner in which the life will leave your body, or the one body of the one closest to you, if you should even think of mentioning this to your creator much less any form of mankind. To know I'm true to my word, today you wore a long brown skirt, matching boots and stripe shirt to work. You had roast beef on wheat bread for lunch with an eight ounces bottle of spring water. When the old lady was giving you a hard time at the counter, you handled yourself very professionally. If you haven't figured it out yet, you are never alone."

He noticed Cassandra's knees could not have sustained her anymore. She read the letter over and over again with a bewildered look on her face. It was obvious that fear had overshadowed her. She double-checked all the doors and windows to make sure they were locked. She checked her security system to make sure it was still working, though it had never malfunctioned before. She jumped and screamed at the bell sound coming from the telephone. She was too frightened to answer and so she didn't. She massaged her forehead with her fingers as a sign of stress.

Michael smiled at the thought that this was the first of many letters to come indicating different times and places. He was not concerned with whether she would have tried to end it. He knew he would have ended her first. He watched as she took two sleeping pills to get through the night. As Michael reminisced, he thought about how much he missed her. He actually liked her. He wondered to himself if she had died in that fire, but there were no human remains according to the fire department. In his heart, he knew she was dead, he just didn't know how and why. God actually took the good ones first, he thought. Well, at least he had no more use for her; Elizabeth was pregnant, his goal was accomplished. As quickly as he thought of Cassandra, he dismissed her from his mind. He replaced it with thoughts of Otis. His rage of Otis' situation engulfed him. He vowed Otis would not suffer at the hands of the "righteous." He assured Otis that he would have had the last laugh. He decided tomorrow he would do a good deed. That cop who stopped by eight years ago was also useful with some information Michael needed. It led him to the Academy. Maybe he would go to his regular job down by the precinct. Maybe he would be a good cop and assisted in taking down some of the bad guys. As he smiled at the concept of helping to take down bad guys, sleep overcame him. Tomorrow was not far ahead; it was already morning.

TWENTY
TWO

Darius had made it back in what appeared to be no time to his Upper Westside apartment. The lack of traffic so early in the morning made the trip uptown a quick one. As he parked the car and headed upstairs, he remembered he had to get some things ready for his trip. He had not seen Maria in a couple of years and seeing her in a day or so was too soon. He had taken out on her life one-million dollars in life insurance and he had intended on praying for her death. *I know her ass belongs to the Angel of Death, so sooner or later, he's going to claim his own and I might as well celebrate in style.* Maria did not have his new cell phone number or any means by which to have contacted him, and he wanted it that way. He knew she was still alive because the money in his account kept dwindling and the landlord confirmed that she was still living there. As the elevator stopped and he waited for the door to open, he breathed loudly. He hated to deal with Elizabeth's situation, but he had to fix the damage. He paused before putting the keys in the door, and noticed that the silence inside overshadowed the human voices. He quickly opened the door and found Diane in one corner sobbing and Julie sitting around the bar in the kitchen with a glass of water. He was afraid to ask.

"Where's Liz?"

"Gone," Julie spurted.

"Gone where exactly?" Darius set his eyes on Diane. He saw that her eyes were red and puffy and she was clearly in no mood to say anything to anyone.

"Darius, she's been like that ever since Elizabeth left."

"And when was that?" He bowed his head and closed his eyes. He instantly knew what had happened. He asked in a low voice. "How?"

"The goddamn picture you had in your room," Diane sprung. "How the hell could you have that shit lying around! What is wrong with you! This is all your fault! All your fault!" She hit him in the chest and continued to bawl. "How could you risk her finding out?"

He grabbed her and tugged her body up against his chest. She cried harder.

"I'm sorry D. I'm so sorry." He held her tighter. He tried not to feel responsible but he could not have helped it. Somehow he had gotten careless and become the prey instead. Michael had him exactly where he wanted him, but as far as Darius was concerned, that was about to change. He gently pushed Diane off his chest. He held her by one hand, walked over to the sofa and pulled her down to have a seat.

"I take it that you were able to get some specimen from Liz," Darius turned his attention to Julie. He had his head back on the sofa, his eyes faced the ceiling, but closed, while the other hand gently held Diane's left hand.

"Yeah. And being that she has no recollection of being with anyone else, we took the liberty of taking some blood for whatever tests and urine so we can do a drug test to see if anything comes up."

"Like the date rape drug. I meant to tell you to do that but I'm glad we were on the same page."

"We looked for other sedatives, such as controlled substances. We can't take any chances here. We don't know how far the person we are dealing with was willing to go. So, we are just doing as many tests for all the kinds of sedatives we can think of, whether they are the ones used in surgery, date rape, or animals. We have to come across something. If not, then we are dealing with the mind of a very sick girl."

"Well, we can cross out the sick part. This shit was planned. Her pregnancy was definitely deliberate to get to me, to try and throw me off guard, so it's definitely a sedative. The motherfucker just didn't plan for one thing."

"What's that?"

"My temporary sterility."

"Somehow, it feels as if Peter is taking forever with the results." Julie said anxiously. "I mean all we need is a call to say yes he has extracted the DNA from the sperm and what drug tests he ran and what are the results."

"But still we need to wait to see how many months along she is. I don't mean to be selfish but I hope she is about four months so she can get an amniocentesis. That's the only route to the father right now."

"Darius...that can be dangerous. Who is to say she will agree?" Julie asked concerned.

"She didn't when I suggested it and I gave her the impression that I will leave it alone, but I can't. When the results come out that she was raped, she will change her mind."

"How can you be so sure?"

"I know her inside and out. Besides, it won't be mine and so she wouldn't really care. Listen, can I speak to you alone in the bedroom please?"

"Ahhh...sure," Julie got up and walked toward the bedroom.

"D, will you please excuse us?" Darius walked into his bedroom. Darius closed the door behind them.

"Talk to me Julie."

"She has definitely been raped; the bruises and tears are recent, fresh like yesterday maybe..."

"Thanks," Darius put up his hand as a way of telling her to stop. "I have heard enough."

"I'm sorry Darius."

"Yah. Ahhh, did you tell Elizabeth?"

"No, I didn't. I figure you wanted to do that."

"How about Diane, did you tell her?" Darius prayed that Julie didn't.

"No. I didn't."

"Good. Thanks again for all of your help. I'm sure I'll be calling upon you sooner than you would like. Come on; let's get back outside before she starts freaking out." He walked to open the door for Julie to reenter the living room.

"Darius," she pulled him back. "There is one more

thing."

"What?"

"She has two red spots on the back of her neck, stun gun."

"What! What the...what the hell?" Darius crunched at the thought of what she might have gone through and not told anyone.

"I think she was shot with a stun gun and she was probably then sedated and raped, being that she can't remember being penetrated." Darius clutched his jaw. *I'm going to kill that motherfucker.*

"Darius? You alright?"

"Fine." He opened the door for her to reenter the living room.

"You know what," Julie walked over to where she was sitting to collect her belongings. "I need to go home and freshen up. If you hear anything before me... call and vice versa."

"Deal."

"Diane, it was nice meeting you and I'll pray that Elizabeth will be okay."

"Thanks, Julie." She walked over to Julie and hugged her.

"While you're standing up, could you please walk Julie to the door for me?" Darius asked Diane as he dropped himself in the sofa, trying to contain his anger. He had trained himself never to have his emotions get the best of him. He was failing miserably. *The complexity of our feelings champ is evidence of the human component that makes us who we are. It's okay to feel. It's okay to cry, to hurt, and to even miss someone when he is gone. It's okay because we know it's temporary as each life is temporary.* Not now dad, he muttered to himself.

"Sure," Diane wiped her eyes, as she walked Julie to the door.

"I'll talk to you later, Darius."

"Later, Julie. Thanks again."

"Don't mention it." As she reached the door, she hugged Diane again. Diane waited at the door until the elevator came. She waved goodbye to Julie and smiled. She closed the door behind her. She remained at the door with her back against it as She thought of Elizabeth.

"I just need to escape for a moment." Darius whispered. "Come here," he said softly as he turned his head towards her and reached out his hand.

"I'm scared for Liz."

"Worrying about Liz right now is not going to change anything D. Believe it or not, she is going to be fine. She probably wanted to be alone, who wouldn't? She will find her way back to one of us if she needs to, but one way or the other, she will be alright. I don't mean to be an asshole about this, but if you are really worried, this is where God comes in, talk to him. Ask him to keep her in his care, comfort, yadi yadi ya…all that stuff. Now, come."

She hesitated.

"Here." He gestured again for her to come and this time she turned her head and looked at him.

Diane walked over slowly to him. Darius patted the seat to the right of him, and indicated for her to sit down. She did. She started to talk about Elizabeth again when Darius got up and knelt down on the floor between her legs. As she continued to talk, he gently put his right hand up under her shirt and caressed her back. He started to unbutton her blouse with his left hand.

"Darius, how can you expect me to do anything at a time like this?"

"You don't have to do a damn thing baby; I'll do it for you." He unbuttoned the last button. He glided his left hand across her belly, up to her stomach and gently pulled the right side of her red bra, and exposed her succulent round breast. As he caressed it; he gently glided his other hand across her back. He covered her breast with his mouth, and at times, used his tongue to bathe the nipple.

"Succumb to pleasure D and forget the pain," he commanded. She obeyed.

She traveled through his hair with her fingers. Darius reached upward and slowly removed her hand from his hair as he stood and immediately sat by her side.

"Stand up." She complied. He turned her around to face him. He pulled her forward, and unfastened her bra. He leaned back with Diane still standing.

"Take off your clothes," he spoke softly, yet in a commanding tone. As she slowly removed her blouse, she allowed it to glide off her arms unto the floor. She slowly unzipped her skirt at the side and let it fall to her ankles and then stepped out of it. She stood there in front of Darius with just her black silk thong. He leaned his head to the right and looked at her with a facial expression, which said, *did I not say all of your clothing?* She proceeded to remove her panties and stood directly in front of him.

"Aren't you going to take off your clothes?" She asked him.

He ignored her question, leaned forward and separated her thighs with his palm. Using his fingers, he parted the lips of her vagina, and caressed it with his hands. As she became moist, he inserted his fingers inside her making a continuous, slow, rhythmic movement. When he was done, he leaned back in the sofa, as Diane stood there.

"Come here." Diane shivered at his command. "Bring your lips to mine." She started to bend forward to kiss him.

"No," he smirked, "not those lips."

Diane inhaled so loudly, it was as if the entire building had heard her. She took a step forward as she climbed on Darius' face. As his lips met the lips between her legs, he grabbed her buttocks as he sucked and ate as if it was his favorite meal. As he did so slowly, Diane's body moved like a worm as her moaning grew. After she climaxed, he slapped her ass as an indication for her to remove herself. He didn't have to say anything. She unbuckled his belt, removed his pants completely off, went on bended knees and caressed his penis with her mouth. As she spread his legs wider, the deeper she went. He was in heaven. Diane continued to serve him for a while. He then lifted up her head, raised her up and stood up.

"Darius. How do you want me?"

"As you are. Wet."

He then held her from behind, grabbed onto both her breasts as he massaged them while he nibbled on the back of her neck. As he moved further down on her back slowly and entered into a kneeling position, his hands simultaneously went from her breasts downward. He continued to kiss her all the way down until his lips suckled with her buttocks and the line in between. He continued downward where he once again massaged her vagina and its lips with his lips and tongue. He bent her over as he stood. He reached down, got a hold of his penis and used it to feel his way inside of her. He stroked back and forth as she experienced orgasms over and over again, until he reached his climax. He then used his left hand, put it under her chin, thrust her head backwards unto him and kissed her passionately.

"Anyone ever told you, you talk too much?" He whispered.

"No," she whispered breathless.

"I find that hard to believe," he pulled out, and dropped his butt in the sofa. "Go clean up baby," he said. She went and brought back a warm washcloth, which she used to clean him up as well. He then lay down on the sofa and brought her to lie next to him. Her naked body was up against his. She was facing the coffee table. By the instant change in her body language, Darius knew she remembered the picture of them he had out.

"I can't…." He knew she was about to complain about the picture.

"Shhhhhhhhh, go to sleep." She listened and they dozed off.

CHAPTER
TWENTY
THREE

Lt. Smith paced around the house trying to gather his thoughts. He was already dressed to return to the hell he called his work. His wife had already left and so his breakfast had been sitting out for hours, being that it was now around 11 in the morning. In a hurry, he grabbed his car keys, dashed out the house, and left the breakfast in the same place his wife had left it. As he drove, the car managed to find itself en-route to 200 Bainbridge Road. Smith could not help but see for himself the kind of people, be it kids, men or women who went in and out the building doing Pierre's dirty work. As he pulled up across the street from the house, he saw a kid, who could not have been more than 13 years old, come out the building. Lucky for Smith, there was nothing on his 2010 silver car that said cop. He followed the kid for a couple blocks. The kid stopped to wait for the bus. As the bus approached, Smith watched the kid board the bus and he followed it. The kid got off the bus at DeKalb Avenue and Pulaski Street and walked to Vasquez's store. Smith decided to take a chance and go to Vasquez's store. Minutes later, the boy walked inside. The kid didn't ask for Vasquez. Instead, he handed the man behind the counter a note. After he read it, the man motioned for the kid to follow him to the back. Smith bought a bag of chips and went back to the car in an effort to not draw attention to himself. As the kid exited the store with a bag, Smith watched him return to the bus stop, where he joined him.

"How you doing kid?"

"Do I know you?"

"No, but I'm about to become your best friend," he put both hands in his pockets as he leaned against one of the posts at the bus stop.

"Who the fuck is you?" The kid stepped back and looked Smith up and down.

Smith pulled an object from his pocket. The kid at first thought it was a pocketknife, but then, Smith flipped it open.

"This is exactly what's wrong with our public school system. No one teaches grammar anymore. NYPD. Who – the fuck – is you?"

"Shit," the kid attempted to scatter, but Smith had already grabbed him.

Smith phone and requested back up. He then re-engaged the kid. "Give me the bag, kid. Now."

"Fuck you, I want my lawyer," the kid said as he tried to pull himself away from Smith.

"Well, the law does give you the right to one of those people. You call them lawyers, and we call them something else, which you are too young to hear. You know what else the law does kid? It gives me the right to snatch this bag away from you."

174

Smith put his gloves on and ripped the bag from the boy's hands. "And the law does give me the right to open it and look at its contents."

He pried the heavy knap sack open and found five pound bags of flour. At least that's what the wrappings indicated. He looked over at the kid who appeared angry, nervous and scared. Smith smiled and used a Swiss knife to pierce through the wrapping and a plastic, and extracted some white powder. As he put a tiny bit on the tip of the tongue, he turned to the kid.

"Now what kind of flour would make my tongue numb? Uum?"

"I don't know what you are talking about," the kid again tried to get away.

Shortly thereafter, two policemen in a patrol car drove up.

"Take him down to the precinct, we'll call his parents from there, and then we can give him his right to his precious lawyer."

"Fuck you, fuck all of you! Maddog is going to cut your fucking tongue out and shove it down your throat, you cocksuckers!" He kicked and screamed.

"Oh, my favorite kind of kid. Arrest him, read him his rights." Smith ordered the cops. He then approached the kid. "Now I know your mama taught you better than that. Look at the bright side, kid. If you have siblings and you share a room, now you will have your own room, all to your lonesome self."

"Fuck you," the kid spat in Smith's face.

"That's your freebie."

Smith took a handkerchief from his back pocket, wiped

his face and discarded it in the trash. He walked to his car. As he sat in the car; he watched the patrol car drive away as he succumbed to disappointment. *Another black kid in the system,* he thought to himself. *Damn.* He headed for the precinct. Many arrests were going to be made today, one way or the other, this steel wall between them and Sambino was going to melt. The kid was the first flame.

TWENTY FOUR

Peter sat in the lab with his head down. The results of the tests had confirmed what he had already believed to have happened to Elizabeth. The tests revealed some sort of anesthetics in her system. Peter just didn't know which one. The only thing he was sure about was that the drug entered her system at least two days ago, though she could not remember. Now, he had to question Elizabeth to try and decipher when the last encounter could have happened. He had to start the drug elimination process, given the longevity of the drug. According to Julie's examination, Elizabeth was recently raped and so as instructed by Darius, Peter extracted the DNA from the sperm in the semen that Julie had extracted from Elizabeth.

"Here we go," he dialed Darius' number.

"Ping," the sound from Darius' laptop awoke him. That sound indicated that either Samurai or the real Mr. Hosten had received an email. As secure as email is intended to be, hackers still have the ability to remotely access and control one's computer or laptop. With such access, the hacker can write email as if from the genuine email account holder, hence presenting a breach of security, and a violation of privacy. This identity fraud naturally can lead to catastrophic events. Moreover, one may try to intercept another's email and respond and delete it prior to the intended recipient having knowledge of it. To prevent such scenario from happening, the government used encryption methods. Due to email messages being encrypted, emails cannot be read or changed prior to the account holder having received it, thus impossible for common hackers, as they do not hold the key to decrypt email messages. The federal government of the United States, more specifically, those who partake in cyber surveillance had the ability to decrypt messages.

DEA Agent Kramer read the message from Samurai to his supplier, "Came by to see you...we gotta talk." Think Darius think...delete this email. Darius was able to have all emails from Samurai's email address to Mr. Hosten rerouted to ensure that no actual communication ever took place with the real Mr. Hosten.

"Sammy, you are not changing plans are you?"

The sound of the vibrating cell phone on Darius' coffee table alerted him. He looked over at Diane, who was still sleeping. He grabbed the phone. He recognized the number on the Caller ID.

"How bad Peter?"

"Positive for some sort of anesthetics which means that it entered her body recently."

"Yeah, right after that stun gun, I'm sure." Darius took a moment to digest that information. "Damn!" Darius walked over and hit the wall. He leaned his head against his right arm that was against the wall and he stared at the floor as he thought. *I'm going to kill this motherfucker.*

"Darius. You there man?"

Peter knew Darius' state of mind at this moment. He had witnessed Darius' application of his version of the truth serum. He recalled Darius' last encounter with Maria some years ago.

"I gotta find Liz, Peter."

"What do you mean find? When did she get lost, exactly?"

"When she found out that her best friend and I are lovers."

"Okay...and the hits just keep on coming."

"Thanks for the reminder that I am fucked up." He dismissed Peter. He did not have the luxury of addressing his betrayal of Elizabeth.

"Hey, that is what friends are for..."

"And I appreciate the friendship. Now moving on... thanks for the meds info and stay put. I'll let you know when I find Liz because I'm sure you will need to speak to her. That's if I don't kill her first for not telling me this oh so important piece of information."

"You are losing focus agent. You have gotten too personal. No one owes you anything. Tell you what? What did she owe you to tell you?" Peter came to Elizabeth's defense.

"Give me a break. You don't think she knew that something wasn't right? You don't think she has been aware for who knows how long that there have been pieces of her life missing that she really can't put her finger on? Don't you think she felt the wooziness when she returned to consciousness from the anesthetics? And how about the stun gun? Are you telling me that her ass didn't realize that she had just experienced some painful pricking which lead to incapacitation and then the loss of memory?"

The pitch in Darius voice steadily grew. "Did she not realize that she missed her period? Damn it Peter, a woman knows when something is wrong! Didn't she feel the soreness in her vagina? Doesn't she go to get that shit checked out? There have been too many coincidences, too many unfamiliar feelings that she was now experiencing, too much for her not to go to somebody!"

"How do you know that she didn't?" Peter remained calm.

Darius noticed that Diane was now awake and was certain that she had heard everything. She was shaking as she rose. She walked over to the bar, poured some rum and took a shot of it. She poised herself before she spoke.

"Liz is schizophrenic. She may have believed she was hallucinating and that Sally had re-emerged to wreck her life and so she wanted to deal with that situation the best way she knows how--to pretend like Sally isn't there." Diane exhaled away the burden of knowledge. "At least now we know that her other personality is not back, so therefore, whatever it is can be fixed."

"What did you just say?"

"Liz is…"

"I heard you. And how long D? Could it be since you knew me that you have been sitting on this information?"

"Don't – yell – at – me. We didn't see the point in telling you or anyone else. It's nothing personal."

"The hell it isn't D, she was only dating me for…"

180

"Oh please. Come off it. Don't act like you were this committed boyfriend who was kept in the dark. In case you have forgotten Roberto, Darius, you were just another fuck remember? That's how you defined your relationship, so why should she invest herself in you? Besides, she didn't want you to see her any differently and she didn't know how long you would have stuck around."

Anger infected Darius. "Who else knows?" Diane remained silent and brushed her hair to one side with her fingers.

"Who else knows?"

"Michael! Alright, Michael! Are you happy now?"

Darius instantly became a mute. Anger was battling him and it was winning. Peter couldn't believe what he was hearing on the other end of the phone.

"Peter?" Darius called to him calmly, "would any kind of sedatives affect her medication for the schizophrenia because I'm sure she is on some." He then turned to Diane.

"Is she on antipsychotics?"

"Yes."

"Which one is she on?" Peter inquired from the other end as he continued. "Is it Geoden, Seroquel, what?"

"Which medication is she taking?" Darius related Peter's question to Diane.

"I believe it's Seroquel."

"Seroquel, Peter," Darius related Diane's answer to Peter.

"I don't think it should, but I would double check with Julie. You know what I am thinking right?" Peter asked Darius.

"Ahh, no, no I don't," he said baffled as he tried to find words as he stared at Diane in disbelief while still losing the battle with anger.

"Maybe whoever did it knew she was schizophrenic and…"

"Yah, and also knows damn well who fathers the child she is carrying because it's the same one who came all up in her. Clearly someone involved in this mess knew she wouldn't go to anyone because she would be thinking another personality is coming back out and so. And if she tries to remain in control, then the other personality would remain suppressed…assuming that Liz has multiple personality disorder."

What Diane had said to Darius moments ago regarding Sally suddenly hit his conscious state of being. He now knew the answer to his question. A perplexed look developed on his face. He's heard that name before at his last party. He has heard it from Elizabeth. He turned around, pointed his index finger towards Diane and walked up to her.

"Who – the hell– is – Sally?" Darius saw Diane look down and said nothing. "Diane, humor me and tell me that Liz has multiple personalities." He spoke to her as if he was chastising a child that has just done something wrong. Darius made the disappointment in his voice clear.

"Darius, I wish I could have made you privy to this information, but as a lawyer, I am trained not to volunteer information."

"Are you kidding me with that statement? Your excuse is attorney-client privilege, which doesn't apply here. I actually went to law school but didn't have to in order to know that. Don't insult my intelligence Diane. I prefer the previous bullshit excuse." Darius was disgusted by her to say the least.

"You know what Diane; I don't need to know anything else." He then turned his attention to Peter.

"Peter, I am going to talk to you later. I have to go find Liz."

"Keep me posted Darius, please."

"I will." Darius hung up the phone.

"I want to come with you." Diane reached out to Darius. Darius ignored her and headed for the shower. Afterward, he headed for the bedroom, and got dressed. Diane was still in the place where Darius had left her. He walked back into the living room with his gun and checked the barrel.

"What does he have on you?" He focused on the barrel, "and don't play with me Diane." He turned and looked at her. His attitude towards her was distant. "I am waiting."

"Michael doesn't have anything over me." She was unable to look Darius in his eyes. Darius stood there trying hard not to slam her against the wall for being so difficult in such a critical time.

"What's up with the protection of Michael?"

"He is my boyfriend, just in case you have forgotten. I am obligated to him. There are loyalties involved here, and you just can't expect me to tramp all over that."

Darius decided that he would not have addressed that loyalty issue especially after she had just spread her legs for him. He walked over to her and bent down slightly so his face could be directly in front of hers.

"I am DEA first, and the man you fuck second. I will get this information one way or the other…"

"So go to the other and get it then."

"Don't be mistaken D, I will get your precious little boyfriend, if I have to take you down to get to him, Ms. Prosecutor, whose job it is to put the interest of the state before the individual." He paused and looked at her, "unless you are down with the individual."

"Fuck you. I resent that accusation."

He rolled his eyes at her and walked away. "There you go again with that resentment shit again. I tell you D, I will forget all this shit, to fuck him up. Not you or anyone else is going to hamper my case. He is a menace to this society and his ass is going down."

"Is he now?" She showed no sign of being intimidated.

The tone and conviction in her voice caused Darius to turn and looked at her. He was bewildered as to her attitude. Something wasn't right. He was missing something. Body language spoke louder than any words. Diane was hiding something critical, and he had missed it along the way. Is he now, is he now…that sounds like I dare you to try. But why the protective role when she gave him up? What the hell? Why send the tip for the DEA to get involved, only not to fully cooperate. What was in it for her? All bets were off the table.

She centered her pupil onto his. "He will kill you if you so much as threaten him or me. It's only a matter of time. Look what he did to Liz for crying out loud. Look how he used her weakness against her. He knew that Sally loved red light districts, so naturally Elizabeth wouldn't think of any other reason as to why she would have awaken there, or any place strange for that matter." Diane felt the wetness invade her eyes.

"Roberto…ahh, Darius, please, you don't want to mess

184

with Michael. He will destroy you and will kill you. He has killed before." She cried. "He will do it again. Darius please, please, if nothing else for me."

"One—you contacted us, and we are here, and we don't leave until our work is done. Two, am I supposed to be moved by this epic story? Tell me counselor, is it your hobby to know of criminal activities and do nothing about them, be it reporting them or having the asshole arrested or are you just into the aiding and abetting of the criminal? With your track record, I see you becoming District Attorney in no time; you are definitely on the right path. For the record, just in case you have forgotten, let me remind you that you are intentionally withholding information from a federal agent." The Roberto she knew was gone.

"Well, I can't tell you Darius, I'm sorry."

"You can't or you won't."

"I won't. I told you, I have to keep my oath to him and him to me."

Darius went to his bedroom and came back out with handcuffs. "Get dressed."
He impatiently waited on her. When Diane was finished, he walked over, turned her around so her back was facing him. He took out his handcuffs and handcuffed her hands together behind her.

"You are under arrest."

"Darius stop playing." He turned her around to face him. "You have the right to remain silent. Anything you say or do can and will be used against you in the Court of Law. If you do not have an attorney, one will be provided for you. Do you understand these rights as I have read them to you?" He spoke to her as if she was a common criminal.

"What are you doing?" The trembling voice inquired.

"Do you understand these rights, as I have read them to you?" She pierced his eyes with hers.

"Yes."

"I will get your precious little boyfriend, if I have to take you down to get to him."

"What are the charges, may I ask?"

"Obstruction of justice and for whatever it is that I haven't come across yet," he walked away. He grabbed his belongings and walked towards the door. "Come on," he commanded as he opened the door.

They walked silently to his car. Darius opened the backdoor and pushed her inside. As he drove off, he contacted his office and informed Revere's assistant that he had someone in custody, and that he was on his way. As he headed out onto the street from the garage, Elizabeth crossed his mind. He had no idea where to find her and Diane refused to help. As he made a right turn, he waited at the traffic light. He casually turned his head to the right. Elizabeth was sitting right there at a café sipping on coffee and reading a book. She looked as if she had no worries. She seemed calm and settled. He maneuvered the car out of traffic and parked illegally next to the café. He said nothing to Diane. He left her in the car and entered the café.

"I'm sure you won't mind if I have a seat, do you?" He asked Elizabeth pleasantly as he dropped down his butt onto the seat and called for the waitress. She came over and Darius turned his attention to her.

"I will have what she's having." At that point in time,

Elizabeth was just staring at him. Astonishing to Darius, she seemed rather pleasant given the situation.

"Liz, I am afraid to ask how you are doing."

But that pleasant appearance ended. "So don't."

"Fair, but because I do care about you, I'm going to ask you anyway. How are you doing?" He felt like an idiot.

"Never been better."

"There's so much, I don't know where to begin." He tapped his fingers on the table.

"So don't."

"Is there a place besides here where we can talk?" He hoped for a miracle.

Her facial expression indicated to him that she believed he was stupid. She turned back to her book and sipped on her coffee.

"Why is Diane in the car?" She was fixated on the pages before her. "She doesn't think I can handle seeing the two of you together?"

"Diane is in the car as my prisoner. She is under arrest for obstruction of justice," Darius did not flinch. Elizabeth looked up. Darius continued. "Knowingly withholding information from a federal officer in a case is a federal offense."

"And what about fucking one?"

"That's legal I think, but I have to look into it."

"Well I take it you are not here for my charm, so what is it that you want?"

"Your cooperation." Elizabeth said nothing. "The tests reveal that you had some form of anesthetics in your system recently, say two days ago or less. You also have two red dots on your neck, evidence of a stun gun, which means it was recent if the red dots are still there. The test Julie did with the rape kit came out positive. You have no memory of anything; you are on the meds for your schizophrenia so I know you are not hallucinating - which means that Sally is not back. What I don't know Liz is why didn't you say anything to anyone?"

"The information one can get from pillow talk, because I sure didn't tell you about my medical problem."

"That's neither here nor there."

"It is to me. It is to me."

"Do you know of enemies you have that would want to hurt you?" He changed the topic.

"Yes. You."

"Liz, for heaven's sake, there is too much shit going on right now for this. After all this, you can beat me up and call me a dog, or whatever, but for now, let's just get to the bottom of this."

"Fine, but after all this is over, you and that little bitch out there can go to hell." For the first time, Darius truly felt physical pain about what he did to her.

"I'm sorry, Liz, I…"

"Yeah yeah, whatever. What do you want to know?" She returned her attention to the book.

"What does Michael have over Diane?"

"She paid him to kill her father, and he put her through law school. Next question." Her eyes never left the pages.

"What?" Darius was discombobulated.

"What's the next question?" Her tone indicated that he was a nuisance.

"Why would she do something like that, an…..and...

188

how…how did she pay him?"

"He molested her and Rebecca when they were kids, and I guess she got sick of it. I don't know their payment arrangement. She's still paying him I think."

"Ahh…" Darius couldn't focus anymore, "ahh, whe-when was this? And …ahh when did she pay him to do this and who the hell is Rebecca?" Darius felt as if he had found himself in a foreign land where he was unfamiliar with everyone, and everything, including the language.

"I just told you that she's still paying him. It's a debt I don't think than can truly be repaid. He did put her through law school, which is additional expense. Rebecca is her younger sister. Aren't you a federal agent, didn't you have us all this checked out, from conception to when we turn ninety years old? How the hell do you not know about Rebecca?"

Darius ignored her question as he knew Diane had one sibling but for some reason everything was looking dark right now.

"What did she give him in turn for those two bargains or did she ahh?"

"Like I said, it's a debt that can't be repaid. In return, she gave herself, forever. She belongs to him and him alone."

"Is that when she and Michael started having problems, when her father was killed?"

"No. They started having problems over some kid named Otis. I don't have all the details. As you must know by now, Diane has worlds. She's secretive, even to us who she allows in."

Darius became so weak that if he were standing, he would

have fallen over. Shortly thereafter, the waitress came with his order. Elizabeth dismissed Darius.

"You are interrupting my reading. I would like for you to leave now. If you need me for the case, unfortunately, you have my cell number."

Darius looked at her and left the money for the waitress. He was about to tell her how they are one in the same with the multiple personalities, except that he had to live with the memories of his. He remembered that wasn't her recent situation. He was about to apologize for all that he had put her through and explained that human casualties were hazards of the job. He didn't get the chance. Elizabeth put up her hand.

"Spare me." As quickly as looked down, she popped up her head. "That morning when you came to my school as a guest speaker...that wasn't by chance, was it?"

"Nothing was ever by chance Liz." For the first time in his career, Agent Kramer was remorseful for a strategy undertaken to complete a mission. He looked down and clasped his hands, as guilt and shame whipped him. He forced his head up to meet hers." If I could take back..."

"Goodbye Agent Kramer," Elizabeth dismissed him and returned to her book.

Darius headed back to the car and stared at Diane through the rear view mirror. He knew she was now aware that he was no longer in the dark. Tears trickled down her face. Darius put on the indicator and headed to his original destination. His phone started to vibrate shortly thereafter. It was Revere, his boss on the other end.

"Yeah boss," Darius was still discombobulated.

"Don't get so entangled with the cop that you forget your ultimate assignment."

"Sir, I have not forgotten. It's extremely difficult to get to them given their status and all. They have camouflaged themselves perfectly in everyday lives; they're not even guarded, just so to avoid attention from themselves. This is the only way I can think of to penetrate the veil, as they say in Corporate America, and get the bastards. Michael led us to Samurai. With all the sweeping for bug devices in Michael's home that he did, he never thought of his cell phone, as it never left his side, except into the hands of the Brazilians, who always returned phones never as they received it. Thanks to my parties, his bugged phone led us to Samurai, who is our only way in.

"We have come too far to be in a hurry now and jeopardize the entire operation. I mean one mess up and the family will take down the entire DEA, be it through lawsuits or by bombs. And, because this is such a delicate situation, I have to move as if they are not even in the picture, but keeping in mind that they are practically the only picture in terms of priority."

"Kramer, you have impersonated Mr. Hosten, the supplier, when you intercepted his encrypted email pretending to be him, and getting secret code, Bread. Sooner or later, they will make contact without your interception. You have got to move quicker before things start to smell funny. You are dealing with lawyers here. I don't need to remind you that you are dealing with the top of the food chain."

"Thanks for the reminder. I will try not to feel insulted," Darius felt the chill run down
his spine. He had forgotten how dangerous the grounds upon

which he was walking were, and he temporarily forgot that Michael was the least of his worries though he was a significant factor. Unfortunately, the damage caused by Darius to the two channels that led to Michael was irreversible.

"Two more things Kramer…"

"What's that?"

"One, based on the conversation between Jim and Diane yesterday, thanks to the bug you placed in her office, it appears that she has been intentionally losing some of her cases. She also wants him to set up his client Otis. We need to find out why the turn against Otis."

Maybe losing the cases was her paying him back, Darius thought, but why flip the switch? Maybe Otis would know. Gotta get to Jim to see if he can get Otis to talk. Damn that attorney-client privilege shit. Maybe he can talk to him.

"Go on, I'm listening," Darius squeezed his forehead.

"Are you alright Darius?" Revere knew the intensity of he and Diane's intimate relationship, as it had all being recorded.

"Yeah, I'm fine, go on. Two…"

"Two, we had already informed Internal Affairs about Michael Walker, being that your cover has been blown. I want you to go down to the precinct to give Lt. Smith advance notice of the investigation that is about to take place in his department. I don't feel that Smith should be left out in the cold. As Walker's boss, he should be aware of what's happening; especially how not knowing could make his job rather difficult, like it has been so far in terms of busting drug dealers. Walker always knew ahead of time what was happening so his people on the streets always received advance notice from him. So I'm sure Smith would appreciate the heads up on this one."

"Okay boss," Darius hung up the phone. He headed down to the precinct with Diane still as his prisoner.

Michael walked into the precinct dancing on air.

"Hey Officer Walker," the officer at the front desk greeted him. "You are looking alright today."

"Yeah, I'm feeling alright."

"Walker," Lt. Smith came down the stairs. "I need you today, we are busting some kids or whoever. We'll need some help with interrogation and everything else," he brushed his fingers in the air, "you know what I mean. I also have the CI coming down now, so I'll have some things for you to do."

"The who?" Michael asked, not having heard what Smith had just said.

"The CI, the confidential informant, the guy that's working for the bad guys but is really on our side, the informant," Smith said as if Michael needed an explanation.

"Oh Walker, I almost forgot," Lt. Smith turned back around, "I also want you on the investigation team for some missing person." He walked away.

"Who?"

"Some woman named Cassandra Willis. When the CI gets here, hopefully we can get some more information."

Michael's disposition suddenly changed. He was now as pale as a dead man standing.

"Yo man, you alright? You don't look too good," an officer said to Michael as he walked by, brushing upon him.

Michael didn't look or feel good. He felt as if the life was leaving his body, but this he guaranteed; he would not be the only one who was lifeless. With the others, it would be literally speaking.

CHAPTER
TWENTY FIVE

Bernard squirmed as the police officer took his fingerprints. He couldn't believe he was in this situation. What would Maddog have done to him or his mama, if he had said anything? Whatever happened, Bernard would have only brought himself down. If they had no information, then Maddog would have been safe and most importantly, his mama.

"Go over there, please, it's time to smile for the camera, this is your Kodak moment," the officer smiled.

As Bernard positioned for the camera, his rage against the cops grew. *These people don't understand that I have to put food on the table. What do they think, that I like to do this shit, and now they are trying to rid me of my bread and butter?*

"Hey kid, what's your name?"

"Fuck me." Bernard extended both his middle fingers.

"How do you spell that?" The officer asked not being amused by Bernard's rudeness.

"Here's the situation kid, you may think you are a man, but the law says you're not. So, since you are not a man, and you are a male, then you must be a boy. And if you are a boy, then we have to contact the parent, the legal guardian, the adult whoever is legally responsible for you. So in essence, your boss won't work, if you know what I mean," he said coldly.

"Leave him alone," a female officer said, "he's just a scared kid, look at him." She was right.

"What's your name? It's okay. I won't let them hurt you. We need to know who to contact, otherwise we have to hold you here till we find someone."

"Let me guess, and then y'all gonna let me go. Woman please."

He hated being a poor kid. He knew if he had money he would never have been arrested. His parents would have received a phone call. He wanted to be just like Maddog who didn't have to go to school, yet had enough money to pay all the teachers in Brooklyn. Maddog always told him that the government's version of education was overrated, and once he knew how to read, write and could count money, he wouldn't need school. Maddog had always taken care of Bernard's family whether it was bringing food or helping with transportation. This was Bernard's way of showing his gratitude especially when he received $50 each trip, excluding bus fare. If he was lucky, he would have done two trips a day. Maddog told him when he was a little bit older, like his 16th birthday, he would be a man doing more manly tasks, making manly money. But that would involve taking risks like a man. Going to the store to get Maddog's packages was a start.

"What's your name honey?"

"Bernard."

"I'm listening." Bernard purposely had not given his last name.

"Tompkins."

"Is your mom your legal guardian?"

"I'm not saying shit without an attorney."

"Okay kid, do whatever you like. I'm not the one that's looking at years behind bars." She walked away.

"Whatever." Bernard thought and thought. For someone who was only 13, he was extremely mature. He could have called Maddog, and have him send a lawyer. He could have then warned Maddog as to what had happened, but then again, the cops didn't know about Maddog so maybe Maddog wasn't in danger, and it would be okay.

"Bernard," the female officer returned, "I need a telephone number for an adult who is responsible for you."

Bernard didn't answer. He had a bigger problem, he did not wish to have his mother know about his whereabouts and he didn't know Maddog's number. The arrangement was to come to Maddog's house every day this week, and if Maddog needed him again, he would have found him. He didn't really know anyone's number except for his mama's and his uncle Louie. He gave the officer his uncle's number and she dialed. Although Bernard's cheeks now had trails of salt water residue, the tears were accompanied by silence.

As per Smith's orders, undercover cops were stationed on Maddog's street. They witnessed three other people who went to Vasquez's store. After those three individuals left Vasquez's store, and they were en route to Maddog's, the cops stopped and confiscated the drugs from one of them. They allowed some of them to return so Maddog would not become too suspicious. One of the undercover cops called Smith to confirm that there were drug transactions going on in Maddog's building. The undercover officer was disguised as a crack head. Shortly after one of Maddog's men left the building, the cop purchased drugs from him. With that information, Smith immediately set out to get a warrant to search Maddog's property. While Smith waited for the call confirming that he had received the warrant, he prepared his men for battle. This was going to be bloody.

CHAPTER
TWENTY SIX

Samurai approached the precinct. He was not in the mood to be a smart ass. He was going inside to tell Smith what he needed to know to take down Michael. This way, Samurai and Mr. Hosten would have gotten rid of the kingpin, Maddog, and the rest of Michael's clients. With Michael out of the way, they would replace Michael's clients with their own and take over his territory. As he walked into the precinct with his shades, he walked up to the officer at the front desk.

"Could you please let Lt. Smith know I'm here?" Before the officer could have answer, Smith came out, and saw Samurai.

"What the hell happened to you? You look like shit."

"Look, let's just get this over with," Samurai was annoyed. "Are we going to your office?"

"After you," Smith motioned him to go upstairs. As they made it upstairs, Samurai sat in the chair, and massaged his eyes. He was exhausted.

"Look what we have for you today Sammy, compliments of the chef," Smith offered him donuts and orange juice.

"Thanks," Samurai appreciated the sugar, but was very much not his upbeat self.

Smith glanced away and saw Michael passing his office.

"Officer Walker, I want you to meet someone." Michael composed himself and walked inside.

"Officer Walker, this is the young man who has been assisting us, our CI, Samurai, and Samurai, this is Officer Walker. He is going to be working with us on the Cassandra Willis and the Sambino issue."

In an attempt to get rid of his headache, Samurai lowered his head and massaged his temples with his fingertips. He lifted his head up to say hi, only to meet Sambino's eyes. Michael reached for his gun, and stopped himself. He wanted to shoot his partner, the traitor, right between the eyes. He held his composure with a smile.

"Samurai, uuh. So you are our CI." Michael's face depicted a deadly smile. Samurai was dumbstruck. Michael knew that Samurai had no idea that he, Sambino, was a cop, much less to be working in that particular precinct.

"Sammy, you alright?" Smith asked as Samurai had begun to perspire.

No black belt was going to stop a bullet that had his name on it. Michael was not going to go through the drama of making a point by a slow death. He was going to walk up to him and put a bullet through his head and his heart to make sure he was dead and he wasn't going to stop even after Samurai was lifeless.

"Sammy?" Smith shook him.

"I gotta aahhh...gotta gotta ahhh...get outta here...gotta get outta here." He tried to get up to run, but could not do so.

200

He was too shaken. He could have no longer looked at Michael.

"Officer Walker," Smith called to Michael, "get Samurai some water."

"With pleasure," Michael smiled.

"No!" Samurai screamed. "No."

"I'll be right back," Smith said as he walked out.

"Walker, stay with him." Smith went out to get some water for Samurai. Samurai could not have faced Michael, and Michael simply stood there smiling.

"You know I was just heading to my office to get everything I need and leave. Do you know why? Don't answer that, I'll tell you. I was saying to myself that it was just a matter of time before the heat gets here and I would not be around to feel it. I was right." Michael took out his gun and rubbed it with one hand with the mouth pointing to Samurai.

"Are you working with the DEA too?" He blew on his gun and kept rubbing it.

"Don't worry, Sammy, soon enough, nothing will matter anymore. After all, how can a dead man have problems right?" Michael smiled. With that, he kissed Samurai on the forehead.

"Enjoy the last air you're breathing mother fucker. I hear it's a precious commodity." As Michael was leaving, Smith came in and offered Samurai the water.

Michael changed his mind about going to his office. He hurried downstairs because now he had bigger problems, to solve. As he headed outside, he ran into Darius who was with a handcuffed Diane.

"Well, well, well, what do we have here? The prince

and the damsel in distress. Though, I think the white horse is missing, and after all you don't want to mess up this fairytale ending," he smiled and mocked them. He stood there and looked at them while Darius looked at him with pure hatred.

"Ah, I see he has you in handcuffs, would that be remnants from last night or…?"

"I am his prisoner Michael."

Michael smirked and walked up to Diane. Darius stepped closer to him.

"You touch her and…"

"You'll do what?" He turned to Darius. "You'll kill me, Mr. DEA?" He spoke in a singing tune as he rocked his body and mocked Darius. "I thought you were going to do that already. Tell me — how is Liz?" Michael smiled.

"Alive, unlike what I can say about you for much longer," Darius was disgusted.

"I'll miss you Roberto," Michael referred to Darius.

He walked over to Diane. "Get over here." She walked over very nervously. "You must feel like the whore that you are. Kiss me." Diane knew that Michael was trying to make a point. She complied with his command.

As she approached, Michael reached out to her. "Let me help you." He reached out his left hand and clasped his palm around the front of her neck and pulled her towards him. As quickly as Michael reached out and grabbed Diane's neck, Darius used his right hand and pounded the hand that Michael had around Diane's neck and used his left to jab Michael under his chin. At this point, both men drew their guns.

"In case you haven't noticed, this is my prisoner and you

can get your cheap kicks later."

Michael angrily remained focus on Darius. "The next time we meet, and there will be a next time, I will kill you."

"Are you threatening a federal officer?"

Michael cocked his gun. "Yes, just in case you couldn't tell, I am. What are you
going to do? Arrest me?"

"No, Michael, what would be the fun in that?" he asked as he cocked his gun.

"You know she could die in the cross fire," Michael said.

"So be it, just as long as you die," Darius was not amused.

Michael laughed. Using the back of his left hand, he smacked Diane across the face. She fell to the ground. Darius never took his eyes off Michael. As much as that gripped at Darius' soul to see Diane like that, he dared not take his eyes off Michael for a second. They both knew that second would be his last.

"Aren't you going to attend to your bitch, Mr. Kramer?"

Darius didn't respond.

"So did you enjoy my used goods, my leftovers?" Michael continued to taunt Darius. "You know when you sucked her mouth, that was my dick you were tasting."

"No, I believe it was actually mine, since mine was the last one in her mouth."

Michael smirked at Darius' comment. "She has got your balls so tightly wrapped up that you can't see what is right in front of your eyes. Take my advice, she is a woman, she is never as she seems. There is always more beneath the surface. Isn't that right Diane?" He never took his eyes off Darius. Darius simply stared at Michael unaffected by what he had just said.

"Damn D," Michael addressed Diane, "you deserve the Oscar for the dumb bitch role you play so well, and don't let anyone tell you differently. You got this nigga fooled. My apologies…this-federal-officer." Michael had a sadistic grin on his face. Diane lowered her head and said nothing.

"You take care Mr. DEA, until we meet again," Michael lowered his gun and put it in the back of his pants. He looked at Diane who was on the ground bleeding. He smiled at her and walked off to his car. He looked back and noticed that Darius had leapt to the ground, and removed Diane's handcuffs. As Darius tried to pull her close to him for comfort, she pushed him away. Michael overheard their conversation.

"Why did you let him go?" Diane wiped the blood off her mouth.

"Strategic move."

Diane giggled as if to laugh at Darius. She pulled herself together. "Am I still your prisoner"

Darius knew letting her go would put her life in danger, but his guts instincts was telling him to release her. Maybe she would lead him to something, he didn't quite know. *You will know it's God when you hear that still small voice, his mother often times told him. And no matter how nonsensical the situation, trust and obey.* He obeyed. "No," he answered her, almost doubting himself.

"Good," she walked away from the precinct. Michael suspected that she was heading home.

Michael's first priority was to go out of state. He looked at the precinct one last time. There was no going back there. He drove off, putting his siren on.

CHAPTER
TWENTY
SEVEN

Uncle Louie rushed inside the precinct with his lawyer friend Samantha.

"I am here to pick up my nephew Bernard Tompkins, Officer Wright is expecting me," he said to the officer at the front desk.

"Have a seat, sir; she will be right with you."

Almost immediately, a female officer came out and the officer at the front desk pointed out Uncle Louie to her.

"I am Officer Wright and you are?"

"Louie Tompkins, Bernard's uncle. This is Samantha Watkins, Bernard's lawyer."

"Hi. Follow me."

Louie and Samantha followed Officer Wright as she took them into the interrogation room. Moments later, another officer brought Bernard inside. He was so embarrassed to see his Uncle Louie. He said hello to him and held his head down avoiding eye contact.

"Hey little man, it's gonna be alright," Uncle Louie said

to Bernard as he went over and hugged him.

"Lookie here, this is Ms. Watkins, your lawyer, she is gonna get you out of here." Bernard barely looked up at her and said hello.

"Take these handcuffs off him man," Uncle Louie demanded of one of the nearby officers. The officers looked at Louie as if Louie had lost his mind.

"Please," Louie became humble. The officer then obliged him.

"I need a moment with my client," Samantha demanded as she reached into her bag for her notepad and pen.

"You heard her, everybody out," Uncle Louie said, as he pulled up his chair next to Bernard.

"Everyone." Samantha reiterated, as she looked at Louie.

"But I'm his," Louie paused and by the look in Samantha eyes, she didn't care if he had just given birth to him. She wanted him out.

"Yo man, if you need me, I'll be right outside, okay little man?"

"Okay Uncle Louie, thanks," he still held down his head. Bernard and his lawyer were now alone.

"Hi, Bernard, I'm Samantha. You may call me Sam, whatever makes you feel comfortable," she tried to look up under his face to meet his eyes. She used her hand and gently pushed up on his chin, assisting him in holding up his head. He noticed her for the first time. Her blond hair was cut in a Bob. Her green eyes were soft and they complimented her pinkish complexion. Her narrow and straight nose matched her gentle straight face. Her soft spoken voice was soothing. Her size four skirt suit was almond and it carried a belt at the high waist.

"Bernard, it's important for you to know that anything you tell me, anything at all is confidential. I cannot repeat it, not even to save my life. Do you understand?" He nodded his head and indicated yes. "Now, do you want to tell me what we are doing here?"

He turned towards her and looked in her eyes. She could tell that he trusted her immediately. He proceeded to tell her everything.

"Bernard," she said softly, "only answer questions that I tell you to answer, okay?"

"Okay Sam."

"Always wait for my cue, Bernard."

"Okay."

Samantha got up, went outside and informed the police officer that her client was ready to talk. Five minutes later, a man walked in the room. One could have told by his facial expression that he was preoccupied. It took him a moment to address everyone in the room, Samantha, her client, and another officer.

"Hello, Bernard, good to see you again," he said as he smiled, and then reached over to Samantha and extended his hand. "I am Lt. Smith and you are..."

"Bernard's lawyer, Samantha," she clasped his hands.

"Why would Bernard need a lawyer? We just want to ask him some questions," Smith pulled out a chair and sat down.

"Evidently someone thinks so. He was handcuffed, fingerprinted, even faced the camera and had his own little jail cell. I would say someone here thinks he needs a lawyer, but then again, there is always false imprisonment," she turned her head to the right and stared at Smith.

"I see why he is your client."

"Well, good. I'm glad someone does, because I don't see why we are here, thus, making him my client."

"You don't see why we are here?" Smith did not hide his disgust. "Funny thing about lawyers Samantha, they are like poisonous snakes. They spit out their venom and just like that what was living is now dead."

"Do you have questions you need to ask my client, because I do have more important matters to which to attend, besides having conversations with police officers."

"We are pressing charges against your client for the criminal possession of a controlled substance, with the intent to sell. So, now you know why he is your client. As for the knowing part, I saw him leave his boss' house, go to accrue the drugs and was on his way back to deliver the drugs to his boss, so I definitely have knowing."

"You can't prove intent and you can't prove that he knowingly was in possession of any controlled substance," Samantha wrote on her pad without looking up.

"Well counselor, lucky for me, once you are in possession of two ounces of a controlled substance, such as cocaine, then you have an intent to sell. The last I checked, he had in his possession 25 pounds of cocaine, which would make 400 ounces if my math is correct."

"See, that's why you are – the cop," Samantha was being arrogant, "because if you were well versed in the law, like say a law-yer, you would know that leaving someone's house doesn't automatically mean that such person is your boss. I leave my mother's house every day, she is not my boss. You don't have anything to prove that the person's house you saw my client exit is the house of my client's supposedly employer, as opposed to my client's friend."

"We have proof that the owner of that house is a drug dealer and your client knows that."

"That's cute," Samantha patronized Smith, "and as I was saying, second, you don't know that it was my client's belief that he was in-fact carrying drugs. And three, being that you never saw him return to the 'drug dealer,' as you put it, he could have been going anywhere. Now as I said, do you have any questions for my client?"

"I do," Carlitta Davis said as she opened the door.

"Hello everyone," she said as she sat down. "I'm Carlitta Davis, the ADA, on this case." She looked at Bernard, "the Assistant District Attorney, otherwise known as the prosecutor."

Bernard noticed that she too was White, but unlike Samantha, Carlitta had red hair. Both ladies weighed no more than 125 and they were approximately five feet six. Although her eyes were also green, they were more fiery than warm. She wore a grey pants suit with a baby blue silk shirt.

Carlitta turned to Samantha. "I understand that you are Samantha Watkins, attorney to you," she looked at Bernard, "Bernard Tompkins."

"Yes, that would be me."

"Counselor," Samantha addressed Carlitta. "Before you proceed, given the nature of the situation, to ensure my client's full cooperation, you and I need to have a conversation."

"I'm listening."

"Full immunity for my client. His testimony will most likely lead to a conviction of a lieutenant or someone in the ranks. You don't want Bernard, he is small cakes."

"I will decide if his testimony will most likely lead to a conviction, and I will decide if he is small cakes."

"No deal, unless you decide now. You don't decide now, then my client will suddenly become a mute. We will risk trial and let 12 not so smart strangers decide if he really knew what he was carrying and what his intentions were. See how well that will go over when we play the sad poverty stricken kid role just trying to figure out what's happening, and, why is he being taken from his momma, and punished for just doing a favor simply for someone who was always good to them. I can go on and on but you and I know, the kid is not who you want. You have bigger fish to fry, so why not start frying it."

"Give me a second, I have to make a phone call and speak to Lt. Smith outside."

Carlitta and Lt. Smith returned around 20 minutes later.

"Very well. Samantha, we have a deal, but if he so much as try to play us, I will have two fishes to fry."

"You may proceed counselor," Samantha smiled.

"Bernard, Lt. Smith has already briefed me regarding your situation. How old are you?" She stroked the pen looking only at the pad.

"13."

"Where do you live?"

"52B Stuyvesant Street."

"Is that in Brooklyn?"

Yes."

"Are you familiar with Bainbridge Road in Brooklyn?"

Bernard looked at Samantha who indicated that it was okay to answer the question.

"Yes."

"How so?"

"Uhh?"

"How are you familiar with Bainbridge Road?"

"It's in my neighborhood, everybody is familiar with it."

"Have you ever been there before?"

"Yes, I told you it's in my neighborhood." Bernard was uneasy in his seat.

"Were you there today?"

Samantha interrupted intentionally to break the mode of things.

"Are we here to ask him how his day was or to get to the point?" She asked annoyed, knowing exactly what Carlitta was doing. Carlitta, whose head was still down, only moved her eyes up to face Samantha's.

"Is there a problem, Ms. Watkins? Have I violated any of his rights?" With Samantha looking straight at Carlitta without an answer, Carlitta got her answer. She put her eyes back down toward the paper.

"Were you on Bainbridge Road today Bernard?"

"Yes."

"What were you doing there?"

"I don't need a reason to walk down any street in my neighborhood." Carlitta ignored that response.

"Did you visit any one in particular today on that street?"

Bernard didn't answer. He remained quiet. Carlitta looked up at him.

"I plead the fifth," he folded his arms.

"What is he doing?" Carlitta turned to Samantha referring to Bernard, "what is this?"

"Bernard, answering this question is not incriminating yourself. You are not admitting to any crime. It's okay, "Samantha touched his hand.

"I still don't want to answer."

"Fine, don't answer. We'll get our answers at the grand jury where your lawyer is not welcome. Either way, we'll get answers." Carlitta stood to leave the room.

"I just need a moment with him before we continue," Samantha said.

"I don't have time for this. Please make it quick," she exited the room with
the officers behind her.

"Bernard, if there is a problem with the questions, I won't let you answer, you have got to trust me on this, alright?" Samantha touched his hand again.

"I do trust you. It's them I don't trust."

"They'll press charges Bernard, and if we can work something out, we will, but you not cooperating will only piss them off and furthermore, it gives the indication that you are hiding something and you are not. You are an innocent kid in all of this, just doing a favor for someone who always helped out your family, not knowing what the favor truly entailed, okay?" Bernard nodded his head.

"We have to come off innocent here, Hon, otherwise, we'll be fuel to the fire, alright?"

"I'm sorry. I'm just scared, that's all."

"I promise, they won't get anything on you. Trust me Bernard." He looked her in the eyes again, and nodded his head.

"Can I go and get them now?" Samantha gently raised his chin. He nodded his head again. Samantha went to get Carlitta, who came in and continued where she left off.

"Did you visit anyone in particular today on Bainbridge Road?"

"Yes"

"Who?"

"Maddog," Bernard hesitated.

"Who's that?"

"A family friend." Bernard felt uneasy.

"How long has he been a family friend?"

"I don't know, you gotta ask my momma that question."

"How long have you known him?"

"It seems like forever."

"How did you meet him?"

"I can't remember. I have always known him as someone in the neighborhood who has always been nice to my momma and me."

"What has he done nice for you and your momma?"

"He would bring us food because he knows my momma can't move too well to leave the house. If my mom needs to go the hospital or anything, he would arrange for his cab friend to take her there and back, if my uncle couldn't do it, stuff like that." He felt an overwhelming appreciation for Maddog.

"Why can't your momma leave the house?" Carlitta was concerned but remained stoic.

"She got some bone disease where when she moves, it hurts." Bernard felt more ashamed of the situation in which he managed to find himself.

"Have you guys ever done anything nice in return for Maddog?"

"No. When my momma asks if there is anything we could do to show our appreciation, he always says just pray for him."

"Is he known to be a nice guy in your neighborhood?"

"Yes, many folks says he is real nice, especially, the old people."

"Why did you visit Maddog today?"

"No reason, I just miss him and I wanted to go say hi."

"Do you just show up or do you have to let him know in advance that you are coming?"

"I have to let someone he knows know I'm coming. You know one of the buddies, tell him I want to come say hi, and if that's okay, he will tell his friend to tell me when and where to come see him."

"Do you see him often?"

"Not as often as I would like, you know he is a busy man. But he always says I should not be a stranger, and if I wanted anything, just come to him."

"And today, you just wanted to visit?"

"He already answered that, move on," Samantha interjected.

"Did you guys do anything when you were over there?"

"We play a couple of video games. He is really cool."

"What kind of games did you play?"

"Violent ones." Bernard wanted to be difficult. Carlitta decided to let that one pass.

"Why did you leave?"

"He asked me to do him a favor."

"What would that be?"

"He asks me to go to this store over DeKalb and Pulaski and ask for Mr. Vasquez, and he is supposed to give me something that belongs to Maddog, and I'm supposed to bring it back to him."

"What is the something?"

"I don't know, I didn't ask Maddog. I am just glad whenever I can do something for him because he is always doing something for me and momma."

"Did you find this Mr. Vasquez person?"

"Yea, I did."

"And?"

"And what? I answered your question. Uou asked me if I found him, and I said yes," Bernard said rudely.

"Have you met Mr. Vasquez before?"

"No."

"So how did you know it was him?"

"I didn't, I mean not really, he was the only one in the store, so I assumed it was him, and so I just handed him the note."

"What note?" Carlitta asked getting closer to her goal.

"The note Maddog gave me to give to him."

"Did you read the note?"

"No! What kind of kid you think I am? My momma raise me better than that," he said proudly and Carlitta managed a smile.

"Did you say anything at all to the man you believed to be Mr. Vasquez, no exchange of words, nothing?"

"Well, yahhh, he says follow me and I did."

"Where did you go?"

"To the back of the store, where he said wait here, and then he lifts up a board off the floor which had some steps leading down into what looks like a small creepy basement. I guess that's where he keeps the stock of his food. He came back up with a bag, a knapsack and he gave it to me."

"Did he tell you what to do with the bag?"

"No. Maddog sent me to get something for him so I knew to take it back to him, that's all to it," Bernard said as if that was obvious.

"Between going for the bag and getting the bag, there were no conversations at all, not even a take care?"

"Well there was one thing," he said not sure if he should have repeated this, "he says what's the password?"

Samantha noticed that Carlitta's disposition changed and she was trying hard not to jump out of her skin.

"And what did you say?" Carlitta waited to exhale.

"Zeus."

"How did you know that was the password?"

"Well, Maddog told me that Vasquez was going to ask me a strange question. I will know it is the strange question because it will be the only question he asks me and he was right, it was strange. Anyways, Maddog also told me regardless of the question, just say the word, Zeus, and the man will give me Maddog's stuff to take to him, and so that's what I did."

"Did you know what was in the bag?"

"Not until that rude ass cop crowded me at the bus stop and snatched the bag away from me."

Samantha knew Bernard was lying. She knew Bernard had been to Maddog's house enough time to see and smell the scent of crack being made. He had seen the little viles around the house. He had seen people come in and out and money exchanged. He knew what Maddog did, because his uncle had shown him enough times. His uncle had shown him different kinds of drugs, how they were taken and so he could not have said that he was never shown. He knew he must avoid them at all cost, especially after he saw the effect of them on the addicts. Maddog underestimated Bernard's intelligence. He did not know he would have picked up on what was happening, like the fact that he knew he was going to get drugs but he didn't care because it was money to help his momma. Bernard had told himself not to take any of the drugs. He told himself not to be like those punks who sold it on the street and get caught. Instead, he would be more like the man in charge, Maddog. Samantha knew because for reasons unknown to her, Bernard told her all in that brief moment of privacy they had.

"Okay Bernard, that's it, thanks for your cooperation," Carlitta said.

"Counselor, we ask that your client speak to no one at all about this conversation, especially not today. If he speaks, he violates the agreement and we will press charges. We have some paperwork for your client or his guardian to sign regarding this agreement. We will also ask that you wait around for a while until we give you the okay to leave, please. This is just a favor.

There are some things happening and it will be better for us if you just give us a moment of your time by staying here at the precinct until everything is clear." Samantha understood immediately, and she agreed.

Carlitta excused herself and stepped outside. Samantha could have seen that Lt. Smith was outside doing something. The door was still opened and so, she overheard their conversation.

"Zeus," Carlitta said.

"That's the magic word for the day. Get a couple of your undercover cops there now. We'll start working on getting a warrant for Vasquez's store today. We only have a small window of opportunity and if this one closes, then it would be almost impossible to get another one."

"Because the password changes daily and more so after all the arrests that are going to be made today, Maddog will find out what is happening and get ahead. Yes, I am with you Ms. Davis."

"Good. Keep me posted."

"I am on the case. I will send a couple of my men to Vasquez's store with the password, Zeus."

TWENTY EIGHT

Darius watched Diane until she was out of sight, and then walked inside the precinct.

"I am here to see Lt. Smith and I do not have an appointment and I cannot wait." He then took out his DEA badge and the officer called Smith right away and informed him.

"Go up the stairs," the officer directed him to the stairs, "and when you get to the top, it is the office that is ahead of you that says Lt. Smith on the door."

Darius thanked the officer and ran upstairs. As he reached Lt. Smith's door, he saw a young man sitting across from Smith. Darius knocked.

"I don't mean to interrupt, but I really need to speak to you," Darius said. Both Smith and Samurai recognized the voice and Smith quickly looked towards the door to greet Darius' eyes. Samurai damn well fell out of his chair at the familiar voice as he turned around at the speed of sound to face yet another nightmare. He grabbed his heart because it was now aching.

"What are you doing here?" Samurai and Smith asked

at the same time. By the way they looked at each other, they realized that they both knew Darius, except that for Lt. Smith, it was by the voice. Darius went inside the office and closed the door behind him, locked it, pulled down the blinds on the door and faced Samurai.

"What the hell happened to you?" He asked in a state of shock as he looked at Samurai as if he was close to death.

"Never mind that." Smith commanded, "Who the hell are you?"

"I'm sorry sir," Darius went over to Smith and extended his hand for Smith to shake it, which he did as he stood up.

"Darius Kramer, DEA," he showed Smith his badge, "but I am going to get back to you in a bit," he turned to Samurai who flew out of his chair.

"Who!" Samurai stood up, "who!"

"Sam," Darius said calmly as he tried to pacify down Samurai.

"You know him?" Smith interjected being confused.

"Okay," Darius turned to Smith, "please sir, ask no more questions. Just sit and listen and things will begin to unfold itself."

Smith shook his head, and reached for Samurai's water, and gulped it. Samurai was losing his mind as he paced back and forth saying "oh my god, oh my god." Perspiration and nervousness flooded him.

"Samurai," Darius reached out to him, "I can explain."

"You are the DEA guy Sambino was talking about! Oh my God, it's you!" Samurai pointed his shaky finger to Darius, as he tried to stop himself from shaking.

"Yea, I am."

"You are the friend, the friend that's a DEA undercover." Samurai continued to pace back and forth looking at the floor. He demonstrated signs of someone who needed a quick fix.

"My name is Darius Kramer, and I am – well – was an undercover who had been assigned to Officer Michael Walker."

At this time Smith choked on the water and as he continued to choke, Darius continued. "Well you know him as Sambino, and he has been my perpetrator now for over three years. I befriended his friends and you, his partner, to get to him." Darius just twisted the truth a little. Smith's eyes popped out of his head when he learned of the relationship between Sambino and Samurai.

"He is a CI, what the hell are you talking about a partner!" Smith refused to stay out of this much longer.

"He is a CI!" He yelled to Darius as he got up.

"No, he is not. He is Sambino's partner, that's why he knows all the details. I am his other partner, who was working with him to take down Sambino. That's why he is in your office detailing you on Maddog and Vasquez so you can take Sambino down, disrupting that operation so we can supposedly move in and take over that territory."

Darius said all this while looking at Samurai trying to inhale oxygen. Smith dropped in his chair.

"I'll be damned," Smith said. Slowly, anger started to creep into him, and he turned to Samurai.

"Is Cassandra Willis bogus?" Smith barely moved his lips.

"No," Darius said, "she is real and that was a lead that

222

would hopefully have led to Michael, building up a case against him, just to add to his impeccable character."

"Michael Walker," Smith mumbled under his breath, "that's why his ass turned pale when he saw Walker in here not too long ago because he was looking at Sambino who had a front row seat in watching his partner do the ultimate betrayal. Shit." Smith snatched the phone and called Carlitta and informed her to get in his office right away.

"Who the hell is that?" Darius asked.

"The ADA on Sambino's case," Smith perused through his desk not having a clue as to what he was looking for.

"Sammy, I know you don't trust me right now, but you have got to listen to me. You have been conspiring with a federal agent. If you don't cooperate, we will take your ass down and that's after I feed you to Michael, not that it matters, because he will most likely kill you anyways. But if you help us, we can offer you immunity and a witness protection program."

"How the hell are you offering deals, isn't that the ADA or federal prosecutor's job?" Smith asked regarding the boldness of Darius.

"This is a federal case. You are talking drug trafficking, drug manufacturing, probably murder across state lines, money laundering and the list I'm sure goes on," Darius said.

Smith became instantly quiet.

"Lieutenant, your mind is actually not playing tricks on you. Snap out of it."

"I'm not helping you with shit," Samurai said to Darius angrily.

Darius walked up to him. "I'm sorry if you are under the

misunderstanding that I am asking you Sammy. Now I'm telling you that you will finish this." He walked away.

"Do you think you are safe right now Sammy? Huh? You don't have a choice but to finish taking Sambino down. I mean I already have enough on him to take him down and definitely on you to take you down, but it is for all our benefit that he comes all the way down. He is going to hunt you down. And he is going to kill you. Do you understand?"

Samurai knew he was right. "I need a cigarette," Samurai said.

"There is no smoking in the building," Smith said.

"I – need – a – cigarette."

"Get him a cigarette Lieutenant," Darius gestured to Smith.

"Shit," Smith pulled out his pack, "he can have one of mine." He threw Samurai one and then offered him a light.

"Shit, I need one myself," Smith lit up his cigarette.

"What do you want to know?" Samurai asked with his forehead in one hand and the cigarette in the other while he sat down, shaking.

"I need to know more about the person who packages the product that's sent to Vasquez and the manufacturing company the drugs are sent from," Darius said.

"What the fuck are you talking about; you are the fucking supplier..."

"I am not your supplier. I never was. I just intercepted at all times and take on the role of your supplier. I still allowed for your drugs to be delivered and business to stay on course to avoid your real supplier getting suspicious. If questions came to you in an email or what have you, we answered for you—remote access. We were you to your real suppliers and to you, we were them. Best adrenaline rush of my career. I need some kind of role recognition for that shit."

"Congra-tu-fucking-lations," Samurai was sarcastic.

"Besides, where the hell am I going to get all that drugs anyway to give you?"

"You are the fucking Drug Enforcement Administration; I thought you manufactured the shit like the feds manufactured money."

"The feds don't manufacturer money, a private company does."

"Whatever...you get my point."

"I don't mean to interrupt this beautiful moment," Smith interjected, but how did you convince a personality type like Walker that you were for real."

"I didn't. He has an insatiable appetite for my other impersonator Roberto's lifestyle, so attracting him was like attracting moth to a flame. The power of the desire to get to the light at all cost, even death, is greater than the will of self-preservation. His greed and ungratefulness wielded him into the trap."

"Makes sense with such a destructive personality why he would want to be in charge," Smith added.

"He wasn't. Sammy here was. Sambino never ordered the drugs or had any contact with the real suppliers, as Samurai here had the real power, he was the real boss. Sambino was able to bamboozle him into partnership because of what he found out which left Sammy here in a vulnerable position. So it's either he was allowed to get in on the action or there would no action at all." Darius touched Samurai's shoulder. "He needed Samurai for the product because of his contacts and he latched on. Samurai didn't mind as with Michael's skills, he made him a lot of money, but not as much as he would make if Michael was out the picture, now that Samurai picked up some skills, and of course a new partner."

"That's some heavy shit Sammy," Smith said in disbelief.

"Yep, that's our Sammy," Darius concurred. "So Sammy, tell us about this manufacturing company?"

"I don't know about the manufacturing company, but we pay someone to ensure that the product is repackaged and sent to Vasquez." Samurai blew out some smoke.

"Are there any drugs there now?"

"Yes. But it won't be for long. Vasquez is due to get his last shipment at the end of the week, which is tomorrow."

Before Darius could say anymore, Smith summoned his officers to seek a warrant, but Darius showed him the wire he was wearing signifying that his people were already on it. Lt. Smith motioned them to do so anyway in case they have to fight over jurisdiction later. It would have to be settled who has more rights, the feds or the state.

"Okay Sammy, there is this lady, her name is Elizabeth and she is somehow carrying a child through Immaculate Conception if you know what I mean."

"Shit," Samurai said.

"This is a picture of her," Darius showed Samurai Elizabeth's picture. "Do you know her by chance?"

"Oh shit. That's that fine chick. I saw her some hours

ago when she left your building. She was gloomy and looked heartbroken. She looked like she was in need of a rescuer, me."

"Oh please," Darius rolled his eyes.

"You are that mother fucker who was banging Sambino's lady and yours at the same time."

"Shut up and answer the question."

"That's some real fucked up shit. You ought to be ashamed of yourself."

"Yea, I am the asshole. I get that part. Do you know anything about her?"

"That's the girl he bragged about how he paid one of his former convicts one hundred dollars a pop for some time until she gets knocked up."

Smith was confused but Darius wasn't. He tried not to succumb to the pain he was feeling for Elizabeth and focused on his determination to kill Michael.

"Ahhhh, did he say how this guy was going to get a chance to do whatever?" Darius was disgusted.

"Yeah, the guy was going to knock her out with some stun gun and some drug thing I'm not quite sure," Samurai waved the cigarette showing his uncertainty.

"Do you know which convict by chance?" Darius was desperate.

"No, he just said one of his released rapists or something like that."

Darius turned to Smith, "I need a list of all his convicted rapists and the ones who are released."

"Done." Smith reached for the phone and delegated. There was a knock on the door and Darius opened it.

"Counselor, this is Agent Kramer," Smith addressed Carlitta, "and Agent Kramer, this is Counselor Carlitta Davis, the ADA on the Sambino case."

"Nice to meet you," Darius extended his hand and she did the same.

"Smith, we have the warrant for 200 Bainbridge and Vasquez's grocery store," Carlitta remarked.

"Great, we need one for the home of Officer Michael Walker. Now sit down." She did and Smith briefed her on what just transpired. She stared at Samurai and shook her head.

"Do you know Maddog?" Carlitta asked Samurai. He shook his head, signifying no.

"Well at least moments from now, we'll know the truth when we haul Maddog in here, being that I don't trust you as far as I can throw you."

She turned to Smith. "Maddog should be getting a visit from some unwelcome guests right about now."

"One more thing," Smith turned to Samurai, "do you know where Cassandra Willis is?" Samurai leaned his head back on the chair and blew smoke up toward the ceiling.

"I could tell you where her body parts are."

Another knock on the door interrupted them. A rookie officer walked inside.

"Sir, I have the information you are looking for regarding Officer Walker," the officer handed Smith the file.

"Thanks."

"Sir, ahhh, I beg your pardon sir, but there is no smoking in the building."

Smith slowly moved his eyes off the file to meet the officer's and by his look, the officer knew to exit and close the door behind him, which he did. Smith opened the file. The list of rape convicts for Walker was small as he was in narcotics. It was a small list, all of one person, Miguel Cruz, who had served five years after a plea bargain and was released not too long ago. The hunt would not be difficult; neither would getting an order forcing Cruz to submit to a DNA test.

CHAPTER
TWENTY
NINE

SWAT (special weapons and tactics) teams were elite tactical units in many law enforcement agencies. Their specialty was to perform high-risk operations that fall outside the scope of performance for the every-day police officer. Dealing with hostage crisis and terrorism as well as serving search warrants in tenable situations and conducting high risks were among their responsibilities. With that, the need for engaging heavily-armed criminals would often times arose and so these teams, in order to be prepared, must themselves be equipped with specialized firearms, and heavy body armor, ballistic shields, entry tools, armored vehicles. SWAT is infrequently called upon for action as the officers were normally deployed to regular duties as these expensively-trained and equipped officers could not be left to sit around, waiting for an emergency.

The New York City Police Department, however, had a different take on that concept. Its equivalence, the Emergency Service Unit (ESU) is one of the few civilian police special-response units that operated autonomously 24 hours a day.

Bam! Bam! Bam! was the sound Pierre Washington heard outside his door at 200 Bainbridge Road. Not expecting anyone and flabbergasted by the thought of someone knocking down his door like that knowing that he was Maddog, he sent one of his men with the order to teach the person at the door some respect. As usual, to be cautious, Maddog had cameras installed all around the property and a 24-hour security system with employees constantly monitoring the scene around his house. All his doors were metal, so there was no knocking down of anything. The police knew this too. They knew that between the cameras and the metal doors, they were not getting in unless invited. Big Bull, one of Maddog's bodyguards opened the steel door. Three people, one male and two females, held bibles and colored pamphlets. They stood in front of the steel guard gate directly before the steel door. Big Bull held on the locked steel gate where the openings were not wide enough to grab somebody.

"Why the fuck are you knocking on my man's door like this, do you not see the fucking bell?" He pointed to the bell they didn't see.

"Bitch what did you say?" One of the ladies said as she stepped back as if she was highly insulted by Big Bull's greeting. She was wearing a loose burgundy dress, noticeable nude stockings and cheap looking brown flat shoes, with an elaborate brown hat with burgundy feathers sticking out. She was dressed as if she was going to church. She looked like a person who had no money, trying to pretend as if she did. She pulled up her brown bag up on her shoulders.

"Bertha!" The other lady yelled at her covering her mouth in disbelief. "Watch your language to the young man; we are here to save lives, not to provoke them."

"Yeah, Bertha, you have been a little bit short tempered today, but we can't be having any of that tongue," the man in the cheap suit who was holding the Bible also commented. He turned his attention to Big Bull.

"Sir, we're sorry, we are just here to hand out some magazines and to ask you if you know Jesus."

"You betta check that bitch, before I check her for you, else she'll know Jesus for sure when she meets him on the other side," Big Bull pointed to Bertha, "and next time ring the fucking bell," he was about to slam the door.

"Well, Mr. Brilliance," Bertha shouted out, in hopes to have gotten his attention, "if your ass was actually bright, you would have known that the mother fucking bell doesn't work. I'm sick of all y'all low lives who is probably gonna burn in hell anyways pretending as if we are taking up your time in your precious no good life, when we're just trying to save it...."

"Bertha!" The other two yelled out holding on to her, "what the hell is wrong with you?"

She brushed them off. "Bitch, you lucky that steel gate is between us, else I would bitch slap your ass," she continued.

That was all Big Bull needed to hear, some *bitch* or anyone threatening him. In a rage, he forgot all the rules, stormed the door open and flew in front of Bertha. Before he got a chance to spew his damage, she used her knee to introduce pain to his testicles. She pulled out the 9 mm gun from under her dress that was secured on her thigh with a holster. Before she was finished knocking him out, the other two rushed inside. Seconds later, the ESU team that was in the two cable vans joined them. Bertha hauled him in the van and handcuffed him, and called for back-up for the other officers. As they rushed inside and yelled police, men, women and kids scattered like mice. Some of Maddog's men fired their guns and the cops fired back. Maddog's first thought was to damage all of the evidence, such as the crack that was being made and the cocaine that was all over the place to be sectioned out. He didn't get the chance. The ESU team was already all over and his other guard had hauled him into the secret spot, a bullet-proof room, which could only be opened from the inside. There was also an exit inside, which led to the back. Maddog's protection did not work that day. The cops had taken over the house, from top to bottom. The cops outnumbered Maddog's people three to one, so there was no escaping. The DEA was on the scene and the joint effort proved effective. All the arrestees were hauled into the vans, including those wounded from the shootings. As ambulances were already on the scene, the wounded were handcuffed while being treated in the ambulance. The authorities could have been in Maddog's house for days given the multitude of evidence. His house was now a crime scene, a prosecutor's dream. They wouldn't know where to begin. Everyone was captured except for Maddog and his other security guard, but that wouldn't be for long. The authorities searched every single room and closet in the house and came up with nothing. No one had exited except for the ones the cops had taken out themselves, and the cops knew because they were at all exits, doors and windows known to them. In an effort to enter the bulletproof room, they would have had to use a bomb to blow the door off, but before they did that, they tried tear gas. Maddog could see what was happening in the entire house from the camera in his bulletproof room. A couple of the officers went down to the basement, and as planned, they prepared to release the gas in the ventilation system so it would have seeped through the entire house, including the bulletproof room, forcing everyone to the closest exit. After the team had successfully placed their gas masks on, they released the gas knowing that it would not have been long before Maddog and his bodyguard started to cough and gag, hence having no other choice but to have opened the door. Sure enough, as the gas seeped into their system, Maddog and his bodyguard tried to escape out another exit. They were greeted with the welcoming arms of the NYPD and the DEA.

After just three hours of furious driving, Michael was in Washington D.C. already, to be more specific, he was at 33 Connecticut Avenue NW. He took the steps up directly to apartment 2A and rang the bell. A five-foot slender, beautiful Latina young lady opened the door. She was wearing a beautiful silk dress that highlighted the shape of her body, matched only by her full lips, dark black hair and dark brown eyes and unparalleled smile. Michael stepped back and took a breath, not expecting what he had just seen.

"Mrs. Darius Kramer?"

Maria loved to hear that name, and showed her elation when she swayed and giggled.

"That's me."

Michael without a moment's notice introduced the 32 caliber gun accompanied by a silencer to her forehead with a hollow point bullet to follow. She fell to the floor and died instantly.

"Compliments of Darius Kramer," he said as he walked away.

He jumped back in his car and headed back to New York. His next stop would be the Blazer's, home to the parents and sibling of Samurai Blazer.

CHAPTER
THIRTY

Finding Miguel Cruz would have been easy. The men's shelter at Atlantic and Pacific Avenue was a skip away. After confirming with Brent, who worked at the shelter that Cruz was now there, cops rushed over. As usual, they parked wherever took them closest to their destination even if that meant the steps. As they entered the shelter, Brent knew instantly why they were there, and volunteered to walk them over to Cruz. He was lying on his mattress on the floor trying to take a nap.

"Are you Mr. Cruz?" One of the officers asked.

"I ain't do nothing man, I was here all day, ask him?" Cruz pointed to Brent.

"Sir, may I see some ID?"

Cruz searched on the mattress that had no sheets, and then in the pocket of his pants that he was wearing. The officers looked at each other and then back at Cruz. He was extremely nervous. He came off as someone who had been doing so many illegal activities that he didn't know which one was coming back to haunt him.

"I...I got it somewhere," he patted down his pants.

"Oh...oh, yeah, it's here," he reached for a dirty, old jacket he had in a plastic bag that he had stuffed under the mattress. He handed the cops his expired license as he was in jail so he couldn't renew it.

"Sir, I have a warrant for your arrest," the officer showed Cruz the warrant.

"What the hell for?" Cruz turned around reluctantly. "Hey man, I ain't do shit!"

The officer went on to read him his rights, which was the last thing Cruz needed to hear. They knew he couldn't afford to get caught for violating his parole because that would mean more prison time. As they left the building, one of the officers thanked Brent. The officers took Cruz to the precinct and into the interrogation room, and left to notify Smith. One of the officers knocked on Smith's door and opened it as instructed.

"Sir, Mr. Miguel Cruz is in the interrogation room."

"Fine, I'm coming down, just wait right here," Smith said in a dismissive tone.

"We – We are coming down," Darius corrected Smith.

"Yeah, we, whatever," Smith waved his cigarette.

"You know that thing will kill you," Carlitta said to Smith, as she referred to the cigarette.

"No, it won't, if this case hasn't killed me yet, nothing will." He put it in his mouth, took another puff, then put it out in the convenient ashtray on the bookshelf behind him.

"This case is far from finished," Samurai uttered convincingly.

"And that's your contribution to this conversation?"

Smith asked Samurai as he raised his eyebrows, while Darius and Carlitta managed to crack a smile.

"I am glad that you find this all funny," Samurai said as he looked shaken and took his last puff. At the same time, Carlitta jumped up.

"What I find funny is…"

"Alright, alright, enough noise at my head. Save it for the courtroom," Smith pushed her back in the chair. "Shit, better yet, save it for Cruz, let's go," he walked over to his door and opened it. He waited for them to leave.

"What about him?" Carlitta referred to Samurai.

"Why do you like to give me work, hmm Davis? You don't think I have enough on my plate? So, now I gotta worry about a grown ass man?"

"Well, it all depends, is he under arrest?" Carlitta prayed that he would be.

"No, not yet, he is too useful." He turned to Samurai.

"This nice officer here is going to see to it that you stay under office arrest until I come back," Smith smiled as he pulled over Officer Wright who was walking by and placed her as Watch Dog. They proceeded with the other officer to meet Cruz. As they arrived outside the interrogation room, Darius took a moment to calm down. He tried to regain his professionalism.

Smith opened the door and they walked inside. "Cruz," Smith paused, "Did I get it right?"

"Yeah, you got it right," Cruz said as he watched Smith go through his entire crime file, including his probation file.

"Look man, I ain't do shit, alright, no shit," he said nervously as he forgot how to stay still in the chair.

Darius' wanted only to jump across the table and break Cruz's neck.

"Do you know an Officer Walker?" Smith paced back and forth around Miguel, who was now about to experience loose bowels. He started to breathe hard.

"Who?" He closed his hands in and out as a sign of nervousness.

"I'll take that as a yes," Smith said.

"Well, he's dead." Smith lied to get a reaction. "He died in the line of fire," Smith pretended as if he was taking a moment to pay respect to Walker.

"Shit!" Cruz screamed out.

"And the interesting thing is, before he died, he grew a conscience, and wouldn't you know it, he wanted to confess to the priest, you know, ask his God for the forgiveness of his sins, particularly the ones that included you."

"I didn't go to him man! He came to me!" Cruz sprang out of his seat.

"I know," Smith hoped that Cruz was telling him the truth.

"He told us that he felt bad getting you involved, he took advantage of you and so he wanted us to promise him that we wouldn't take you down."

"And!" Cruz yelled nervously.

"Well, we told him not to worry, he had better things to think about as he was about to leave us, but for some reason, he was insistent on fixing it. He said you would cooperate and we should ask you for the details."

"Why me?"

"Because he wouldn't have much time to finish it man, what else?"

"Oh yeah, the dead thing," Cruz said as he became suddenly subdued.

"He was alright," Cruz bent his head and used his right index finger to make the cross on his upper body while he said "Hail Mary" and then kissed his hand.

"Did you just say the Hail Mary? You had the nerve to say the Hail Mary?" Smith asked in disbelief.

"Yeah man, may his soul rest in peace."

"Gimme a fucking break." Darius was disgusted.

"I'm sorry about your friend and all, but I'm gonna need a lawyer you know to protect my rights and all," Cruz said boldly.

"Everyone, get out," Darius frowned. He turned to look at Smith.

"Please," he said as if he was being polite.

"Okay, since you asked nicely," Smith said, "ADA Davis, and officer, after you," he opened the door and they exited. They could still see everything through the mirror from the other side. Before Cruz knew it, Darius violently knocked him off the chair, busting his lips in the process. Darius stomped on Cruz and he crunched over in pain that was followed by a kick. He jerked Cruz's body inches from his face.

"Every time I hear the word lawyer from you, I'm going to fuck you up, you got that Cruz?"

"Yeah!" Cruz screamed in pain as he spat out a tooth.

"Now, do you need a lawyer?" Darius leaned over Cruz. He didn't answer.

"Mother fucker, I say do - you - need -a - law - yer?"

240

Darius repeated as he punched Cruz in the eyes with each syllabus.

"No!" Cruz screamed out in pain.

"I didn't think so. See, this is how it is going to work. I'll ask questions, you will answer. If I have to ask twice, I will kick you in your balls twice for each time I have to ask twice, got it?"

"Yeah," Cruz nodded while crunched on the floor, with his eyes now disfigured, "yeah."

Darius started his interrogation. "Did Walker hire you?"

"Yeeahhhh,"

"When?"

"Around four months ago?"

"How did it happen?"

"A couple days after I got out on parole, he approached me. He told me he got something for me to do but not to worry because if I ever got caught, he would clear me even if he had to destroy the evidence. He said if I didn't do it, he would see that I continued being someone's bitch and then end up dead shortly after." Cruz coughed.

"But worse than that, he would see to it that the person closest to me would become someone's bitch. He would make sure that what I did to that chick I got busted for, would be the same thing that happened to me, so I...I...I just did what he said."

"You believed him!"

"Yeah, I did. You had to see his eyes, it's as if he had no soul and so I knew he meant every word he said."

"Have you ever seen this woman before?" Darius showed him Elizabeth's picture.

"Damn," Cruz sniffled, "yeah, that's the woman."

"What did he have you do?"

"I had to penetrate her repeatedly, till she got pregnant," Cruz tried to sound proper.

"Did he pay you?"

"Yes, one hundred dollars each penetration."

"How many times did you do it?"

"I made a little over a grand, so I guess around that much."

"You raped her over and over again at least 10 times. Is that what you're telling me?" Darius grabbed Cruz up off the floor but Smith rushed in, and pulled him off.

"Fuck!" Darius threw a chair in rage. "What else?" He didn't even wait for an answer. Pain ripped through him, and left him empty. He flew in front of Cruz and with all his might threw him against the wall and pulled out his gun. "Penetrate this mother fucker."

"Noooooooooooooooooo!" Smith reacted swiftly and he and the officer jumped on Darius and others rushed in to hold him down.

"I'm sorrrrrrrrrrrry!" Cruz cried, "I had to do it or else he would have someone close to me raped, I couldn't...." Cruz broke down and cried. "I couldn't...."

As officers fought to get Darius out the room, he yelled, "You are going to have an accident mother fucker! An accident called death!"

Outside, the officers slowly let Darius go and he stormed into the men bathroom. One of the same officers who had brought Cruz to the precinct, and who had witnessed Darius' interrogation of Cruz, followed behind him. Darius locked himself in the stall and cried. The officer left him there and returned to the interrogation room.

"How did you do it?" Smith asked Cruz as he offered him the chair.

"He gave me a stun gun and ahh," Cruz wiped the blood from his eyes, "ahh, and then I injected some drug thing in her to knock her out."

"What drug thing?"

"I don't know the name. Each time, he would give me the syringe with the thing already in it."

"Where did he get it?"

"From this lady, I don't know her name."

"Can you describe her?"

"No, I never saw her face, I just knew she works in a hospital."

"How do you know that?"

"The first time I was supposed to meet the lady…"

"What lady?" Lt. Smith bluntly interrupted him.

"The lady that he would have me meet on occasion, the one that would give me the thing that he would have me use on the other woman. Anyways, he told me that if the woman smelled funny, don't worry; it's just hospital smell. He cracked a smile but I believed him. I don't think he meant to tell me but he may have gotten relaxed or something, and then realized that."

"Why do you say that?"

"Because right after, he says 'forget I said that', and he never mentioned her again."

"How many times you met her?"

"Few times, I don't know exactly how many times."

"Where did you meet her?"

"In Prospect Park. I always meet her there, or she would drop it off there and I pick it up right after, but she would wait to make sure I got it before she left."

"When was the last time, you raped the other one?"

"Yo man, you gotta put it like that?" Cruz felt remorse, but Smith felt no sympathy for him.

"Couple days ago," Cruz held one of his eyes.

"Did you break into her apartment?"

"No. Officer Walker told me where she would be. So, I waited for her to come home. It was night. When she was about to go in her house, I looked around, made sure it was safe and I shot her with the stun gun. I then took her to a spot in East New York because Officer Walker told me to do it. He said that the place was sentimental to her."

"What do you mean sentimental?"

"I don't know man; I was just following an order."

"Where in East New York?"

"I had specific instructions to take her over to where the whores do their thing." Smith shook his head as he retrieved the court order.

"We have a court order to force you to do a DNA test."

"Yo man, I'm sorry, I didn't mean to-"

"Shut up." Smith got up and left the room. He would have updated Darius. On his way to finding Darius, he went to one of the detectives who were working on finding Cassandra Willis. He informed him that they must pay particular attention to anyone named Cassandra Willis who worked in a hospital. The officer showed his acknowledgment and nodded his head.

CHAPTER
THIRTY ONE

Smith noticed that Maddog's Lawyer was already at the precinct waiting for Maddog when the cops dragged him inside. Maddog must have contacted his lawyer while he was hiding away in the escape pod in his room. His lawyer was a white man, in his fifties and he was definitely a legend. That explained why he charged Maddog three hundred and fifty dollars an hour. As the cops hauled his client inside, he approached them.

"I am Robert Gingsky, Mr. Pierre Washington's attorney. Do not question him in my absence."

"Well damn, we didn't even get to central booking yet, or even charge him yet, and you are here already," one of the officers mimicked.

"As I said, do not question him in my absence, on anything whatsoever."

As they brought Maddog to the interrogation room, Miguel Cruz was still inside.

"It's a bit crowded in here, isn't it?" Maddog smiled. The cops ignored him while one of them directed Cruz out.

"Have a seat sir, and we will send your lawyer inside," an officer said to Maddog and then disappeared. As the officer reached outside, he left the door ajar. Miguel Cruz turned to him.

"I want to press charges against that crazy cop who beat me up and against the police department."

Just as he was finished, Smith walked over. "What cop? I can assure you that no cop beat up on you. You weren't even here in the interrogation room. No one knows what you are talking about. But, it makes sense, it's your illusion from the LSD you've been sniffing. And let me tell you, you keep up with those illusions and someone is going to start investigating you, and discover the drugs you would have been taking. You will be locked up for sure," Smith paused "for your penetration charges."

Cruz looked away. He knew he was screwed.

"Follow me sir," Smith said to Cruz as they headed to Smith's office. Darius, Samurai, and Carlitta were waiting there. As they approached Smith's office, his door was slightly ajarred. Smith saw a lady whom he had never met.

"I am Lt. Smith and you are…" he waited for an answer as he extended his hand to her.

"I'm Julie." She extended her hand. "Agent Kramer contacted Mr. Peter Viesser and I and requested for us to meet him here."

"Well Julie, this is Miguel Cruz, we will be taking his blood today for DNA testing." Smith turned towards Miguel.

"So Mr. Cruz, if you could have a seat right here, we'll be done in no time. And don't worry Mr. Cruz, because we have probable cause, you know an overwhelming reason that you are in fact the one who raped Elizabeth Webster. Also, a nice judge gave us permission to take your blood. It's called accumulating evidence against you." Smith smiled.

Cruz was so scared as Darius kept staring at him. Cruz had never seen Samurai before but from the way Samurai looked, he was not in a good shape either. Julie directed Cruz to give her his hand and then she took the blood. Peter was not too far away to collect it. As soon as Peter returned to the office from the bathroom, Julie handed him the blood even before he could have introduced himself to Smith. After a quick introduction, he left and hurried to the lab. Smith called in an officer to his office and directed him to put Cruz in a cell and call his probation officer.

"Oh by the way," Smith said to Cruz as he was leaving, "you are under arrest for the multiple rapes of Elizabeth Webster. Anything you say, can and will be used against you in the court of law, if you do not have an attorney, one will be provided for you, do you understand these rights as I have read them to you?"

"Mother fucker!" Cruz kicked and screamed.

"I know how the DNA test is going to come out, so I'm just doing this ahead of time, so I don't have to leave what I'm doing to personally read you your rights, so consider it official in an hour or so." Smith slammed the door in front of Cruz and listened to him as he kicked and screamed on his way to the cell.

"Now, Sammy," Smith turned to Samurai, "where are Cassandra Willis' body pieces?"

"They are planted around Officer Walker's house, from his back yard, to the front; you will have to do some excavating. That's where he wanted to keep her to ensure that he would always have an eye on her and no one would ever find her."

Everyone's mouth in the room dropped except for Darius.

"How do you know this?" Darius was not amused.

"Does it matter?" Samurai stood up. "Now, give me my fucking immunity and let me get out of here. I have had enough of this place, this town and definitely enough of you."

"I have never seen you like this before Sammy, so authoritative, so in control, so devoid of fear and this air of arrogance that looms over you is quite refreshing. It will make it easier to take your ass down. I now understand why you and Sambino are partners. You are basically one in the same. It's hard for me to tell who is who right now." Darius smirked.

"It must be fucked up to know that you, the defenders of society, don't have a clue about shit." Samurai eyes danced. "Sammy, I sensed that you are trying to get rid of Michael and then turn around and try to take care of me. That would be suicidal, though I would applaud you for your creativity." Samurai managed a deadly smile and fixed his eyes on Darius. Carlitta interrupted their tense moment.

"I know - I know, we need an order from the court to dig up his yard," she said before Smith could tell her.

"Sharp, aren't we?" Smith referred to her. "Mr. Kramer, Ms. Davis, shall we?" Smith opened the door.

"What about him?" Carlitta asked referring to Samurai.

"Sammy, my boy has been the highlight of my week, so he gets to stay here with these two officers to keep him company. He doesn't get a jail cell, he gets first class treatment, isn't that right Sammy?" Smith patted Sammy on the back, but Sammy didn't respond to Smith. As they left to go to the interrogation room, Samurai called out to Darius.

248

"Hey DEA!" Darius turned around. "What the hell took you so long?" Darius didn't understand the question so he brushed off Samurai and they headed down to the interrogation room.

"Could you guys please close the door?" Samurai asked one of the officers in the room with him. "I don't want the whole world to see me in here, I mean what if one of those guys you have just arrested notices me and …"

"Alright, we get the point, you don't want to be noticed by any of them, it could ruin your CI status," one of the officers said.

As the officer was about to close the door, Samurai moved as if at the speed of light. He reached out and put his left hand around the other officer's mouth and jammed a pick he always carried, straight through the officer's throat, which stopped him from screaming. Just as quickly, he spun the officer around, snatched his gun from the holster and pointed it at the other officer.

"Don't fucking move," Samurai said, "don't even think about it."

Before the officer could have flinched, Samurai broke the neck on the officer in his hand and flew in front of the other officer with the gun pointed in his face.

"Turn around," Samurai demanded in a low voice.

As the officer faced the door, Samurai snapped his neck and broke it. He stepped over the officer, left the room, closed the door behind him and walked out as if nothing had happened. He no longer had the appearance of someone who was still shaken. An officer, who was casually passing by, witnessed all of what happened in a glance. The blinds were partially opened. Before that officer could have done anything, Samurai, the partner of Sambino as well as the Confidential Informant for the NYPD, was gone.

CHAPTER
THIRTY TWO

Maddog was in the interrogation room with his lawyer, ready to fire away at the ADA and the cops. Smith and the rest of the gang walked in and before they could have situated themselves, Mr. Gingsky made his announcement.

"My client will not answer any questions, so unless you are going to press charges, we are leaving."

"Hold your horses," Carlitta announced, "before you jump on us from your high throne, here is the deal. We give you immunity, you tell us everything. We are not interested in you, just the one above you…"

"And," Smith interjected, "you get the hell out of my neighborhood."

"Yeah and you get the hell out of his neighborhood," Carlitta added, "and if you don't, then the deal is off and we'll get you, and we will."

Maddog didn't even look at his attorney. "Deal."

"Great, so let's roll," Carlitta sighed. "Okay, I am just going to cut to the chase…ahhh, how are you informed that a shipment is coming in."

"I get a call directly from Sambino, well he says he is Sambino."

"Have you ever called him?"

"No, he always call me, and that's not often. If I need to reach him, I do it through the person who he assigned. He works at the place where the goods are packaged. Well that's the rumor anyways.

"You don't have any contact with Vasquez?"

"No. When I get a phone call, I know that Vasquez already got his phone call because it's going to his store."

"Do you know who contacts Vasquez?"

"No. I suspect it's Sambino, but I don't know. See, he doesn't trust anyone so it is rare that he would have someone do something for him."

"I see. Are there any drugs now to be sent to Vasquez?"

"I don't know. I still had some left to get from Vasquez, but don't know if he got that package already."

"Is there anything that you know that we don't know?"

"I don't know. I don't know what you know."

She looked up at him as if he was being a smart ass. "We are going to place you under protective custody until after the trial or whatever. We'll put you up in the place of your choice, and if you are interested in the witness protection program, we'll set you up, if not, you're on your own."

"What about my guys who work for me?"

"What about them?" Carlitta showed that she could have cared less about them. They were all going down.

"Have you met Sambino?" Maddog asked.

"Yes. I think so. I'm not quite sure. Everything just seems like one long day. I couldn't tell you what day it is."

"Damn! You caught that Japanese mother fucker!" Maddog uttered in disbelief! How y'all do that!"

At the end of the word Japanese, Darius, Smith and Carlitta stopped dead in their tracks and slowly turned around to look at Maddog.

"Ja-pa-nese," Smith said slowly having received the shock of his life. His CI was Sambino. "That's what he meant when he said what took Darius so long to figure it out." *'I now understand why you and Sambino are partners. You are basically one in the same,'* he remembered Darius saying to Samurai. He looked at around. Everyone was in a state of shock, except for Agent Darius Kramer. He had known all along.

"Revere was right," Darius said, "I lost focus of my true mission. I will see you later," Darius prepared to leave.

"Where are you going?" Smith asked.

"To close my case."

"Yep," Maddog continued, "Japanese, half black, whatever. I mean that's how Jabed describes him. Yo man, I would love to meet that mother fucker and shake his hand."

"Come on," Smith said to an officer as they too sprinted out of the interrogation room upstairs toward Smith's office.

As Darius pried the office door open, he discovered two dead officers. He immediately told an officer to get Smith upstairs right away and put out an APB on Samurai.

"That won't be necessary," Smith said as he fell against the door in disbelief. There were two Sambinos.

"Call your men about going over to where Maddog's

contact works. Get the address from him." Smith said barely finding the words to speak."

"That won't be necessary," Darius said as he exposed the wiring that he was wearing. "They are already on their way.

CHAPTER
THIRTY
THREE

By this time, information had leaked to the media and coverage of Officer Walker being the notorious drug lord, Sambino, had hit every newspaper, television and radio station. Diane was right—somebody from Roberto's party was going to hit the news. It was hours later and Michael was now in New York. He listened in his car as the media ripped him to threads for the alleged murder of Cassandra Willis. Michael, having been what he had been through yesterday and today, was not even surprised that Samurai had framed him for her murder, especially because he had told Samurai of Cassandra. From the looks of it, Samurai never stopped until he found Cassandra Willis, the anesthesiologist. Michael just didn't see the necessity in Samurai framing him. Just have me killed, he thought. Tired of being the latest celebrity, Michael turned off the radio and inserted his favorite classical piece.

As he approached the Blazer's apartment in Morningside Heights, still known to many as Harlem, and the home of Columbia University, he didn't even look for a place to park.

Being a police officer, he simply pulled up at the building, parked and walked inside. He showed the doorman his badge, informed him he was there on police business and he was going to the fourth floor. An apartment number wasn't necessary as the Blazers occupied the entire floor. The doorman as usual, called upstairs and informed the Blazers that a detective was there to see them. When they asked what it was about, Michael informed the doorman to tell them he could not discuss police business in front of anyone else due to privacy but rest assured, they would want to let him inside, and so they did.

As he got on the elevator, the doorman pressed the fourth floor button and used his keys to activate it. As the elevator door closed, Michael nodded his head to the doorman showing his gratitude. When the doorman was no longer in view, he took out his gun. He made sure the silencer was on and held the gun behind his back with both hands. The elevator door opened directly into the apartment. He noticed Mrs. Blazer and concluded that her Japanese features contradicted her surname. She, as opposed to the hired help, was walking toward him. That meant one thing, she had given the hired help the day off and so there was no one to attend to the guest. Mrs. Blazer walked over to the elevator to welcome him. She approached him with concern, extended her hand, and started to introduce herself. Michael ended that introduction with a hollow point bullet to her forehead. It took the life from her body instantly. She fell to the floor.

"Nice to meet you," Michael said and stepped over her.

"Babe," her husband called to her as he walked down the stairs. "Which tie should I wear to the event tonight? I am confused as to which...." Mr. Blazer came to a shocking halt

256

when he saw Michael helping himself at the bar.

"Who the hell are you?"

"Where are my manners?" Michael said as he put down the bottle of gin. "I am Detective Walker, a friend of your son, Samurai." He extended his hand and shook Mr. Blazer's, hand. By this time, he had put the gun in the back of his pants and used his shirt to cover it.

"Oh yes, Samurai's friend. You are the young man who I saw Samurai with one day and who went out of his way to tell me that you think my company was doing remarkable work in the community and you wanted to personally thank me for putting Bedford Stuyvesant's interest first." Mr. Blazer at this time released his hands of Michael's and put his hands in his pockets, clearly detecting his uneasiness. "Not too many people have shown the extent of gratitude as you have," he said nervously and wandered what else did Detective Walker know.

"I bet they don't." Michael stared at Mr. Blazer with a deadly grin on his face.

"So, you are here with Samurai?" From Mr. Blazer's body language, Michael felt that Mr. Blazer was uneasy.

"Yes, I'm here with Samurai – in spirit," Michael said as he quickly pulled out his gun and released a bulled in Mr. Blazer's forehead. "And I am also here to kill you."

He walked over to the bar, picked up his gin and dropped in the comfortable leather chair in the corner. He put his head back, occasionally took a drink, closed his eyes and then waited for Samurai. Samurai had to visit his parents eventually, Michael thought. Lucky for his brother, he was not home and part of Michael hoped he stayed away.

THIRTY FOUR

Darius felt the vibration of his phone. He looked down and saw Peter's number.

"Talk to me?"

"Where are you?"

"On my way to Michael's house to meet what is left of Cassandra Willis. The order to excavate came in and I am sure the media is all over his property by now. Maybe I can do some damage control. This is still an investigation after all."

"I am sure their viewers seeing different body parts live on TV the moment they are discovered, is more exciting than securing a crime scene." Peter was silent. Darius didn't even have to ask.

"How bad?"

"The DNA matches Miguel Cruz." Peter stopped as he tried to contain himself.

"And…." Darius tried not to be snappy with Peter knowing how sensitive Peter could get, "just spill it man, what is it?"

"And," Peter said, "Clearly, she is carrying small as it was hard to tell but she is about 14 weeks pregnant."

"How the hell do you know that?" Darius wished his reasoning would be bullshit.

"Julie told me. Elizabeth had contacted her to find out if Julie knew how far along she was and so they met up and Julie had a sonogram done."

"When was all this? When was I going to be informed of any of this?"

"It happened when everything in your world was going upside down as it still is. Besides, Elizabeth just wanted a favor, and she didn't feel as if it had to involve you. You're not exactly on her likable list right now so her not having anything to do with you at this point is because she feels she has to do certain things herself and so she does them reluctantly. Besides Julie would have given you this information anyway, as she knows you need it."

"Does Liz know any of this information?" Darius hoped she didn't.

"Not yet. Why?"

"I fear what she might do with this information being that no one would be giving her an abortion at this stage of the game. She would however, find a way to get rid of it still."

"The danger to her life is becoming more real, isn't it?" Peter's voice dropped as if in a whisper.

"Fuck!" Darius screamed. "Fuck!"

"Excuse me Agent Kramer," Peter heard someone call out to Darius.

"Yeah, what is it?" Darius asked as Peter listened on the

phone. "This sick fuck."

"What is it Darius?" Peter asked alarmed.

"Sambino's name is written all over her body parts. Her limbs are separated from her body."

"Darius, you alright man,"

"That mother fucker Cruz is about to have an accidental death right there in that jail cell. That's after his asshole is ripped to pieces by a train of men, followed by separation of his legs and arms."

"You are talking crazy Darius."

"Am I? Listen, I gotta go. I know you are relieved that you are not the one who has to break the news to Liz."

"You know it. Let me know how she is doing Darius."

"I will. Talk to you later."

"Later." They hung up the phone with each other.

He decided to go to Elizabeth's house, taking a chance that she would be there, and she was. In what seemed like no time at all, Darius knocked on Elizabeth's door. Elizabeth opened the door. The smell of the alcohol that seeped through her threw Darius back for a moment.

"You don't drink," Darius tried to take the bottle of vodka from Elizabeth, who just looked at him as if he was stupid.

"I do now," she chucked down some more.

"Jesus! You're killing yourself," he tried to get the bottle from her.

"Leave me the fuck alone!" She walked away. What do you want?" She snapped. Darius realized it was pointless to argue. He proceeded to tell her everything about Michael, Miguel and Cassandra. He explained how she was Michael's bait to get to Darius and to get back at him for having an affair with Diane. Elizabeth fell to the floor from shock.

"I feel as if I am on a ferris wheel that is going faster and faster with no way of stopping." As she vomited, she bawled.

"What did I do?" She cried. "What have I done to Michael for him to have done this to me?" She continued crying as she folded into herself on the floor.

"Liz," Darius said gently as he tried to hold her.

"Get off me," she yanked away from him. "This is all your fault. Just get out! Get out!" He respected her wishes as he hoped that would have given her even a lit bit of satisfaction. Darius was devastated.

"I am so sorry Li—," he stopped himself. Elizabeth was right. There was nothing he could have said or done to have made up for anything. He closed the door behind him. *Martha Brae River, where the hell are you?*

THIRTY FIVE

Michael decided not to wait any longer so he gave himself a head start. Using the Blazer's home phone, he called Samurai. "Mom, I know you are calling to check on me. I am fine, but I can't talk now, I'll catch up with you later."

"Your momma can't come to the phone right now Sammy, but I'll be sure to pass the message along when I see her on the other side." Samurai gasped.

Michael heard the slamming of cars. He knew Samurai just had an accident, probably slammed into someone.

"Or your daddy either," Michael continued. "Now Sammy, you may not want to get any ideas or call anyone. The media would have a field day with the information I have left here for them. That would only smudge your parents' flawless image and we wouldn't want that, now would we, being that they are such respectable citizens of our society and all. Excuse me- were. Besides, it wouldn't be too nice for younger brother to have to deal with the mess his parents had created, including you. It's bad enough that he will be living in this world-all-alone."

Samurai hung up the phone. Michael knew he was rushing over. As Samurai had his own set of keys, he wouldn't need the doorman. Almost one hour later, he was on the fourth floor. As the door opened to his mother's fallen body, Samurai fell down on her and screamed in agony.

"I should have killed you long time ago," Samurai sobbed.

"You mean like the moment I found out that your parents had an alliance with the cartel, or is the cartel, whatever…" Michael said being sarcastic.

"My parents were not the cartel," Samurai said sternly.

"The fuck they weren't. They were the owners of the manufacturing company, who had a partnership with some Nicaraguan to get its shit to this great country of ours!" Michael yelled with no care in the world.

"When it hits American soil, Sammy, the Nicaraguan did his part, so now the Blazer's had to do their part, which is to get it repackaged. Who the hell would have suspected two extremely successful attorneys would be the masterminds behind aiding with the destruction of the youth in Bedford Stuyvesant? " He paused. "The quarter million tax deduction for pro bono attorneys to get off the dealers and the users—as they are essential to the business and the clinic to treat the addicts to whom they supply the drugs…are brilliant moves. I would dish out all that money in Bed-Stuy to protect my investment too, especially if it comes with a tax benefit.

"You are crazy…" Samurai said with conviction.

"Bed-Stuy was their particular target because we are supposed to be expendable, right mother fucker."

"How the hell did you find out about the company, and even if that is the case, what the hell did they do to you to warrant killing them? They were innocent for God's sake," Samurai painfully laid his mother gently down as he stood.

"Okay Sammy, let's attack those concerns of yours one by one shall we?" Michael tapped his lower right cheek with his gun as he remained seated. "One, how did I find out about the company, let's see. One of the fools who delivered "flour" to Vasquez one night pleasantly honored my request, when he witnessed one of my bullets leaving my gun barrel and miraculously exiting through the back of the other's head. You know me; I had to make a statement without saying a word. Anyways, enough of that... after I took out the first idiot, I commented to the other idiot how beautiful his wife and children must be. Let's just say he took me to the promise land, otherwise known as the manufacturing company that actually receives the drugs from Nicaragua. A trip to Nevada and the rest was like stealing candy from a baby. A few more empty gun barrels and I knew who owned, well in this case, what company owns the manufacturing company."

"Why else do you I think I approached you?" Michael got up, took his drink with him and made a step towards Samurai.

"We made a perfect partnership--you would need someone on the inside of the law to make your job easier, hence me becoming a cop. We were supposed to be partners, Sammy, Sambino and Sambino. That is the name of our little enterprise, or have you forgotten. Sambino was to have two faces, make it a bit harder for the feds or the locals or who the fuck else to figure out. And just in case you haven't figured it out yet, I don't need a reason to wipe a mother fucker off the face of the planet. I just need to know that wiping them out will bring my enemy closer to me, as in the Blazers for example." He smiled.

"You are right Sammy, they were innocent being that they didn't do shit to me, but what can I say? He waved his gun not taking his eyes off Samurai, while at the same time sipping on his drink. In fact, they handed me my freedom—multimillionaire, while I'm still young and robust."

"My father was right," Samurai said, "I played around with you too much, I should have handled you long time ago instead of trying to take you down later."

"But see your daddy was smart, he knew it would be hard to kill me and why," Michael suddenly caught on to what Samurai said, "oh shit, your father wanted me dead because I found out the family secret, didn't he?" Michael stopped as Darius came to his mind instantly.

"Shit," Michael walked over.

"Fuck," he laughed. "Your family is Darius' original perpetrators, aren't they? He couldn't get to your parents just yet, because they were too much of a passive player. But, you were very much active and of course we are partners so I, of course, incidentally would be linked too, and me being Sambino and all, well one of them anyways, was just an extra bonus. Darius played you like the bitch that you are and you think he was after me, and I guess he was. You at no time knew you were the bigger target and it was I who was the bait believe it or not. So, that mother fucker decides why not kill two birds with one stone. He used me to get to you. You would have ultimately helped him to take me down, and then you would try and take him out.

But, that wouldn't have worked, because after you helped him out, he would have already turned around and taken you down, ultimately leading to your parents."

Michael was like a kid in the candy store as he uncovered Darius' strategy. Michael wished he could have seen Darius if nothing else to give him much respect. It all made sense to Michael now.

"Darius befriended Elizabeth because she was more approachable than Diane and then he used Diane to get to me. He's been studying our little circle of connection for a while now, and how convenient it was to penetrate that circle that just happened to lead to you, hence, momma and poppa Blazer... four degrees of separation. Yo, I'm his biggest fan," Michael chuckled.

Samurai noticed his father lying in blood across the room and as much as he wanted to move, he felt paralyzed.

"Wow!" Michael continued, "the mother fucker is not so dumb after all Sammy, he has actually outsmarted us all, except that he believes that I am named Sambino and not our little foreign company."

Michael saw that Samurai couldn't believe that he was the perpetrator all this time. Samurai made a step towards Michael and Michael stepped forward with his gun already cocked. Samurai studied the situation he was in and tried to figure out how to kill Michael. Michael decided to help him and quickly threw his glass of gin directly at Samurai. As Samurai focused on dodging the glass, Michael seized the opportunity-- Samurai's lack of attention on him. Without hesitation, he discharged a hollow point bullet into Samurai's head. As Samurai's lifeless body laid on top of his mother, Michael pumped several more into his brain.

"You can't figure out how to kill me Sammy, so stop trying," he said. "Oh one more thing," he said as he turned, "compliments of Sambino and Sambino, motha fucker."

CHAPTER

THIRTY SIX

When Darius left Elizabeth, he called Diane who ignored her phone as he believed she would. So, he went where he knew she was. As he rang her bell, he realized how tired he was and truly broken from this assignment. He vowed this would be his last. *What doesn't kill you son will make you stronger;* he heard his father's voice from a far distance. Diane opened the door and of course Darius was not surprised to see the alcohol.

"What is this, abuse liquor day?"

"What do you want? I know you are here for your job so let's just get to it."

"Fine. I need you to give me access to Michael's accounts in the Cayman Islands. I know you have some information."

He was right, during some of their moments of pleasure, she had talked too much about some strange account discoveries she had made, and how she was going to do her own little investigation on her boyfriend because there had got to be more to him than what she saw. She said one day she would have actually followed through with it. She took Darius to the box of data on Michael she had been collecting for a while now. She was alone many times at Michael's while he went to work, so she had made use of herself in his apartment. She knew pass codes and passwords that he didn't even realize. Never underestimate a woman. Darius was in disbelief at the wealth of information upon which he was looking. *What was in this for her? Why so easily disposed of the man to whom she claimed she had an obligation?*

"How do you know so much detail Diane? He asked suspiciously. "It's one thing to know a little here or there, but you know it like it is yours." He was prepared to read her body language, not hear her words.

"I told you..."

"Ya, I know what you told me but you have pass codes and account numbers of not just any account, but Cayman Islands accounts. That's not something that just lies around."

"What are you saying?" She placed both her hands on her hips.

Defensive posture...umm, interesting, he thought. "Ok, I apologize. Didn't mean to accuse you of anything, it's the detective in me, can't help it."

"Forget about it."

"But I am curious," Darius continued, "did you always have access to this information?"

"No," she said calmly.

Uum, she told the truth for a change. "When did you get so lucky?"

"If you can call it luck...but about four years ago."

Another truth. That was about the time she contacted

us. Interesting…something in the account or not in the account prompted her to contact us. "I see."

"What's up with all the questions? Do I need a lawyer? Am I under arrest again?"

"Diane, you reached out to us, so logically one would assume that you would want to help us."

"Not necessarily," she walked away.

"Evidently. Though there is something to say about seeing an ADA at a grand jury."

"Screw you," she snapped.

"Right now is not a good time as time is definitely of the essence," he came right back at her.

"Why are you doing this?" She asked painfully.

One of the neighbors across from Maria's apartment noticed blood seeping from under the door. She ran and called the cops and the superintendent. They went over to the apartment. After they constantly knocked and got no response, they opened the door forcefully. They discovered Maria dead. When the cops asked who was responsible for her, the superintendent told them of her husband, and at that time, they instructed him to call Darius.

Darius' phone vibrated. He was shocked to see that it was his superintendent in D.C. He had given him the number and insisted not to give it to anyone including his wife.

"Mr. Harris, to what do I owe this surprise?"

"Mr. Kramer, sir, I have some bad news."

"Just get to the point, Mr. Harris."

"Sir, uhhh," Mr. Harris stuttered.

"What is it?" Darius snapped.

"Your wife, sir, she is dead. A bullet to her forehead in her own apartment," he sniffed.

"Thanks," Darius spoke callously and hung up the phone. *Thank God for life insurance,* he thought to himself, *she came in handy after all.* He knew the cops would be calling him to inform him to identify the body.

"I have to go to D.C. Diane. I have to go identify Maria's body."

"Who is Maria?"

"My wife," he said as if she had just asked him the time.

"Are you going to be alright?" He asked Diane who just stood there and stared at him. He knew she was amazed that he was not moved by the fact that he just told her that he was married but of course, why not, why the hell not?

"It's not what you think, I'll explain later. All you need to know is that Michael killed her and he is going to try and kill you too. I'll talk to you later." He gathered the information she had given him. "You know D," he turned around, "if I had to go through all of this again to find you, I would. You are the only woman I ever loved. You are the only one who ever gave my life meaning, even in the midst of all this darkness."

He closed the door behind him as she succumbed to the pain. As he walked to the car, his mind turned to Maria as he headed out to D.C. Who would have thought his next trip to D.C. would be to identify her body? He so wished she had a different life, but more importantly, a different husband. He believed everyone deserved to be happy. Maybe the next life would bring her happiness and peace of mind. Now, he would enjoy the million. He wondered if he would have missed her and he forced himself to go back to the days they first met in college. It was easier that way to think nice thoughts about her. He didn't even realize an hour had gone by since he left Diane and was on the New Jersey Turnpike South when his phone vibrated again. This time it was Michael. Darius answered the phone.

"There goes my dying wish that the next time we had any kind of contact would be the moment before you depart from this world," Darius said.

"Let me guess, by your hands, right? Whatever happened to 'hello,' 'how are you doing,' 'I was just about to call you. 'Now, folks just skip straight to 'I'm gonna kill ya.'"

"What do you want?" Darius was not entertained.

"Just called to say sure missed ya at the Samurai's departure thing we had. He would have loved it if you were there to give your condolences, though I don't know who you would have given it to, being that everyone else is where he is; you know in heaven of course."

Darius pulled the car over and knocked his head back and forth on the steering wheel. Michael had just assassinated a family and this killing spree was not about to stop.

"Why?" Darius asked disgusted. "Ahh, they were bad people, they needed to go. I mean you more than anyone else knows that. Consider it my part in cleaning up the planet," Michael's tone indicated a grin.

"Not that it matters, but why Maria?"

"Why not? The interesting question you need to ask is why not yet Diane? But that is about to become a sentence in the past tense. I just called to say I hope it was all worth it."

"Shit!" Darius said as he now made his way to the New Jersey Turnpike North heading back to New York. He was on his way to Diane.

CHAPTER

THIRTY SEVEN

"Liz, please pick up the phone, pleaseeeeeeee," Diane begged on Elizabeth's answering machine.

"I have to tell you something really important," she just knew Elizabeth heard and chose to ignore her.

"Okay I know you are listening, so I will just say my piece. I have a bad feeling so I am leaving town, probably for good. I'm going to disappear, try and create a new life for myself. I will always let you know where I am, you will be the only person. I am going to pack now, and I'll call you." She paused. "Liz if you don't hear back from me within a couple hours," she tried compose herself but it didn't work, "then I was taken by Michael and he is going to kill me, probably the same place he killed my father, you know where," she sniffled.

"Liz, uhh, about Darius, I never expected to fall in love with him. I never expected to feel alive. He does for me what no one else ever did or will ever be able to do. I risked your friendship when I loved him, which I swear was from the first moment I saw him." Diane couldn't get to finish her thought because the tape was finished, so she called back.

"Remember that time I told you I just met my soul mate, my angel, the one? I was just sitting on the bench across from the Parthenon in Prospect Park and there he was. Our eyes met and it was over. I've never felt so scared before because for once I was not in control and I didn't understand what was happening, but I knew I wanted it to happen for the rest of my life. Well, remember I called you right after and you blew me off. I also told Michael about where I was and how I saw an angel in human form. That's why months later, when you introduced me to him; it was as if I had seen a ghost. He was my free spirit and there you were introducing him to me as the guy you were casually seeing." She was uncontrollable.

"Then and there, my world crashed, because I loved this guy and he was with you and I was with Michael and there was nothing I could do about it. I didn't even know his name or what he was like. Anyways, I don't know what life has in store for me but I wanted to clear the air. I wanted my best friend in my life but I always wanted to know what it's like to really live, feel alive and with him, I lived. I am saying all that, because I would give him up to have you back in my life," she cried some more.

"That's how much I love you Liz, and I am so sorry. I want to be there for you and the baby or whatever you decide to do, but please just don't shut me out." Diane was unable to finish her message. Her telephone line was cut and shortly thereafter Michael was at her door.

"If you don't open up, I'll kill her, and if you try to use your cell phone to call your pimp, Mr. DEA, I'll kill her." Diane knew he was talking about Elizabeth and he was not lying. She looked around, nothing seemed to matter anymore. She thought of Darius and then of Elizabeth. As she reluctantly opened the door, Michael dragged her to his car.

"Didn't think you would meet your father so soon, huh, D?" He looked across at her. She refused to give him the satisfaction of crying.

"I never loved you," she said. "After Darius, I realized that I have never truly loved before. But you know it's only fitting, to lose life right after you discover it."

She felt Michael's rage.

"Yeah well I'm sure you two will have a lot to talk about in the life after death."

They both decided to be quiet the remainder of the way. Diane closed her eyes, and thought only of Darius.

At this time, Darius was speeding up the New Jersey Turnpike. He was going 100 miles per hour. His concentration was interrupted by the voice on his phone that was saying "you've got voicemail." He could not have figured out how he missed the call. Hoping it was Diane, he listened. It was Elizabeth.

"Darius, I just got a message from Diane, and I think she is in trouble. I am pretty sure that Michael has her. My feelings are not wrong on this. You will be able to find her at 660 Kingsville Court, Riverdale, Bronx, the penthouse. Now, finish this."

"I'm ahead of your Liz," he said to himself, "but thanks for the address."

Michael broke the silence between him and Diane in the car.

"You know, I had Miguel, the father to Elizabeth's bastard child meet Cassandra at the exact bench you were when she saw – your angel. Ironic isn't it, that meeting place was the beginning of your life and of Liz's death."

Diane flashed back to that night when Elizabeth called her from the red light district. How Michael must have gloated when Diane and Elizabeth believed that it was Sally who had returned. She thought of the night of the broken vase and how she had wondered how it was that Michael had allowed her to get away with behaving and speaking to him in a certain manner. She thought of the night of Roberto's party, the moment she told Michael that Elizabeth was pregnant. She thought about the many times the four of them went out and how Michael must have felt knowing that she was sleeping with his enemy, a man he once called friend. All of this destruction to get to one man. Then the betrayal ripped through her like a tornado. She remembered Darius' words, *"You were not a part of my mission, just the best incidental from it."* She sobbed. She was necessary to get to Michael and Elizabeth was necessary to get to her. The moment she first saw him in the park was not a coincidence. He needed her to notice him.

"If I could, I would kill you myself," she said to Michael as she now stared out the window. "Only if I could."

"Just once you know you can't, we are on the same page."

"If I may have one last wish, may it be that you never speak another word to me, just do what you came to do and get it over," Diane pleaded with a simple sentence.

"And what makes you think I give a fuck about what you want? You clearly don't give a fuck about what I want," he said passively. She exhaled and closed her eyes. Before she knew it, Michael was taking off the handcuffs. He dragged her out the car and handcuffed her to him.

"Just in case you have any ideas, remember I am attached to you. And if you try any shit, I'll snap your fucking neck."

The apartment building was as picturesque as its neighborhood, which was filled with the people who earned seven digits income. Michael looked all the way up as he was on the top floor. He always liked penthouses, he believed it added to the rush and he could have always threatened to throw someone out the window. They walked inside, greeted the doorman who knew Michael and then they headed upstairs. The elevator opened up to the stillness and silence in the air. Michael turned the key in the lock and waited a moment before he stepped inside.

"I almost forgot how much I love this place, though I don't think we should be here because it's still a crime scene," he smiled.

"Sit down," he said harshly as he pushed her down in the chair and proceeded to take off the handcuffs. He tied her to a chair. He went and opened the window behind him so fresh air could circulate the apartment.

"One last kiss baby," he said to her, as he grabbed her viciously and kissed her. "So, this is how we end up?"

He knelt down in front of her, being genuine. "I told you that you were slipping and I am actually surprised that you fell because I taught you better than that. I don't know what the fuck you were thinking getting involved with the enemy because I know you had to have known at some point that you were sleeping with the enemy." He grabbed her face and squeezed with all his might.

"What was it D? You got so caught up with the dick that you missed all the signs or was it that you knew all along and it was fuck Michael time, fuck our partnership, fuck what we had, just fuck everything, right D?" He pushed the chair over backwards and then grabbed her up by the neck bringing the chair to its original position.

"I liked you my whole life it seems and it's fair to say I will always like you," he said calmly as he headed to the kitchen.

"The shit you did to Otis will not go unpunished. I don't get the impression that you did everything in your power to be the ADA on that case or to see to it that the assigned ADA lost that case."

"Go fuck yourself, you and Otis."

He looked back at her and smiled. He pulled out his cell phone and dialed.

"Yeah, keep looking out and if things don't go as planned, get Mr. Otis Raymond the package." Just as quickly, he ended the call.

Diane swallowed hard. She imagined what was in that package going to Otis. Although she knew in her heart she would die, she worried about Darius and Elizabeth. She should have reached Rebecca.

"Just in case you are curious D, I am going to get the knife to start the butchering process. I am telling you D, it will be fun. If you don't believe me, ask your old man. Oh yeah, I forgot. He's dead, isn't he?" He smiled.

"I'm sorry D" he said, "you leave me no choice."

Diane did not respond. She knew there was nothing she

could have said or done to have him change his mind. He would not have forgiven her. She had betrayed him in more than one way and there was no turning back from that. To get it over with, she decided to incite him.

"You don't have the guts to kill me."

"You know, I was going to go and pull out my "Oh Fortuna" piece but I think I'll just get to the point," he walked back to her.

"Darius is going to find me."

"Is that before or after I kill you?" He pointed the 32 calibre to her head and was about to pull the trigger.

BUM . The loudest noise Diane had ever heard was just made as Michael flew backwards out the window and down 29 stories. Diane screamed so loud, the entire building would have shaken if it could have done so.

"That would be before," Elizabeth said answering Michael's question, still holding the gun in that direction as if Michael was still there.

"Liz, oh God!" Diane was startled.

"I left immediately after your message. I knew I had to get here before Michael. I hid in the apartment and slowly made my way out." She now turned to look at Diane as she was still staring in the direction where Michael was before.

"I was determined to save your life."

"How? How did you, how did you get in?"

"Well, we knew the doorman and the superintendent for years, so I was no stranger to them. I just convinced him that you and I were throwing Michael a surprise party and I needed to get in to set up the place."

The turn of the door lock by the superintendent and the quick entrance thereafter caused Diane and Elizabeth to turn in that direction. Darius instantly slouched and dropped his gun to the side when he saw Elizabeth.

"Don't worry Liz, it's defense of others or self-defense or whatever, just give me the gun," he said softly as he approached her. He noticed Diane, forgot what he was doing and rushed over and started to untie her. Elizabeth looked over at them and smiled.

"I am going to miss my friend. Thanks Diane for making my life worth living." She looked down at the gun and back up.

"You really do love him, and vice versa," she said to Diane with a painful smile.

"Liz, is the baby okay?" Diane asked as she tried to help Darius untie the ropes.

"Soon enough, that won't matter," Elizabeth said still smiling.

"Darius, I'm leaving so promise me you will take good care of her. She is my sister after all." Diane did not believe it. She could not have waited to get over there and hug Elizabeth.

"Diane," Elizabeth called to her.

"Yeah," Diane looked up at her with a smile.

"I wish the two of you the happiness we have been seeking all our lives." They were both so touched by her kindness. They just simply looked at her with remorse all over them.

"Don't ever forget me okay Diane," Elizabeth in a split of a second, put the gun to her head and pulled the trigger.

"Nooooooooooooooooooooooooooooooooooooooooooooo ooooooooooooooooooooo!" Diane screamed in agony.

She dashed over there to try and catch her body. It was too late. Elizabeth was dead. Diane grabbed Elizabeth's body in her arms like a baby, and rocked her while she hollered. Darius held her just as equally shaken. She was holding the body of her dead friend. The body of the ex-boyfriend not too far away. It was over.

CHAPTER
THIRTY
EIGHT

Lt. Smith sat in his office, and felt lifeless. Samurai, his parents--the Blazers, Officer Walker, Cassandra, Cruz, Elizabeth, all gone. He could have cared less about Cruz when he heard about his accidental death. He felt it for the others, including Samurai. In a sick way, he liked the kid. Though he never knew Darius for long, he was happy he was still alive. He promised to stay in touch.

The cage was indestructible, as were all the contents within it. It was long enough to house the two metal shelves cots that were positioned one above the other. Upon each cot, a mattress was covered with a hard grey plastic. There was no ladder adjoining the two. The bottom cot, the nearby toilet and simply pulling oneself up was the way to the top cot. The occupant who was afraid of nothing, including bringing or receiving death occupied the lower cot. The cage was wide enough to allow the occupant to take no more than three steps to reach the tan metal toilet that had no lid. The toilet was cemented to the floor. A tan metal structure accompanied it. It was affixed to the faded green impenetrable cement wall. This structure had a dual role feature. It was a fountain as well as a sink. In the corner, to the left of the toilet was a rectangular reflective metal gray shelf used as a desk. It too was affixed to the cement wall. In front of it, a metal chair was bolted to the hard cold concrete floor. The smell of disinfectant filled the air. Natural lighting was absent, as was a clock or anything to indicate the time of day or night. The encased lighting on the wall came on the same time in the morning and went out the same time at night. Dull, black vertical and horizontal iron rods guarded the entrance. They would open without notice and shut without notice.

The occupants of such cage were told when to eat, sleep, bathe, leave or enter the cage. The occupants were told when they could or could not do, and when they would or would not do. It was around four in the afternoon. The occupant on the lower cot used both of his hands as an extra pillow, placing them under his head. He stretched his six- foot body across the cot and threw his right leg across his left. He fixed his light brown eyes between the spaces of the iron rods. He looked in all directions. He looked in silence. Such silence was broken by mail call. The occupant on the lower bunk, like all others on that cage block, heard the same echo, different words at around four in the afternoon. Sometimes the words would repeat themselves on different days. The occupant on the lower cot has not heard a word to his liking in days. As far as he was concerned, his only family died few days ago, and so he would not hear a word to his liking in a long time to come.

Raymond!"

The occupant on the lower cot was wrong. Disbelief caught him off guard. He crinkled his face and slowly moved his hands forward as he eased upward and sat. He put his right leg on the floor and kept the other stretched on the cot. He rested his right arm on his right leg and his left hand respectively. As if in slow motion, he gazed with caution at the slot on the iron rods. He watched as a small package emerged from the slot onto the cage's floor. Curiosity propelled him to it. He carefully grasped the package and glided to the cot. He reached for the cot to ensure that he would not fall as he sat. He was weak in the knees. As customary in the cage, all mails that were delivered to any occupant was already opened. More important to Otis Raymond than the contents within the package was the sender. He turned his attention to the addresser. He gasped.

"Michael?" He uttered softly. Instantaneously, he felt a burning sensation in his throat and eyes. His chest tightened and his vision dimmed temporarily. The last time Otis experienced something similar was when he received word of Michael's death. Prior to that, it was his mother's death. This time however, there was something that was not quite the same. These sensations were mixed with others. Strangely, they were the exact opposite. As the tears emerged, so did the smile. As the pain caused him to sink, delight jolted him. He closed his eyes and hung his body over the package. He swayed his body and whispered, "thank you Michael, thank you." Without having gone further, Otis Raymond knew in his heart, he had in his possession, the keys to his freedom. With anticipation, he pried open the package. There was a detailed account of past events with names, dates and times, pictures of Diane, and Darius; a to-do list in codes; and there were specific instructions for his attorney. There were numbers for his attorney to call and people to see and new evidence to collect to reverse Otis' conviction. There was a complaint with the New York State Bar against an attorney named Diane Roberts to be filed. For Otis' convenience, there were a few stacks of bills in a bank account that carried the face of Benjamin Franklin. It was more than enough to pay the highest paid attorney if necessary. As Otis read the detailed accounts pertaining to him being framed by Diane, he ushered an uncomfortable laugh. It became louder when the words on the page revealed why the package didn't arrive much sooner. His eyes carried him to a name he has never known-Rebecca. Otis sighed at Michael's final command.

"Finish this."

CHAPTER
THIRTY NINE

Agent Darius Kramer sat in the apartment once occupied by Roberto. Exhausted mentally and drained spiritually, his case still wasn't over. There was one final curtain to close and it was the most painful of all. The role of Diane Roberts would come to light momentarily. Darius had all the computer hardware in both Michael's and Diane's apartments and offices secured. A forensic analysis had taken place and Michael's accounts were seized and turned over for further investigation. The results of the investigation showed that Otis had worked only from Michael's computer at his home. Thanks to the power of the United States federal government, and the bank account information Diane handed over to Darius, the bank in the Cayman Islands cooperated with the investigation. Being that all of Michael's assets were linked to money laundering and profits from the illegal sale of controlled substance, his millions were seized. Darius browsed over the expected discoveries, until he came to a sudden stop. For the past four years in a row, the deposited amount suddenly increased by approximately

7.5%. Darius rushed over the painting on the wall. He lifted it, and with care put it on a nearby table. He felt the area where it once hung, and snap the center of it. A squared section of the wall protruded. With his index finger, he glided underneath and swung the movable section of the wall to the left, leading him to a vault. He inserted the code and retrieved the file he had accumulated thus far. The amount of narcotics received by the Blazers from Nicaragua and distributed didn't increase. The price of the product didn't increase, and the demand for the product didn't decrease. Darius rushed back to the file from the forensic accountant. It showed that Michael always received the same amount of revenue…but wait. Something was off. Way off. Darius saw for the first time since he had been reviewing the accountant's results what he hadn't seen before. The revenue that Michael received from Samurai was less than what was deposited in the Cayman Islands. *What the hell? Where was the rest of the money?* He dragged his eyes to the page that took him to the deposited amount as of four years ago. The deposit to the Cayman Islands, though it wasn't all the funds, drastically increased, which could only mean one thing.

Buzz, his phone rang. He ignored it. Buzz. It rang again. He ignored it. Buzz…

"What!"

"Did I catch you at a bad time?" Revere, his boss felt as if he just interrupted a deep conversation of some sort.

"Sorry, I just…sorry… what's up?"

"Otis Raymond got a package…"

"And…" Darius was distracted by what he was seeing in the files before him. He sent a text to the accountant to find out where the other money was going. He fell back by the quick response that such information was already in the report that he had...but Darius didn't see it, or maybe he didn't want to see it.

"And a copy of all its contents is being delivered to you," Revere paused, "I'm sorry Darius."

"Uhh huh," Darius said not having heard a word of what Revere just told him. "Whatever you say boss." He closed his phone.

He walked to the bedroom. Approximately 72 hours ago, he held a party, he was surrounded by laughter. Elizabeth smile lit the room, Michael still had a "friend," in Roberto, and he made love to a woman his soul had come to yearn. Darius walked back to where he and Diane once laid...her black panties were still there, unclaimed. He sobbed. He felt this way once when the inevitable was near.

"Come on champ, no tears...you now have to take care of you and mommy for me, ok."

"Don't leave me daddy, please...please don't leave me" *Tears flooded his cheeks.*

"Never Darius, never. But you will learn to move on. You will learn to find the sweetness in life again. You must, otherwise tragedy and death have won."

"I hope so daddy..." the burning sensation in his throat made it hard for the words to come out. *"I hope that you will never forget me, I hope that you will forever love me, I hope..."*

"Shhh...I do love you, and I always will. I could never forget you as I will always be with you right here," he tapped on Darius' heart. *"Do you know what I hope Darius?"*

"What daddy?"

"I hope you will find love, family, friends in abundance, good days with laugher, sunshine and serenity. And even when the thunderstorms in life come your way, I hope you can find peace beyond all understanding. I hope you can find the lesson in every trial because that is one thing, Darius, in some form or another, we all must bear."

'That's a lot of hoping dad."

His dad gently swept his hand across Darius' face, *"someone once said 'hope is the thing with feathers that pierces in the soul and sings a tune without cords, and never stops at all.'"*

The inevitable goodbye was here. Darius hoped it would all be over soon.

One week later, Diane buried Elizabeth. Darius, Peter, Julie and Mr. Revere were also there for support. As Diane and Darius bid their last farewell to their friend, Diane did not have the strength to walk back to the limousine, so she leaned on Darius. He leaned against the limousine.

"Let's walk to the bench," he held his head down and took her hand.

"What's going on?"

"I am tired. I am worn. I am heavily burdened, and I am going to miss you with every fibre of my being."

"Are you leaving for good because the case is over?" She too held her head down. She lifted it back up with desperation in her eyes, "I was hoping…"

"Shhh," he placed his index finger over her lips. "I'm sorry that Michael stole from you," he stood.

"What!" She jumped.

"I'm sorry he deprived you of hundreds of thousands...
7.5% less to be exact, and he used Otis to do it."

"What!" Diane couldn't believe what she was hearing.

"The 13th Amendment is a bitch isn't it?"

"What the hell are you talking about?"

"It says that slavery is abolished except for those who are incarcerated, hence property of the state, property of master."

Diane had a blank look.

Darius continued, "As prisoners such as Otis has no rights, all letters are read before delivered, all packages inspected before delivered, all phone calls recorded..."

"I know about the 13th Amendment Darius. I don't need a lecture from you. Get to the point," she snapped,

"He received a package from the deceased."

"Oh God, no," she placed her hand over her mouth and froze.

"But truth be told, I didn't need to look at that either, as the investigative report from our forensic accounting told all. You sent us the tip about Michael only because you discovered that he went back on your original deal of you getting 10% of whatever he earned to you now getting 2.5%. And from what I understand it, that 10% was income for losing cases, and you know the rest of it."

"No," she made repeated steps backwards.

"You knew so much about him because you were his silent partner." Darius moved slowly towards Diane. "Why didn't you just come to me? We could have worked out a deal."

"I didn't know who you were!" She yelled in fear. Her entire world, the one to which Elizabeth wasn't privy had shattered. "No," she whispered as she cried.

"I gave you ample time D...you protected him. You didn't protect us."

"No, no, no..." she stomped her feet. She came toward him and hit his chest repeatedly, "no, no no..."

He looked up at the black cars that were across from him next to the limousine. He nodded his head, and few agents came out. Revere also came out. Diane looked around and saw them heading their way.

"Please Roberto" she pled, "please...it's me...please."

"I hope you will find love, family, friends in abundance, good days with laugher, sunshine and serenity. And even when the thunderstorms in life come your way, I hope you can find peace beyond all understanding. I hope you can find the lesson in every trial because that is one thing in some form or another, we all must bear." He put his face up to hers and held her cheeks, "I hope one day sooner than we both know, you will be free. Goodbye Diane."

"Noooooooooooooooo!!!!" She tried to pull him back.

He removed her hands from his arm, and walked steadily away with his heart and chest pounding, throat burning and tears no doubt flowing. The last case of his career was over. He heard the sounds from one of the officer coming from behind, though he dared not look.

"Ms. Diane Roberts, you have the right to remain silent. Anything you say can and will be used against you in the court of law. If you can't afford an attorney, one will be provided to you. Do you understand these rights as I have read them to you?"

CHAPTER
FOURTY

Darius watched as they emptied the apartments Roberto and Mr. Hosten once occupied. He took whatever personal tokens he could from both places, including the framed picture of he, Diane, Elizabeth and Michael at Roberto's last party. At the end of the day, he walked away with two framed pictures, heartache and pain. He headed to the field office in Long Island to pack whatever items he had there and to submit his resignation letter. To Darius, that was the longest drive he had ever undertaken.

"Hey, hey, hey agent," Revere walked up. He too was sad for Darius, but he would put that aside today.

Darius quickly glanced in the direction of his desk where something had just fallen from Revere's hands.

"Compliments from the guys in the office." Revere watched as Darius picked up the printed confirmation of his gift. "Try too hard not to think of us," he smiled, while the other agents rushed and jumped on Darius.

"Darius, Darius, Darius," was the chant in the room. Laughter and stories of their time together saturated the office.

Darius laughed and he laughed and he laughed. It was the kind of laughter that brought pain. *"I hope you find friends in abundance, good days with laugher."*

⌇⌇⌇

Bing was the sound of PA system.

"The captain has asked that you please fasten your seatbelt, as we will be landing shortly," the woman with a twang spoke. It was music to Darius' ear. It was a gift well needed. He closed his eyes and smiled as a sign of his gratitude.

"We would like to take this opportunity to say to our first time visitors, welcome to Jamaica." Darius exhaled with delight when he saw the blue Caribbean Sea below.

"And," the melodious voice continued, "for those of you who are returning," she paused, "welcome home."

The line of warm black faces all too willingly to help the tourist rushed to Darius as he took off his shades, lifted his head backward and allowed the sun to bathe him.

"This is what I call paradise," he said to himself.

He then thanked and dismissed the natives politely and walked to the rent-a-car location where a topless white jeep awaited him. He threw his only luggage—a light carry-on bag, in the back seat and pulled out his map.

The scenery heading from Montego-Bay was breathtaking. Palm trees lined the street for miles. Resorts, hotels, craft stalls, shops, and Caucasian tourists were in view. As his scenery became less touristic, Darius watched as the water beat upon the rocks as it came crashing in. Fishing boats painted in red, yellow or green rested upon the sand or most times docked at a board-walk, where one or two persons sat and dangled their feet. Bungalows never seemed more welcoming. There were fish huts where older men with locks and salt and pepper beard cooked fish and other local cuisine. Children ran around and played on the sand as if it was their playground.

The raw like scent from the sea became his companion, and he sifted it in with humility. The wind created the cool breeze. He accelerated as he turned up the volume and rocked to the beat of "Three Little Birds," by Bob Marley. *I hope you will find sunshine and serenity.* After a good distance, he glanced through the rear view mirror. A sign blew in the wind. It carried the words, "Welcome to Trelawny." The Martha Brae River wasn't too far away.

Made in the USA
Charleston, SC
21 March 2013